"I KNEW YOU'D SHOW UP," HE SAID.

My throat felt tight and raw. I couldn't think of anything to say, and couldn't have gotten the words out even if I had.

He hung the cue stick on the wall rack and walked toward me.

I was frozen in place, temporarily speechless, just the way I'd been on the road outside of town an hour or so earlier.

Tristan pushed a button on the boom box, and our song began to play. "Dance with me," he said, and pushed me into his arms.

"How did you know I'd come here?"

"Easy," he said. "This was home. I knew you couldn't stay away." He kissed me, a light, nibbling, tasting kiss.

from "Batteries Not Required"

**Read more by your favorite authors
in these collections**

Linda Lael Miller
Sun, Sand, Sex

Jill Shalvis
Bad Boys Southern Style

Lucy Monroe
Bodyguards in Bed

Kate Angell
Unwrapped

Published by Kensington Publishing Corporation

LINDA LAEL MILLER

JILL SHALVIS

HE'S THE ONE

LUCY MONROE

KATE ANGELL

KENSINGTON BOOKS
http://www.kensingtonbooks.com

KENSINGTON BOOKS are published by

Kensington Publishing Corp.
119 West 40th Street
New York, NY 10018

All Kensington titles, imprints and distributed lines are available at special quantity discounts for bulk purchases for sales promotion, premiums, fund-raising, educational or institutional use.

Special book excerpts or customized printings can also be created to fit specific needs. For details, write or phone the office of the Kensington Special Sales Manager. Attn.: Special Sales Department. Kensington Publishing Corp., 119 West 40th Street, New York, NY 10018. Phone: 1-800-221-2647.

Kensington and the K logo Reg. U.S. Pat. & TM Off.

ISBN-13: 978-0-7582-1095-1
ISBN-10: 0-7582-1095-7

First Kensington Books Mass-Market Paperback Printing: July 2013

eISBN-13: 978-0-7582-8901-8
eISBN-10: 0-7582-8901-4

First Kensington Books Electronic Edition: July 2013

10 9 8 7 6 5 4 3 2 1

Printed in the United States of America

CONTENTS

BATTERIES
NOT
REQUIRED

Linda Lael
Miller

The last thing I wanted was a man to complicate my life. I came to that conclusion on the commuter flight between Phoenix and Helena, Montana, because my best friend Lucy and I had been discussing the topic, online and via our BlackBerrys, for days. Maybe the fact that I was bound to encounter Tristan McCullough during my brief sojourn in my hometown of Parable had something to do with the decision.

Tristan and I had a history, one of those angst-filled summer romances between high school graduation and college. Sure, it had been over for ten years, but I still felt bruised whenever I thought of him, which was more often than I should have, even with all that time to insulate me from the experience.

My few romantic encounters in between had done nothing to dissuade me from my original opinion.

Resolved: Men lie. They cheat—usually with your roommate, your best friend, or somebody you're going to have to face at the office every day. They forget birthdays, dump you the day of the big date, and leave the toilet seat up.

Who needed it? I had B.O.B., after all. My battery-operated boyfriend.

Just as I was thinking those thoughts, my purse tumbled out of the overhead compartment and hit me on the head. I should have realized that the universe was putting me on notice. Cosmic e-mail. Subject: *Pay attention, Gayle.*

Hastily, avoiding the flight attendant's tolerant glance, which I knew would be disapproving because I'd asked for extra peanuts during the flight and gotten up to use the restroom when the seat belt sign was on, I shoved the bag under the seat in front of mine. Then I gripped the arms of 4B as the aircraft gave an apocalyptic shudder and nose-dived for the landing strip.

I squeezed my eyes shut.

The plane bumped to the ground, and I would have sworn before a hostile jury that the thing was about to flip from wing tip to wing tip before crumpling into a fiery ball.

My stomach surged into my throat, and I pictured smoldering wreckage on the six o'clock news in Phoenix, even heard the voice-over. *"Recently fired paralegal, Gayle Hayes, perished today in a plane crash outside the small Montana town of Parable. She was twenty-seven, a hard-won size 6 with two hundred dollars' worth of highlights in her shoulder-length brown hair, and was accompanied by her long-standing boyfriend, Bob—"*

As if my untimely and tragic death would rate a sound bite. And *as if* I'd brought Bob along on this trip. All I would have needed to complete my humiliation, on top of losing my job and having to make an appearance in Parable, was for some security guard to search my suitcase and wave my vibrator in the air.

But, hey, when you think you're about to die, you need *somebody*, even if he's made of pink plastic and runs on four "C" batteries.

When it became apparent that the Grim Reaper was otherwise occupied, I lifted the lids and took a look around. The flight attendant, who was old enough to have served cocktails on Wright Brothers Air, smiled thinly. Like I said, we hadn't exactly bonded.

Despite my aversion to flying, I sat there wondering if they'd let me go home if I simply refused to get off the plane.

The cabin door whooshed open, and my fellow passengers—half a dozen in all—rose from their seats, gathered their belongings, and clogged the aisle at the front of the airplane. I'd scrutinized them—surreptitiously, of course—during the flight, in case I recognized somebody, but none of them were familiar, which was a relief.

Before the Tristan fiasco, I'd been ordinary, studious Gayle Hayes, daughter of Josie Hayes, manager and part owner of the Bucking Bronco Tavern. *After* our dramatic breakup, Tristan was still the golden boy, the insider, but I was Typhoid Mary. He'd grown up in Parable, as had his father and grandfather. His family had land and money, and in ranch country, or anywhere else, that adds up to credibility. I, on the other hand, had blown into town with my recently divorced mother, when I was thirteen, and remained an unknown quantity. I didn't miss the latest stepfather—he was one in a long line—and I loved Mom deeply.

I just didn't want to be like her, that was all. I wanted to go to college, marry one man, and raise a flock of kids. It might not be politically correct to admit it, but I wasn't really interested in a career.

When the Tristan-and-me thing bit the dust, I pulled my savings out of the bank and caught the first bus out of town.

Mom had long since moved on from Parable, but she still had a financial interest in the Bronco, and the other partners wanted to sell. I'm a paralegal, not a lawyer, but my mother saw that as a technicality. She'd hooked up with a new boyfriend—not the kind that requires batteries—and as of that moment, she was somewhere in New Mexico, on the back of a Harley. A week ago, on the same day I was notified that I'd been downsized, she called me from a borrowed cell phone and talked me into representing her at the negotiations.

In a weak moment, I'd agreed. She overnighted me an airline ticket and her power of attorney, and wired travel expenses into my checking account, and here I was—back in Parable, Montana, the place I'd sworn I would never think about, let alone visit, again.

"Miss?" The flight attendant's voice jolted me back to the present. From the expression on her face, I would be carried off bodily if I didn't disembark on my own. I unsnapped my seat belt, hauled my purse out from under 3B, and deplaned with as much dignity as I could summon.

I had forgotten why they call Montana the Big Sky

Country. It's like being under a vast, inverted bowl of the purest blue, stretching from horizon to horizon.

The airport at Helena was small, and the land around the city is relatively flat, but the trees and mountains were visible in the distance, and I felt a little quiver of nostalgia as I took it all in. Living in Phoenix for the decade since I'd fled, working my way through vocational school and making a life for myself, I'd had plenty of occasion to miss the terrain, but I hadn't consciously allowed myself the indulgence.

I made my way carefully down the steps to the tarmac, and crossed to the entrance, trailing well behind the other passengers. Mom had arranged for a rental car, so all I had to do was pick up my suitcase at the baggage claim, sign the appropriate papers at Avis, and boogie for Parable.

I stopped at a McDonald's on the way through town, since I hadn't had breakfast and twenty-six peanuts don't count as nourishment. Frankly, I would have preferred a stiff drink, but you can't get arrested for driving under the influence of French fries and a Big Mac.

I switched on the radio, in a futile effort to keep memories of Tristan at bay, and the first thing I heard was Our Song.

I switched it off again.

My cell phone rang, inside my purse, and I fumbled for it.

It was Lucy.

"Where are you?" she demanded.

I pushed the speaker button on the phone, so I could finish my fries and still keep one hand on the wheel. "In the trunk of a car," I answered. "I've been kidnapped by the mob. Think I should kick out one of the taillights and wave my hand through the hole?"

Lucy hesitated. "Smart-ass," she said. "Where are you really?"

I sighed. Lucy is my best friend, and I love her, but she's the mistress of rhetorical questions. We met at school in Phoenix, but now she's a clerk in an actuary's office, in Santa Barbara. I guess they pay her to second-guess everything. "On my way to Parable. You know, that place we've been talking about via BlackBerry?"

"Oh," said Lucy.

I folded another fry into my mouth, gum-stick style. "Do you have some reason for calling?" I prompted. I didn't mean to sound impatient, but I probably did. My brain kept racing ahead to Parable, wondering how long it would take to get my business done and leave.

Lucy perked right up. "Yes," she said. "The law firm across the hall from our offices is hiring paralegals. You can get an application online."

I softened. It wasn't Lucy's fault, after all, that I had to go back to Parable and maybe come face-to-face with Tristan. I was jobless, and she was trying to help. "Thanks, Luce," I said. "I'll look into it when I have access to a computer. Right now, I'm in a rental car."

"I'll forward the application," she replied.

"Thanks," I repeated. The familiar road was winding higher and higher into the timber country. I rolled the window partway down, to take in the green smell of pine and fir trees.

"I wish I could be there to lend moral support," Lucy said.

"Me, too," I sighed. She didn't know about the Tristan debacle. Yes, she was my closest friend, but the subject was too painful to broach, even with her. Only my mother knew, and she probably thought I was over it.

Lucy's voice brightened. "Maybe you'll meet a cowboy."

I felt the word "cowboy" like a punch to the solar plexus. Tristan was a cowboy. And he'd gotten on his metaphorical horse and trampled my heart to a pulp. "Maybe," I said, to throw her a bone.

"Boss alert," Lucy whispered, apparently picking up an authority figure on the radar. "I'd better get back to my charts."

"Good idea," I said, relieved, and disconnected. I tossed the phone back into my purse.

I passed a couple of ranches, and a gas station with bears and fish and horses on display in the parking lot, the kind carved out of a tree stump with a chain saw. Yep, I was getting close to Parable.

I braced myself. Two more bends in the road.

On the first bend, I almost crashed into a deer.

On the second bend, I braked within two feet of a loaded cattle truck, jackknifed in the middle of the highway. I had already suspected that fate wasn't on my side. I knew it for a fact when Tristan McCullough stormed around one end of the semi-trailer, ready for a fight.

My heart surged up into my sinuses and got stuck there.

The decade since I'd seen him last had hardened his frame and chiseled his features, at least his mouth and lower jaw. I couldn't see the upper part of his face because of the shadow cast by the brim of his beat-up cowboy hat.

What does Tristan look like? Take Brad Pitt and multiply by a factor of ten, and you've got a rough idea.

"Didn't you see the flares?" he demanded, in that one quivering moment before he recognized me. "How fast were you going, anyway?" It clicked, and he stiffened, stopped in his tracks, a few feet from my car door.

"No, I didn't see any flares," I said, and I must have sounded lame, as well as defensive. "And I don't think I was speeding." My voice echoed in my head.

He recovered quickly, but that was Tristan. While I was pining, he'd probably been dating rodeo groupies, cocktail waitresses, and tourists. While I was waiting tables to get through school, he was winning fancy belt buckles for the school team and getting straight A's at the University of Montana without wasting time on such pedantic matters as studying and earning a living. "Back around the bend and put your flashers on. Otherwise, this situation might get a whole lot worse."

I just sat there.

"Hello?" he snarled.

I still didn't move.

Tristan opened the door of the rental and leaned in. "Get out of the car, Gayle," he said. "I'll do the rest."

My knees were watery, but I unsnapped the seat belt and de-carred. Four stumpy French fries fell off my lap, in seeming slow motion. It's strange, the things you notice when the earth topples off its axis.

Tristan climbed behind the wheel and backed the compact around the bend. When he returned, I was still standing in the road, listening to the cattle bawl inside the truck trailer. I felt like joining them.

"Are they hurt?" I asked.

"The cattle?" Tristan countered. "No. Just annoyed." He did that cowboy thing, taking off his hat, putting it on again in almost the same motion. "What are you doing here?"

For a moment, I was stumped for an answer. His eyes were so blue. His butternut hair still too long. Everything inside me seized up into a fetal ball.

"Gayle?" he prompted, none too kindly.

"The Bucking Bronco is up for sale, as you probably know. My mom sent me to protect her interests."

The azure gaze drifted over me, slowly and thoughtfully, leaving a trail of fire in its wake. "I see," he drawled, and it sounded like more than an acknowledgment of my reasons for returning to Parable, as if he'd developed X-ray vision and could see the lace panties and matching bra under my linen slacks and white cotton blouse. My blood heated, and my nipples went hard. When we were together, Tristan had had a way of undressing me with his eyes, and he hadn't lost the knack.

I flushed. "How long until you get this truck out of the way?" I asked. "I'd like to get my business done and get out of here."

"I'll just bet you would," he said, and a corner of his mouth quirked up in an insolent ghost of a grin.

He leaned in, and I felt his breath against my face. More heat. "You're real good at running away."

My temper flared. "Whatever," I snapped. If he wanted to make the whole thing my fault, fine. I wouldn't try to change his mind.

His gaze glided to my left hand, then back to my face. "No wedding ring," he said. "I figured you would have married some poor sucker, out of spite. Maybe even had a couple of kids."

"Well," I said, "you figured wrong."

"No boyfriend?" There was a note of disbelief in his voice, as though he thought I couldn't go five minutes without a man, let alone ten years.

I straightened my spine. The pitiable state of my love life was nobody's business, least of all Tristan McCullough's. "I'm in a committed relationship," I said. "His name is Bob."

Tristan's mouth twitched. "Bob," he repeated.

"He's in electronics," I said.

Something sparked in Tristan's eyes—humor, I thought—and I hoped he hadn't guessed that Bob was a vibrator.

Get a grip, I told myself. Tristan might have known where all my erotic zones were, but he wasn't psychic.

Feeling bolder, now that I knew I wouldn't spontaneously combust just by being in Tristan's presence—provided he didn't *touch* me, that is—I cast a disgusted glance toward the trailer, full of unhappy cows. "So, how long did you say it will take to get this truck off the road?"

"You already asked me that."

"Yes, but you didn't answer."

He looked irritated. "I called for some help.

There's a wrecker on the way. Guess you're just going to have to be patient."

I approached the trailer—the cattle smelled even worse than they sounded—and noticed that a set of double wheels at the front had slipped partway into the ditch. Beyond it was a drop-off of several hundred feet.

My stomach quivered. "I really hope they don't all decide to stand on one side of the trailer," I said.

Tristan was right beside me. He looked pale under his rancher's tan. "Me, too," he said.

"What happened? I thought you were this great driver."

He scowled, did the hat thing again. Before he had to answer, we heard revving engines on the other side of the truck. We ducked between the trailer and the cab and watched as a wrecker and about fourteen pickup trucks rolled up.

An older man—I recognized him immediately as Tristan's grandfather—leaped out of a beat-up vehicle and hurried toward us. "We gotta get those cows out of that rig before they trample each other," he called. He squinted at me, but quickly lost interest. Story of my life. Sometimes, I think I'm invisible. "Jim and Roy are up on the ridge road, unloading the horses. We're gonna need 'em to keep the cattle from scattering all over the county."

Tristan nodded, and I looked up, trying to locate the aforementioned ridge road. High above, I saw two long horse trailers, pulled by more pickup trucks, perched on what looked like an impossibly narrow strip of land. I counted two riders and some dozen horses making their careful way down the hillside.

"What's she doing here?" the wrecker guy asked Tristan, after cocking a thumb at me.

I didn't hear Tristan's answer over all the ruckus. Oh, well. I probably wouldn't have liked it anyway.

"Get out of the way," Tristan told me, as he and the guys from the flotilla of pickup trucks up ahead got ready to unload the cattle. I retreated a ways, and watched as he climbed onto the back of the semi-trailer, threw the heavy steel bolts that held the doors closed, and climbed inside.

An image came to my mind, of the whole she-bang rolling over the cliff, with Tristan inside, and I almost threw up the twenty-six peanuts, along with the Big Mac and the fries.

The horsemen arrived, and several of the men on the ground immediately mounted up. Tristan threw down a ramp from inside.

"Watch out them cattle don't trample you!" the grandfather called. He'd gone back to his truck for a lasso, and he looked ready to rope.

Over the uproar, I distinctly heard Tristan laugh.

A couple of cows came down the ramp, looking surprised to find themselves on a mountain road. The noise increased as the animals came down the metal ramp. The trailer rocked with the shifting weight, and the wheels slipped slightly.

"Easy!" Grampa yelled.

"I'm doing the best I can, old man!" Tristan yelled back.

The trailer was big. Just the same, I would never have guessed it could hold that many cattle. They just kept coming, like the critters bailing out of Noah's Ark after the flood, except that they didn't travel two by two.

Before long, the road was choked with them. There was dust, and a lot of cowboys on horseback, yelling "Hyaww!" I concentrated on staying out of the way, and wished I hadn't worn linen pants and a white blouse. On the other hand, how do you dress for something like that?

Tristan came down the ramp, at long last, and I let out my breath.

He wasn't going to plunge to his death in a cattle truck.

I found a tree stump and sat down on it.

I lost track of Tristan in all the fuss. The cattle were trying to get away, fanning out over the road, trying to climb the hillside, even heading for the steep drop on the other side of the road. The cowboys yelled and whistled and rode in every direction.

All of a sudden, Tristan was right in front of me, mounted on a big bay gelding. A grin flashed on his dusty face. "Come on," he said, leaning down to offer me a hand. "I'll take you into town. It'll be a while before the road's clear."

I cupped my hands around my mouth to be heard over the din. "What about my car?"

"One of the men will bring it to you later."

I hadn't ridden a horse since the summer of my American Cowboy, but I knew I'd get trampled if I tried to walk through the milling herd. I went to stand up, but my butt was stuck to the stump.

Tristan threw back his head and laughed.

"What?" I shouted, mortified and still struggling.

"Pitch," he said. "You might have to take off your pants."

"In your dreams," I retorted, and struggled some more, with equal futility.

Grinning, Tristan swung down out of the saddle, took a grip on the waistband of my slacks at either side, and wrenched me to my feet. I felt the linen tear away at the back, and my derriere blowing in the breeze. If I'd had my purse, I'd have used it to cover myself, but it was still in the rental car.

My predicament struck Tristan as funny, of course. While I was trying to hold my pants together, he hurled me bodily onto the horse, and mounted behind me. That stirred some visceral memories, ones I would have preferred to ignore, but it was difficult, under the circumstances.

"I need my purse," I said.

"Later," he replied, close to my ear.

"And my suitcase." I'm nothing if not persistent.

"Like I'm going to ride into town with a *suitcase*," Tristan said. "It could spook Samson."

"Why can't we just borrow one of these trucks?"

"We've got a horse." I guess he considered that a reasonable answer.

Tears of frustration burned behind my eyes. I'd hoped to slip in and out of Parable unnoticed. Now, I'd be arriving on horseback, with the back of my pants torn away. Shades of Lady Godiva.

"Hold on," Tristan said, sending another hot shiver through my system as the words brushed, warm and husky, past my ear.

He didn't have to tell me twice. When he steered that horse down into the ditch—one false step and we'd have been in free fall, Tristan, the gelding, and me—I gripped the saddle horn with both hands and held on for dear life. I would have closed my eyes, but between clinging for dear life and controlling my bladder, I'd exhausted my physical resources.

We bumped up on the other side of the trailer and, once we were clear of the pickup trucks, Tristan nudged the horse into a trot.

I bounced ignobly against a part of his anatomy I would have preferred not to think about, and by that time I'd given up on trying to hold the seat of my slacks together. He was rock-hard under those faded jeans of his, and I sincerely hoped he was suffering as grievously as I was.

Parable hadn't changed much since I'd left, except for the addition of a huge discount store at one end of town. People honked and waved as we rode down the main drag, and Tristan, the showoff, occasionally tipped his hat.

We passed the Bucking Bronco Tavern, now closed, with its windows boarded up, and I felt a pang of nostalgia. Mom and I weren't real close, but I couldn't help remembering happy times in our little apartment behind the bar, with its linoleum floors and shabby furniture. My tiny bedroom was butt up against the back wall of the tavern, and I used to go to sleep to the click of pool balls and the wail of the jukebox. I felt safe, knowing my mother was close by, even if she *was* refereeing brawls, topping off draft beers, and flirting for tips.

Behind the stores, huge pines jutted toward the supersized sky, and I caught glimmers of Preacher Lake. In the winter, Parable looks like a vintage postcard. In fact, it's so 1950s that I half expected to blink and see everything in black-and-white.

I had reservations at the Lakeside Motel, since

that was the only hostelry in town, besides Mamie Sweet's Bed and Breakfast. Mom wouldn't have booked me a room there, since she and Mamie had once had a hair-pulling match over a farm implement salesman from Billings. Turned out he was married anyway, but as far as I knew, the feud was still on.

Tristan brought the horse to a stop in front of the Lakeside, with nary a mention of the B&B, another sign that Mom and Mamie had never had that Hallmark moment. He dismounted and reached up to help me down.

I didn't want to flash downtown Parable, but my choices were limited. As soon as I was on the ground, I closed the gap in my slacks. Tristan grinned as I backed toward the motel office, my face the same raspberry shade as my lace underpants.

The woman behind the registration desk was a stranger, but from the way she looked me over, she one, knew who I was, and two, had heard an unflattering version of my hasty departure on the four o'clock bus.

I bit my lower lip.

"You must be Gayle," she said. She was tall and thin, with short, dark hair. I pegged her for one of those people who live on granola and will risk their lives to protect owls and old-growth timber.

I nodded. I had no purse, and no luggage. I'd just ridden into town on a horse, and I was trying to hold my clothing together. I didn't feel talkative.

Suddenly, she smiled and put out a hand in greeting. "Nancy Beeks," she said. "Welcome to the Lakeside." She ruffled through some papers and slapped a form down on the counter, along with one of those giveaway pens that run out of ink when you write the third item on a grocery list. "You're in Room 7. It overlooks the lake."

After glancing back over my shoulder to make sure no one was about to step into the office and get a good look at Victoria's Secret, I took a risk and signed the form. "My stuff will be arriving shortly," I said, in an offhand attempt to sound normal.

"Sure," Nancy said. Then she frowned. "What happened to your pants?"

She'd probably seen me on the front of Tristan's horse, and I didn't want her jumping to any conclusions. "I—sat in something," I said.

She nodded sagely, as though people in her immediate circle of friends sat in things all the time. Maybe they did. Country life can be messy. "I could lend you something," she offered.

I flushed with relief, claiming the key to Room 7 with my free hand. "I would really appreciate that," I said. There was no telling how long it would be before my car was delivered, along with the suitcase.

"Hold on a second." Nancy left the desk, and disappeared into a back room. I heard her feet pounding on a set of stairs, and she returned, handing me a pair of black polyester shorts, just as a minivan pulled into the gravel parking lot out front.

I practically snatched them out of her hand. "Thanks."

A husband, a wife, and four little kids in swimming suits got out of the van, stampeding for the front door. I eased to one side, careful to keep my butt toward the wall. Out of the corner of my eye, I thought I saw Nancy grin.

"Heck of a mess out on the highway," the husband announced, as he stepped over the threshold. He was balding, clad in plaid Bermuda shorts and a muscle shirt. The effect of the outfit was brave but unfortunate. "Cattle all over the place. We had to wait at least twenty minutes before the road was clear."

"Where's the pool?" one of the kids yelled. All four of them looked ready to thumb their noses and jump in.

Their mother, a harried-looking woman in a saggy sundress, brushed mouse-brown bangs back from her forehead. "There isn't a pool," she told the children, eyeing me curiously as I sidestepped it toward the door, still keeping my back to the wall. "You can swim in the lake."

"Excuse me," I said, and edged past her to make a break for it, the borrowed shorts clutched in one hand.

Room 7 was around back, with the promised view of the lake, but I didn't bother to admire the scenery until I'd slammed the door behind me, peeled off my ruined slacks, and wriggled into the shorts.

Only then did I take a look around. Tile floors, plain double bed, lamps with wooden bases carved to resemble the chain-saw bears I'd seen in the gas station parking lot. There was a battered dresser along one wall, holding up a TV that still had a channel dial. The bathroom was roughly the size of a phone booth, but it was clean, and that was all that mattered. I wouldn't be in Parable long. Sit in on the negotiations, sign the papers, and I'd be out of there.

I splashed my face with cold water and held my

hair up off my neck for a few seconds, wishing for a rubber band.

Going to the window, I pulled the cord and the drapes swished open to reveal the lake, sparkling with June sunlight. There was a long dock, and I could see the four little kids from the office jumping into the shallow end, with shouts of glee, while their mother watched attentively.

I felt a twinge of yearning. The Bronco backed up to the lake, too, and Mom and I used to skinny-dip back there on Sunday nights, when the tavern was closed and the faithful were all at evening services.

I was tempted to call her, just to let her know I'd arrived, but I decided against it. There would be a charge for using the phone in the room, and my budget was severely limited; better to wait until my stuff arrived and I could use my cell. I had unlimited minutes, after all, and besides, she probably wouldn't hear the ring over the roar of the Harley engine. My mother, the biker chick.

The lake was really calling to me by then. I would have loved to wander down to the dock, kick off my sandals, and dangle my feet in that blue, blue water, but I couldn't bring myself to intrude on the swimming party. Anyway, I figured being at the fringe of that happy little family would have made me feel lonelier, instead of lifting my spirits.

I was sitting on the end of my double bed, leafing through an outdated issue of *Field & Stream*, when the telephone jangled and nearly scared me out of my skin.

"Hello?" I said uncertainly.

"Just thought I'd let you know your car is here,"

Nancy told me. "It's parked in the lot, and I have the keys here in the office."

I thanked her and rushed to reclaim my suitcase and purse.

When I got back to the room, I took a shower, scrubbing the pitch off my backside, and put on clean jeans and a tank top. My cell phone, nestled in the bottom of my bag, was on its last legs, making an irritating bleep-bleep sound.

I turned it off, plugged it in for a charge, and peered out the window again. The minivan family was still in the water. The dad had joined them by then, but the mom still sat on the dock, smiling and shading her eyes with one hand.

I grabbed my purse, locked up the room, and stopped by the office to return Nancy's shorts. I suppose I should have washed them first, but that seemed a little over the top, considering I'd worn them for half an hour at the outside.

Leaving the rental car in the lot, I set out on foot for the Bucking Bronco. I was hoping for a peek inside, though I don't know what I expected to see.

Passing cars slowed, so the driver and passengers could gawk, as I walked toward the tavern. Strangers always get noticed in towns like Parable—if I could be considered a stranger. Most likely, people remembered me as the poor girl who thought someone like Tristan McCullough could really be interested in her.

I waved cheerfully and picked up my pace.

Reaching the Bronco, I noted, without surprise, that the front doors were padlocked. I tried looking through the cracks between the boards covering the windows, but to no avail. I went around back, hoping for better luck.

Here, there were no boards and no padlocks. I turned to scan the sparkling lake for watching boaters, but there were none to be seen, so I tried the door.

It creaked open, and I stopped on the threshold. I thought I heard music, soft and distant. The jukebox? Impossible. The Bronco had been closed for several years, according to Mom, and the electricity must have been shut off long ago.

Still, my breath quickened. I stood still, listening. Yes, there was music. And the familiar click of pool balls.

Ghosts? The only people who would have haunted the Bronco were Mom and I, and we weren't dead.

I stepped inside, hesitantly, my heart hammering. I wasn't scared, exactly, but something out of the ordinary was definitely going on. My curiosity won out over good sense, and I followed the sounds, swimming through a swell of memories as I passed through the little apartment. Mom at the stove, stirring a canned supper and humming a Dolly Parton song. Me, curled up on the ancient sofa, studying.

The door between the apartment and the bar stood open.

The music brought tears to my eyes. Tristan and I used to dance under the stars to the song that was playing. For a moment, I was transported back to our favorite spot, high on a ridge overlooking his family's ranch, with that old, sentimental tune pouring out of the CD player in Tristan's truck. I felt his arms around me. I remembered how he'd lay me down so gently in the tall, sweet-scented grass, and make love to me until I lost myself.

I took another step, even though everything inside me screamed, *Run!*

There was a portable boom box on the dusty bar, and Tristan stood next to the pool table, leaning on his cue stick. He was wearing the same dusty clothes he'd had on before, and his hat rested on one of the bar stools.

"I knew you'd show up," he said.

My throat felt tight and raw. I couldn't think of anything to say, and couldn't have gotten the words out even if I had.

He hung the cue stick on the wall rack and walked toward me.

I was frozen in place, temporarily speechless, just the way I'd been on the road outside of town an hour or so earlier.

Tristan pushed a button on the boom box, and our song began to play. "Dance with me," he said, and pulled me into his arms.

I stumbled along with him. He used the pad of one thumb to brush away my tears.

I finally found my voice. "I didn't see your horse outside," I said.

He laughed. For all that he'd been herding cattle, he smelled of laundry detergent and that green grass we used to lie down in, together. "Gramps took him back to the ranch," he said. "I walked over here from the office. Left my truck there."

"How did you know I'd come here?"

"Easy," he said. "This was home. I knew you couldn't stay away." He kissed me, a light, nibbling, tasting kiss.

I should have resisted, but the best I could do was ask, "What do you want?"

"We have some unfinished business, you and I," he said, and caught my right earlobe lightly between his teeth.

A thrill of need went through me. "We don't," I argued, but weakly.

I felt the edge of the pool table pressing against my rear end. That was nothing compared to what was pressing against my front. "You cheated on me," I murmured.

He kissed me again, deeply this time, with tongue. The floor of the tavern seemed to pitch to one side, like the deck of a ship too small for the waves it was riding.

"You cheated on *me*," he countered.

We'd had that argument just before I left Parable, ten years before, but the circumstances had changed. There had been a lot of yelling then, and I'd thrown things.

Tristan slid a hand up under my tank top, and I didn't stop him. I don't know why. I just didn't. I groaned inside.

He pushed my bra up, cupped my breast, chafing the nipple with the side of his thumb, and kissed me once more.

I am not a loose woman, but you'd never have known it by the way I responded to Tristan's kisses and the way he caressed my breast. I was wet between the legs, and I could already feel myself opening to take him inside, even though I had no intention of letting him get into my jeans.

He unsnapped them, pushed the zipper down, then tugged my tank top down to bare my breast.

When he took my nipple into his mouth, I cried out, buried my hands in his hair, and held him close.

I felt his chuckle of triumph reverberate through my breast, but I still didn't stop him. *Just a minute more*, I remember thinking. *Just a minute more, and then I'll push him away and slap his face for him.*

"Oh, God," I said instead.

He hooked a thumb in the waistband of my jeans and panties and pulled them down, in one move. Without releasing my breast, he hoisted me onto the pool table, eased me back onto the felt top, and reached inside to find my sweet spot.

I gasped his name.

He pushed up my top, and my bra, took his time enjoying my breasts.

My vision blurred. *Just a minute more . . .*

"Remember how it was with us?" Tristan asked throatily, kissing my belly now. My jeans and panties were around my ankles by then. "Remember?"

I'd tried to shut the memory out of my mind for ten years, but I remembered, all right. At a cellular level.

Tristan stopped long enough to pull off my shoes and toss my pants aside. Then he was nibbling at my navel again, and I felt his fingers glide inside me.

I wish I could blame him, but I was the one who lifted my heels to the edge of the pool table and parted my legs.

I held my breath, waiting. There was a debate going on inside my head.

Tell him to stop.

Just a minute more . . .

The debate was nothing, compared to the riot in my senses. The weather was mild, but my skin burned as the passion grew.

Tristan parted me, took me into his mouth.

I moaned.

He teased me with the tip of his tongue. Made me beg.

He sucked again, then went back to flicking at me.

I bucked on that old pool table, and when he knew I was ready to come, he slipped both hands under my buttocks, raised me high, and ate me until I exploded. I had one orgasm, then another, deeper and harder. I lost count before he finally eased me down onto the felt again, and even though I was dazed with satisfaction, I knew it wasn't over.

I sensed that he was unbuttoning his jeans, un-wrapping a condom, putting it on.

He moved sleekly into me, and that was when I caught fire again. He'd worked me over so well that I wouldn't have thought I had another orgasm in me, but I did.

Tristan put his hands behind my shoulders and lifted me up, so I was sitting on him. I wrapped my bare legs around his hips and held on tight. I knew from experience that this ride would be wilder than anything the rodeo had to offer.

"God, you feel good," Tristan rasped, kissing me again. "So good."

He raised me, then lowered me slowly along his shaft. I gave a sob, tilted my head back, and closed my eyes.

"Look at me," he said.

I was under a spell by then, rummy with need. I did as he asked.

I had three more orgasms before Tristan laid me down again, on the pool table, and thrust hard, one, twice, a third time. We came together, me sobbing and clinging, drenched in perspiration, Tristan with his head flung back like a stallion taking a mare. He gave a muffled shout, and stiffened against me, driving deeper than ever.

When it was over, he braced both hands against the side of the table, on either side of my hips, breathing heavily.

"Is it like that with Bob?" he asked.

That was when I slapped him, hard.

He stepped back, grinning, but the look in his eyes was hard. He handed me my jeans and panties and stepped back, after pulling me to my feet. I scrambled into my clothes, jammed on my shoes. I wanted to slap him again, but a part of me was ashamed of doing it once, let alone a second time. I'm not a violent person, and I don't believe in hitting people.

"You bastard," I said. Then I fled, across the tavern, through the apartment, out into the backyard, letting the screen door slam hard behind me. The lake was right there, shimmering with azure blue beauty, and I wanted to drown myself in it.

Behind me, the door hinges squeaked.

"Gayle." Tristan's voice. I knew without looking that he was in the doorway.

I wasn't planning to turn around, but I did. Hadn't planned on letting an old boyfriend screw me on a pool table, either. Did that, too.

Tristan was leaning against the door jamb, just as

I'd imagined, rumple-haired and too damned attractive, even then. "I'm sorry," he said.

I stared at him. I'd expected something else, I don't know what. Mockery, maybe. More seduction. But certainly not an apology.

"I shouldn't have mentioned your boyfriend."

I almost defended Bob, before I remembered he was a vibrator. "You proved you could still make me lose control. Let's leave it at that, okay."

"Is he going to be mad?"

I suddenly saw the humor in the situation, even though I knew there were fresh tears on my face. "There'll be a buzz," I said.

Tristan looked confused, which was fine by me. "You're planning to tell him?"

I nodded. I was on a roll. "He'll be rigid about it."

"Did it ever occur to you that he might not be the right man for you, if it was that easy to get hot with me?"

So much for nonviolence. I would have slapped him again if he hadn't been well out of reach. "Maybe it's not a great relationship," I said, "but at least Bob doesn't cheat on me."

Tristan shoved a hand through his hair, and his jawline hardened. But, then, he wasn't in on the joke. "No, but you cheat on him. Some things never change."

I tightened my fists. "No," I snapped. "Some things never do."

With that, I headed for the rocky beach that runs along the edge of the lake. I was both relieved and disappointed that Tristan didn't follow.

The motel was a half-mile hike, but I was so distracted that I hardly noticed. Fortunately, the Fun Family had left the swimming area, so I didn't have to worry about anybody seeing me with my hair messed up and my eyes puffy from crying furious tears.

I pulled my key from the hip pocket of my jeans, let myself into the room, and immediately took another shower.

I wanted to hibernate, but the Big Mac had worn off, and I knew the Lakeside didn't offer room service. I dressed carefully in the only other set of clothes I had, besides the prim business suit I planned to wear to the meeting with the other owners of the Bronco and the new buyers, a cotton sundress. I'd briefly scanned the papers, and knew the gathering was scheduled for ten the next morning; I would worry about the where part later.

Determined to restore some semblance of dignity, I put on makeup, styled my hair, and left the motel again.

There was still only one restaurant in Parable, a hole-in-the-wall diner on Main Street, across from the library. I had to pause on the sidewalk out front and brace myself to go in.

I was the girl who had done Tristan McCullough wrong, and I knew the locals remembered. By now, some of them might even know that I'd just done a pool-table mambo with the golden boy, though I didn't think Tristan would stoop so low as to screw and tell. Just the same, I'd be lucky if they didn't throw me out bodily.

I was starved, and the only other place I could get food was the supermarket. That would mean going back to the motel for my rental car, shopping for cold cuts and chips, and huddling in my room to eat.

No way I had the strength to do all that.

I needed protein. Immediately.

So I forced myself to go in.

The diner hadn't changed much since the last time I'd been there. Red vinyl booths, a long counter, a revolving pie case. There was no hostess, and all the tables were full.

I took a stool at the counter and reached for a menu. I could feel people staring at me, but I pretended I had the restaurant to myself. Oh, I was a cool one, all right. Unless you counted a tendency to boink Tristan McCullough on a pool table with little or no provocation.

"Help you, honey?"

I looked up from the menu and met the kindly eyes of an aging waitress. She seemed vaguely familiar, but I didn't recognize her name, even when I read it off the little tag on her uniform.

Florence.

"I'll take the meat loaf special," I said, looking neither to the left nor right. "And a diet cola. Large."

"Comin' right up," Florence assured me, and smiled again.

I relaxed a little. At least there was one person in Parable who didn't think I ought to be tarred, feathered, and run out of town on a rail. Make that two—Nancy Beeks, over at the Lakeside, had been friendly enough.

The little bell over the door tinkled as someone entered, and the diner chatter died an instant death. I knew without turning around that Tristan had just walked in, because every nerve in my body leaped to instinctual attention.

Damn him. He wasn't going to leave me alone. He'd gotten past my well-maintained defenses without breaking a sweat. He'd made love to me in an empty tavern. What more did he have to prove?

He took the stool next to mine, reached casually for a menu. He'd showered, too, I saw out of the corner of my eye, and put on fresh clothes—Levi's and a blue chambray shirt. "Fancy meeting you here," he said, without looking my way.

"Like it's a surprise," I retorted.

Florence set my diet cola down, along with clean silverware. "That special will be ready in a minute, sweetie," she told me, before turning her attention to Tristan. "Hey, there, handsome. You stepping out on me, all slicked up like that?" she teased.

To my satisfaction, color pulsed in Tristan's neck. "Would I do that to you, Flo?"

She laughed. "Probably," she said. "Who's the lucky gal?"

"You wouldn't know her," he replied, smooth as could be. "The meat loaf sounds good. I'll have that, and a chocolate milk shake."

Flo glanced at me, then looked at Tristan again. Somehow, she'd connected the dots. She smiled broadly and went off to give the order to the fry cook.

"How long are you going to be in town?" Tristan still wasn't looking at me, but I figured he wasn't asking the customer on the other side of him. The man had the look of a longtime resident.

"As long as it takes to finalize the sale of the

Bronco," I answered, because I knew he wouldn't leave me alone until I did. Tristan was a hard man to ignore. The reference to the tavern made me squirm, though, because I couldn't help remembering how many orgasms I'd had, and how fiercely intense they'd been. I hadn't exactly kept them to myself.

"Shouldn't be long," he said, still staring straight ahead, as if he'd taken a deep interest in the milk shake machine, already churning up his order. "The other owners are eager to sell, and the buyer is ready to make out a check."

"Good," I replied, and took a sip of my diet cola. At the moment, I wished it would turn into a double martini. I could have used the anesthetic effect.

He turned his stool ever so slightly in my direction, but there was still no eye contact. Like everybody in the diner didn't know we were talking. "I suppose you've talked to Bob by now," he said.

Bob was in my dresser drawer, under four pairs of panties. "Of course," I said lightly. "Bob and I are honest with each other."

"Right. By now, he's probably on his way here to punch me in the mouth."

"Bob isn't that sort of man." Bob, of course, wasn't *any* sort of man.

"I'd do it, if I were him."

I smiled to myself, though I was shaken, and there was that peculiar tightening in the pit of my stomach again. "He's not the violent type," I said.

Flo set my plate of meat loaf down in front of me. Hunger had driven me to that diner, but now I had no appetite at all. Because I knew Tristan and everybody else in the place would make something of it if I paid my bill and left without taking a bite, I picked up my fork.

"And I am?" Tristan asked tersely.

"You said it yourself," I replied, with a lightness I didn't feel. I put a piece of meat loaf into my mouth, chewed and swallowed, before going on. "If you were in Bob's place, you'd punch him in the mouth."

"What does he do for a living?"

"I told you," I answered smoothly. "He's in electronics. Mostly, though, he just concentrates on keeping me happy."

"I'll just bet he does."

I wanted to laugh. I ate more meat loaf instead.

Tristan looked annoyed. His voice was an edgy whisper. "What kind of man doesn't mind when somebody else boinks his woman?"

"Bob gets a charge out of things like that," I said. It wasn't the complete truth. I didn't have to plug him into the wall like I did my cell phone. He ran on Duracells.

"I can't believe you'd settle for a man like that," Tristan snarled. He glowered at Flo when she brought his milk shake and silverware, and she retreated quickly, though she was grinning a little. "Don't you have any pride?"

The meat loaf turned to cardboard, and stuck in my throat. I took a gulp of cola to avert any necessity of the Heimlich maneuver. "Funny you should ask," I replied quietly, "after what just happened at the Bronco."

At last, Tristan turned far enough to face me. He

looked straight into my eyes. "You don't love this Bob bozo," he said bluntly. "If you did—"

At my panicked look, he stopped. For all I knew, the people on both sides of us were listening to every word we said.

Flo came back with his meat loaf, but he pulled some bills out of his Levi pocket and tossed them on the counter without even looking at her or the food. "Come on," he said. Then he grabbed my hand and dragged me out of the diner.

I dug in my heels when we hit the sidewalk. "I wanted to finish my dinner," I lied.

"I'll fix you an omelet at my place," he said. There was a big, shiny SUV parked at the curb. He opened the passenger door and practically tossed me inside.

"I am not going to your place," I told him. But I didn't try to escape, either. Not that I could have. He was blocking my way. "What we did at the Bronco was a lapse of judgment on my part. It's over, and I'd just as soon forget it."

"We need to talk."

"Why? We had sex, it was good, and now it's history. What is there to talk about?" Was this me talking? Miss Traditional Love and Marriage, hoping for a husband, two point two children and a dog?

Tristan stepped back, slammed the car door, stormed around to the other side, and got in. His right temple was throbbing.

"Maybe that's all it means to you," he bit out, jamming the rig into gear and screeching away from the curb, "but to me, it was more than sex. *Way* more."

My mouth dropped open. We were hovering on the brink of something I'd fantasized about, with and without Bob—or were we? Maybe I was out there alone, like always, and Tristan was leading me on. It didn't take a software wizard to work out that he wanted more sex.

"Like what?" I said.

He turned onto a side street, and brought the SUV to a stop in front of a two-story house I used to dream about living in, as a kid. It was white, with green shutters on the windows and a fenced, grassy yard. There were flower beds, too, all blooming.

And the sign swinging by the gate read TRISTAN MCCULLOUGH, ATTORNEY AT LAW.

"Never mind like what," he snapped, while I was still getting over the fact that he was a lawyer. "Things didn't end right between us, and I'm not letting this go till we talk it out!"

I was a beat or two behind. Last I'd heard, Tristan was planning to major in Agriculture and Animal Husbandry. Instead, he'd gone on to law school.

Sheesh. A lot can happen in ten years.

I'd been into survival. He'd been making something of his life.

The contrast hurt, big-time. I sat there in the passenger seat like a lump, staring at the sign.

Tristan shut off the engine, thrust out a sigh, and turned to face me squarely. His blue eyes were narrow, and shooting little golden sparks.

"Impressed?" he asked bitterly.

I flinched. "What?"

"Isn't that why you left Parable? Because you

thought I'd turn out to be a saddle bum, following the rodeo?"

"I thought," I said evenly, "that you would work on the ranch. Family tradition, and all that."

He sighed again, rubbed his chin with one hand. He'd showered and changed clothes between the Bronco and the diner, but he hadn't shaved. An attractive stubble was beginning to gleam on the lower part of his face.

"I keep getting this wrong," he muttered, sounding almost despondent. I wasn't sure if he was talking to me, or to himself.

I wanted to cry, for a variety of reasons, both simple and complicated, but I smiled instead. "It's okay, Tristan," I heard myself say. My voice came out sounding gentle, and a little raw. "We never did get along. Let's just agree to disagree, as they say, and get on with our lives."

"As I recall, we got along just fine," he said. I could tell he didn't want to smile back, but he did. "Until one of us said something, anyway."

I laughed, but my sinuses were clogged with tears I wouldn't shed until I was alone in Room 7, with a lake view. "Right."

"How's Josie?"

The question took me off guard. "Fine," I said.

"She was a kick."

"Still is," I said lightly. "She's into bikers these days."

Tristan brushed my cheek with the backs of his fingers, and I had the usual cattle-prod reaction, though I think I hid it pretty well. "Got to be better than Bob," he said.

I felt a flash of guilt. "Listen, about Bob—"

Tristan raised an eyebrow, waiting.

I couldn't do it. I just couldn't bring myself to admit that Bob was a vibrator. It was too pathetic. "Forget it," I said.

"Like hell," Tristan replied.

A stray thought broadsided me, out of nowhere. Tristan was a lawyer, and most likely the only one in Parable, given the size of the place. Which probably meant he was involved in the negotiations for the Bucking Bronco.

"Who's buying the tavern?" I asked.

It was his turn to look blank, though he recovered quickly. "A bunch of investors from California. Real estate types. They're putting in a restaurant and a marina, and building a golf course across the lake."

"Damn," I muttered.

"What do you care?" he asked.

"You're representing them, and my mother knew it."

"Well, yeah," Tristan said, in a puzzled, so-what tone of voice.

"She *knew* I would have done anything to avoid seeing you."

"Gee, thanks."

"Well, it's true. You broke my heart!"

"That's not the way I remember it," Tristan said.

I unfastened my seat belt, got out of the SUV, and started for the Lakeside Motel. By now, my phone would be charged. I intended to dial my mother's number and hit redial until she answered, if it took all night.

I had a few things to say to her. We were about to have a Dr. Phil moment, Mom and I.

Tristan caught up in a few strides. "Where are you going?"

"None of your damn business."

"I did *not* break your heart," he insisted.

"Whatever," I answered, because I knew it would piss him off, and if he got mad enough, he'd leave me alone.

He caught hold of my arm and turned me around to face him. "Damn it, Gayle, I'm not letting you walk away again. Not without an explanation."

"An explanation for what?" I demanded, wrenching free.

Tristan looked up and down the street. Except for one guy mowing his lawn, we might have been alone on an abandoned movie set. Pleasantville, USA. "You know damned well *what!*"

I did know, regrettably. I'd been holding the memories at bay ever since I got on the first plane in Phoenix—even before that, in fact—but now the dam broke and it all flooded back, in Technicolor and Dolby sound.

I'd gone to the post office, that bright summer morning a decade ago, to pick up the mail. There was a letter from the University of Montana—I'd been accepted, on a partial scholarship.

My feet didn't touch the ground all the way back to the Bronco.

Mom stood behind the bar, humming that Garth Brooks song about having friends in low places and polishing glasses. The place was empty, except for the two of us, since it was only about nine thirty, and the place didn't open until ten.

I waved the letter, almost incoherent with excitement. I was going to college!

Mom had looked up, smiling, when I banged through the door from the apartment, but as she caught on, the smile fell away. She went a little pale, under her perfect makeup, and as I handed her the letter, I noticed that her lower lip wobbled.

She read it. "You can't go," she said.

"But there's a scholarship—and I can work—"

Best of all, I'd be near Tristan. He'd been accepted weeks ago, courted by the coach of the rodeo team. For him, it was a full ride, in more ways than one.

Mom shook her head, and her eyes gleamed suspiciously. I'd never seen her cry before, so I discounted the possibility. "Even with the scholarship and a minimum-wage job, there wouldn't be enough money."

For years, she'd been telling me to study, so I could get into college. She'd even hinted that my dad, a man I didn't remember, would help out when the time came. Granted, he hadn't paid child support, but he usually sent a card at Christmas, with a twenty-dollar bill inside. Back then, that was my idea of fatherly devotion, I guess.

"Maybe Dad—"

"He's got another family, Gayle. Two kids in college."

"You never said—"

"He was married," Mom told me, for the first time. "I was the other woman. He made a lot of promises, but he wasn't interested in keeping them, and I doubt if that's changed. Twenty dollars at Christmas is one thing, and four years of college are another. It would be a tough thing to explain to the wife."

The disappointment ran deep, and it was more than not being able to go to college. "You led me to believe he was going to help," I whispered, stricken.

"I thought I could come up with the money, between then and now," Mom said. She looked worse than I felt, but I can't say I was sympathetic. "I wanted you to think he cared."

I turned on my heel and fled.

"Gayle!" Mom called after me. "Come back!"

But I didn't go back. I needed to find Tristan. Tell him what had happened. And I'd found him, all right. He was standing in front of the feed and grain, with his arms around Miss Wild West Montana of 1995.

I came back to the here and now with a soul-jarring crash, glaring up at Tristan, who was watching me curiously. He'd probably guessed that I'd just had an out-of-body experience. "You were making out with a rodeo queen!" I cried.

Tristan looked startled. "What the hell—?"

"The day I left Parable," I burst out. "I came looking for you, to tell you I couldn't go to college like we planned, and there you were, climbing all over some other girl in broad daylight!"

"*That's* why you left? Your letter said you met somebody else—"

"I lied, okay? I wanted to get back at you for cheating on me!"

"I *wasn't* cheating on you."

"I *saw* you with Miss Rodeo!"

"You *saw* me with an old friend. Cindy Robbins. We went to kindergarten together. The vet had just put her horse down, and she was pretty shook up."

It was just ridiculous enough to be true.

I *really* got mad then. Mad at myself, not Tristan. I'd been upset, that long ago day, because I'd just learned my dad was a married man and my mother was his lover, and because I wasn't going to college. I hadn't stopped to think, or to ask questions. Instead, I'd gone to the bank, withdrawn my paltry savings, dashed off a brief, vengeful letter to Tristan, explaining my passion for a made-up guy, and caught the four o'clock bus out of town, without so much as packing a suitcase, let alone saying good-bye to my mother.

Rash, yes. But I was only seventeen, and once I'd made my dramatic exit, my pride wouldn't let me go home.

"Hey," Tristan said, with a gruff tenderness that undid me even further. "You okay?"

"No," I replied. "I'm *not* okay."

"There wasn't any other guy, was there?"

I shook my head.

He grinned. I was falling apart, on the street, and he *grinned*.

"Bob's not a guy, either," I said.

"What?" Tristan did the thumb thing again, wiping away my tears.

"He's a vibrator."

Tristan threw back his head and laughed, then he pulled me close, right there in front of God and everybody. "Hallelujah," he whispered, and squeezed me even more tightly.

He walked me back to the Lakeside Motel, and I might have invited him in, if the minivan family hadn't been there, swimming again. They smiled and waved, like we were old friends.

"Later," Tristan said, and kissed me lightly.

With that, he walked away, leaving me standing there with my room key in one hand, feeling like a fool.

I finally let myself in, locked the door, and took a cold shower.

When I got out, I wrapped myself in a towel, turned on my cell phone, and dialed my mother's number. I was expecting the usual redial marathon, but she answered on the second ring. I heard a motorcycle engine purring in the background.

"Hello?"

"Mom? It's me. Gayle."

She chuckled. "I remember you," she said. "Are you in Parable?"

"Yes, and you set me up."

"Sure did," she replied, without a glimmer of guilt. "The meeting's tomorrow, at Tristan's office. Ten o'clock."

"Thanks for telling me."

"If you'd bothered to read the documents, you would have known from the first."

"It was a sneaky thing to do!"

"I'm a mother. I get to do sneaky things. It's in the contract."

I paused. My mother is no June Cleaver, but I love her.

"How are you?" I asked, after a couple of breaths. My voice had gone soft.

"Happy. How about you?"

"Beginning to think it's possible."

"That's progress," Mom said, and I knew she was smiling.

The Harley engine began to rev. Biker impatience.

"Gotta go," Mom told me. "I love you, kiddo."

"I love you, too," I said, but she had already disconnected.

I shut off the phone, curled up in a fetal position in the middle of the bed, and dropped off to sleep.

When I woke up, it was dark and somebody was rapping on my door.

I dragged myself up from a drugged slumber, rubbing my eyes. "Who is it?"

"Guess." Tristan's voice.

I hesitated, then padded over and opened the door. "What do you want?"

He grinned. "Hot, slick, sweaty sex—among other things." His eyes drifted over my towel-draped body, and something sparked in them. He let out a low whistle. "Lake's all ours," he drawled. "Wanna go skinny-dipping?"

My nipples hardened, and my skin went all goose-bumpy.

"Yep," I said.

He scooped me up, just like that, and headed for the lake, leaving my room door wide open. I scanned the windows of the motel as he carried me along the dock, glad to see they were all dark.

I'm all for hot, slick, sweaty sex, but I'm no exhibitionist.

The lake was black velvet, and splashed with starlight, but the moon was in hiding. Tristan set me on my feet, pulled off the towel, and admired me for a few moments before shedding his own clothes.

Then he took my hand, and we jumped into the water together.

When we both surfaced, we kissed. The whole lake rose to a simmer.

He led me deeper into the shadows, where the water was shallow, over smooth sand, and laid me down.

We kissed again, and Tristan parted my legs, let me feel his erection. This time, there was no condom. He slid down far enough to taste my breasts, slick with lake water, and I squirmed with anticipation.

I knew he'd make me wait, and I was right.

He turned onto his back, half on the beach and half in the water, and arranged me for the first of several mustache rides. Each time I came, I came harder, and he put a hand over my mouth so the whole world wouldn't know what we were doing.

Finally, weak with satisfaction, I went down on him in earnest.

He gave himself up to me, but at the edge of climax, he stopped me, hauled me back up onto his chest, rolled me under him. He entered me, but only partially, and the muscles in his shoulders and back quivered under my hands as he strained to hold himself in check.

I lifted my head and caught his right earlobe between my teeth, and he broke. The thrust was so deep and so powerful that it took my breath away.

I'd thought I was exhausted, spent, with nothing more to give, but he soon proved me wrong. Half a dozen strokes, each one harder than the last, and I was coming apart again. That was when he let himself go.

I don't know how long we laid there, with the

lake tide splashing over us, but we finally got out of the water, as new and naked as if we'd just been created. Tristan tossed me the towel, and pulled on his jeans. We slipped into my room without a word, made love again under a hot shower, and banged the headboard against the wall twice more before we both fell asleep.

When I woke up the next morning, he was gone, but there was a note on his pillow.

"My office. Ten o'clock sharp. After the meeting, expect another mustache ride."

Heat washed through me. The man certainly had style.

I skipped breakfast, too excited to eat, and at ten straight up, I was knocking on Tristan's office door. The buyers and other owners had already arrived, and were seated around the conference table. Tristan looked downright edible in his slick three-piece suit, and even though he was all business, his eyes promised sweet mayhem the moment we were alone.

The crotch of my panty hose felt damp.

The negotiations went smoothly, and when the deposit checks were passed around, I glanced down and noticed my own name on the pay line, instead of Mom's.

"There's been a mistake," I told Tristan, in a baffled whisper.

"No mistake," he whispered back. "Josie signed the whole shooting match over to you."

I stared at him in disbelief.

The meeting concluded amiably, and in good time. Everybody shook hands and left. Everybody but Tristan and me, that is.

Tristan loosened his tie.

I quivered in some very vulnerable places.

"Ever made love on a conference table?" he asked. He locked the door and pulled the shades.

"Not recently," I admitted.

"Not even with Bob?"

I laughed. "Not even with Bob."

Tristan took the check out of my hand, damp from my clutching it, and drew me close. He felt so strong, and so warm. "If you plan on having your way with me," he said, "you're going to have to make a concession first."

"What kind of concession?"

"Agree to stay in Parable."

I loosened his tie further, undid the top button of his shirt. "What's in it for me?" I teased. I thought I knew what his answer would be—after all, it was burning against my abdomen, practically scorching through our clothes—but he surprised me.

"A wedding ring," he said.

I tried to step back, but he pulled me close again.

"It seems a little soon—" I protested, but my heart felt like it was trying to beat its way out from behind my Wonder bra.

"I've been waiting ten years," he answered. "I don't think it's all that soon." He caught my face in his hands. "I loved you then, I love you now, and I've loved you every day in between. The engagement can be as long or as short as you want, but I'm not letting you go."

My vision blurred. My throat was so constricted that I had to squeeze out my "Yes."

"Yes, you'll marry me?"

I nodded. The words still felt like a major risk, but they were true, so I said them. "I love you, Tristan."

He gave me a leisurely, knee-melting kiss. "Time we celebrated," he said.

I took the lead. Forget foreplay. I wanted him inside me.

I unfastened his belt and opened his pants and took his shaft, already hot and hard, in my hand. And suddenly, I laughed.

Tristan blinked. Laughter and penises don't mix, I guess.

"I was just thinking of Bob," I explained.

He groaned as I began to work him with long, slow strokes. "Great," he growled. "I've got a hard-on like a concrete post, and you're comparing me to a vibrator."

I teased him a little more, making a circle with the pad of my thumb. "Ummm," I said, easing him into one of the fancy leather chairs surrounding the conference table and kneeling between his legs.

"Oh, God," he rasped.

"Payback time," I said.

He moaned my name.

I got down to business, so to speak.

Tristan took it as long as he dared, then pulled me astraddle of his lap, hiked up my skirt, ripped my panty hose apart, and slammed into me. I was coming before the second thrust.

That's the thing about a flesh-and-blood man.

They never need batteries.

CAPTIVATED

Jill Shalvis

Chapter One

She'd really screwed up this time, even more so than usual, and that was saying something. Ella Scott shifted to swipe the hair out of her eyes, but her right wrist caught on the handcuff, rattling the steel, jerking on the tile towel rod that she was cuffed to. With a sigh, she used her left hand, then lifted her head and surveyed the situation.

Having worked the past straight month without a day off, she'd come to her Baja cottage for a desperately needed weekend to herself. But thanks to her surprise goons, she now stood between the shower and the toilet, handcuffed at chest level to the towel rack, wearing only the towel she'd managed to wrap around herself one-handed, with no key to get free, nothing at all within reach that could help her.

Such was the life of the incurably curious. She'd actually managed to parlay that lifelong curiosity into a career, not as a criminal, as her mother had feared, but as an insurance investigator. Except that now, for the umpteenth time, she'd dipped her nosy nose in where it hadn't been welcome, and here she stood in her least favorite position—that being completely helpless.

She'd been cautioned. Threatened, actually. Told time and time again that if she kept at this case, she wouldn't like the consequences. Having been warned too many times to remember by other, more unsavory types before, she hadn't given it a single thought.

Seems maybe she'd been a little premature in that.

But damn, it should have been so easy, a few days off. Some R and R. She'd arrived via plane, then rental car, and had taken a nice swim in the warm Mexican Pacific waves until her muscles quivered before hopping into the shower.

After that she'd planned to lie on the deck and watch the sun set over the ocean and contemplate why, when she'd finally found a job she enjoyed, it didn't satisfy her the way she'd thought it would.

But it'd all been interrupted by two beefy morons who'd hauled her naked and slippery and screaming out of the shower. Luckily for her, they hadn't been interested in her body, hadn't been interested in anything other than handcuffing her to the shower rod, still dripping wet. And even then, they'd only cuffed the one hand, promising her to send someone in a few days to free her.

And that's when she'd known. They weren't rapists or murderers, but *thieves*. They'd been from the yacht company she'd been investigating for suspicious loss of property. Two separate multimillion-dollar boats had been sunk in the past sixteen months. Her company had found nothing suspicious with the first downed ship, and the insurance company had been forced to pay out. Just two weeks ago, in fact.

Then the second boat had gone down for the count in Santa Barbara, and now Ella was closing in on why. Bad drug deals, and a greedy yacht owner wanting it all. She'd been watching their third yacht, the *Valeska*, all week, but had been unable to get aboard because there'd been activity on it.

Now she was due to present her suspicions to the D.A.'s office, soon as she made one more trip to Santa Barbara, where she was going to get on the *Valeska* come hell or high water.

Clearly, the suspects didn't want her to get to the D.A.'s office, at least not before they skipped town with the money from the insurance from the first boat and any physical evidence. Chances were that had already happened, and they were long gone.

Ella shook her head. She should have taken that job at Target out of college like her mother had wanted. Sure, she looked awful in red, but she'd be willing to bet no one would bother to break and enter her place because of *that* job, or handcuff her naked to her own towel rack.

Unless she wanted them to.

A slight breeze blew in the open window, breaking the brutal summer heat as the sun sank. Oh, God, the sun was sinking, and the severity of her situation sank in. It was Saturday evening. Next week was a long time away. God knew she wouldn't starve, not with the five extra pounds she'd been carrying around since puberty—okay, *ten*, damn it. Still, the amount of time looming ahead felt long, and never having been big on self-discipline, she was already hungry.

She could reach the shower and the toilet. The sink was across from her, a leg's length away. Above it was the mirror that assured her she was as frightening-looking as she'd imagined, her hair air-dried and a complete frizz bomb, her face not wearing a lick of makeup. *Ack*. She decided not to look at herself again.

Beneath the toilet was a cabinet which, if she stretched, she could just toe open. A box of tampons, two extra rolls of toilet paper, and a tube of toothpaste. Gee, *yum*.

She looked out the window. The cottage was isolated, down a long, sinuous stretch of highway surrounded by bush-lined high desert hills, punctuated by dense groves of date palms and citrus trees and little else.

The sun sank away, the daylight faded, and Ella felt anxiety pit in her stomach. But even stretching her leg out to bionic contortions, she couldn't reach the light switch.

And the dark came.

She'd spent a good amount of her childhood chasing after her three older brothers, and feeling invincible because of them. She'd wear her blankie as a cape and pretend she was a superhero who could fly through wind and sleet and snow, who could do anything.

She didn't feel so invincible now.

Then came a noise. The front door closing. *When had it opened?* Heart in her throat, she froze. Or rather her body froze. Her towel did not. It slipped yet again. She grabbed it with her left hand and hastily tucked the corner back between her breasts, her heart tattooing a crazy beat against her ribs.

No other sound, but she could *feel* someone on the other side of the door.

Listening.

Breathing.

Oh, God. She couldn't scream, couldn't even draw air into her lungs.

The handle on the bathroom door began to turn.

Ella stared at it, her life flashing before her eyes. She hadn't watered her plants. She hadn't tried skydiving. She hadn't reconciled her checking account!

The door creaked open.

She stuffed her uncuffed hand against her mouth to hold back her panicked whimper at what was about to happen to her. What would they tell her family? No one had even known she was coming here, not her parents, her brothers, not even—

"Ella?"

At that low, husky, almost unbearably familiar voice, she squinted into the shadows of the opened door, thinking, *Oh, no.* No, no, no, no, no.

But indeed, the form was tall, wide in the shoulders, narrow in the hip, the body built like the long-distance swimmer he used to be. "*James?*"

The shadow stepped into the bathroom and came to an abrupt halt. Not a shadow at all but the one man she hadn't wanted to see her like this, the one man she hadn't wanted to see, period.

Her mouthwateringly sexy, break-her-heart-and-stomp-on-it husband.

Make that almost ex-husband.

Chapter Two

Ella let out the pent-up breath she'd been holding and tried to look normal. As if being handcuffed in nothing but a slipping towel was anywhere close. But she couldn't pull it off, so she sucked in a breath and went for calm, cool, and collected, or at least the appearance of it.

And reminded herself that as far as the worst-case scenario went, this wasn't it. Close, but not quite. After all, she hadn't been raped, tortured, or killed before the goons had left her, right? She was still breathing, which was a good thing, so she kept that in front of her.

James let out a sound that managed to perfectly convey his surprise and unhappiness at the sight of her.

The fading light fell over him favorably, but *any* light fell over the man favorably. Then he flipped on the switch and the fluorescent bulbs had her blinking like an owl. "Hi," she said.

He just looked at her. His nearly black hair was

cut short as always, but no matter the length, it had a mind of its own. His melt-me chocolate eyes could reveal everything in his heart, or nothing at all, depending on his mood. They were pretty stingy at the moment. He had his cop face on, allowing only his tough competence to show as he moved in closer to prop up the wall with a shoulder, his arms crossed casually over his chest. A deceptively relaxed pose. "I'd appreciate it if you wouldn't play sexual games with your boyfriend on my weekend for the house," was all he said.

She registered the urge to knock her head against the wall. He hadn't actually yet signed the divorce papers she'd sent him, which technically made them only separated, but that *he'd* been the one who'd left still rankled. And that it had been her job to drive him away made explaining her current problem a tad bit difficult, because she really hated when he was right. "I don't have a boyfriend."

He lifted a disbelieving brow but relaxed. It was a marginal lessening of the tension in his shoulders that no one else would have noticed, but she'd known him for a very long time and could read his body like a book.

"If there's no boyfriend, what's this?" He gestured with a jerk of his chin to the way she was cuffed to the rack. "An early Christmas present?"

"Ha, ha," she said, and jangled the cuff. "A little help?"

He took his gaze on a slow roll up her body, starting at her bare feet, past her legs, which she'd thankfully shaved—*No.* Just because he'd been the first, *and the last*, man to drive her to the edge of sanity with a debilitating combination of love and lust and like and more lust, she did *not* care if her legs were shaved for him. Damn, but he could still get to her like no one else, which really topped the cake.

His gaze continued on its tour, landing on her breasts, which were spilling over the edge of the slipping towel, then her throat, and finally her face, his own impassive.

She couldn't blame him there. She'd taken that single, horrified glance in the mirror. She knew her long, curly, blond hair had long ago rioted, resembling an explosion in a mattress factory. She knew she looked like a ghost without blush and lip color. She was just surprised he hadn't gone running for the hills.

But then again, nothing scared James. He stood there in black jeans, black athletic shoes, black T-shirt well fitted to that mouthwatering body, looking like sin personified.

"What the hell are you doing here, Ella?"

Good question, she thought, and since she had no intention of telling him the truth, that she was a complete idiot, she racked her brain for a good excuse. "*Me?* Just . . . hanging." She added a grin, and hoped he bought it.

But he'd never bought the bullshit she'd been able to feed just about anyone else. He stepped closer, a mixed blessing for her. She felt a huge relief, because though he was a lot of things, including a rat bastard, he was incapable of leaving her here trapped and helpless. Or so she hoped.

And then there was her panic, because now she could see him up close and personal: the dark day's growth on his jaw, the way his eyes were like two fathomless pools she could drown in, his tight jaw . . . and then there was his scent, which made her want to press her nose to his throat and inhale. Pathetic.

Once upon a time he'd been everything to her, her greatest fantasy, her most amazing lover, her best friend, and she missed him, mourned him like a missing limb, and if he looked close enough he'd know it. Not wanting that to happen, she dropped her head down, but he only stepped even closer, and her forehead brushed his chest. He was warm and hard with strength, and beneath the shirt his heart beat steady. The waistband of his jeans were loose, low on his washboard abs. She had good reason to know his body looked just as perfect without the clothes, and that he knew exactly what to do with it to drive her insane with wanting.

Why did he have to be so damned perfect?

Why couldn't he have love handles? Or bad breath? Okay, maybe not love handles or bad breath, but it'd be nice if *he* could screw up once in a while instead of it always being her.

"Ella."

Right. He wanted answers. "It's complicated," she said demurely.

"Uh-huh." He tipped up her chin. "Keep going."

Her towel slipped another half inch. Before she could pull it back up, her left hand was in James's, held above her head against the wall in a gentle but inexorable grip. "Look at me, Ella."

She stared at his Adam's apple and hoped the towel was still covering her nipples. His thighs bumped her bare ones and said nipples hardened with hope because they knew exactly how good he could be to them. "Why?"

"Because we both know you can't look me straight in the eyes when you're lying, Super Girl."

A nickname she'd acquired from her various escapades, usually nearly fatal. He kept his other hand on her jaw, holding her head, leaving her stretched and bound like an offering. "M-maybe I really am an early Christmas present."

He stared at her, his eyes no longer the flat, cool cop's eyes. Now they were filled with frustration, temper, and a good amount of the heat and love that had always caught her breath. "It's only June."

"Merry Half Christmas." But he didn't cave, he never caved. "Okay, fine," she said, grumbling. "So I ran into a little problem with a case."

"Surprise, surprise. What was the problem?"

"I found proof that a multimillion-dollar yacht we'd insured and lost this year was purposely destroyed. It didn't click until their second, and more expensive, yacht was destroyed last week."

"Drug runners?"

She nodded. "A few deals in a row went bad. They were hurting for money. Now we think they sank the boats for the insurance money."

"And?"

"And I'm working on getting proof."

His eyes narrowed. "Let me guess. Your suspects are planning to hightail it out of town with the cash from the first boat, and you got in their way."

She bit her lip.

"Jesus Christ, El." Temper dropped, replaced by instant concern as his hands slid down to her arms. "Did they hurt you?"

"No."

His expression was no longer a cool cop's, but fierce and terrified. "Did they—"

"Nothing. They did nothing but cuff me." And okay, maybe they'd made a joke about her being a true blonde. "I'm fine."

He let out a low breath, fighting for control as the muscles bunched in his jaw.

She knew it was more than this particular situation. Her job was the basis of any fight they'd ever had—her putting herself in danger, sometimes stupidly. Him hating it.

He ran a finger over the cuffs on her wrist. "Hell of a mess you've got yourself into."

"Do you have a key or something?"

"Or something," he murmured, and looked her over again, slowly. "You sure do look like my idea of Christmas, all naked and . . ." He ran a callused finger over the edge of her towel, his knuckles brushing over the plumped-up curves of her breasts. "Restrained." His melting eyes met hers and her knees nearly buckled at the memories his words caused.

It'd been their first Christmas together, and she'd bought him two new silk ties, which he'd used not around his neck but for her wrists in his bed. He'd had his merry way with her, and then in return had let her bind him.

The memories made her ache. "Can you just set me free?"

Another slow pass of his finger over the edge of the slipping towel, and though she didn't lower her gaze and look, he was helping the thing fall, damn him. "*James*."

"Yeah, I could set you free."

Relief rushed through her. Short-lived, as it turned out.

"Soon as you tell me one thing." His slow exhale fanned the hair at her temple, warming her ear, causing a delicious set of goose bumps to raise over her skin.

Her eyes wanted to drift shut. In their marriage, one thing that had never wavered was this . . . this hunger, this unquenchable need.

Truth was, she missed his arms around her at night; she missed his big, solid presence in their bed. He had a way of making her forget everything but what he could make her feel, and what he made her feel was like a walking orgasm. The man oozed sex appeal, and that hadn't changed. "Um . . . what do you want me to tell you?"

He ran his hand up her free arm, once again lifting hers over her head, entwining their fingers. His thighs bumped hers, and it took every ounce of self-control she had—which wasn't much on a good day—not to rub against him like a cat.

"Tell me that you really don't want to be married anymore," he murmured, and curved his fingers into hers now so that they were holding hands rather than him restraining her. "Tell me you really want me to sign those divorce papers you had sent to my work."

That was so far from what she expected, she blinked. "You were the one who left me."

"Mmm," he said noncommittally, tracing the pads of his rough fingers over her skin. Just that small touch and her world spun. Her free hand automatically went to his arm for stability, even though she couldn't have fallen if she'd wanted to. Her fingers dug his ropey, satiny shoulders. She was close enough to see into his dark, dark eyes, and what she saw there made her go still and quivery at the same time.

"El."

Just that, just her name on his lips, and everything faded away except the excitement that always shimmered between them no matter what they were dealing with. He tipped her face up and their mouths were only a breath apart. With a soft sigh, she leaned into him. A sound escaped him, one of frustration, of need, and then he hauled her close, wrapping his arms tight to her body. "This is crazy," he muttered, and rubbed his jaw to hers. "Stupid crazy."

She nodded. She knew it, knew also if he dipped his head a fraction of an inch and kissed her, it'd be a mistake. It'd taken her this whole time to even begin to get over him, she couldn't do it again, she just couldn't—

"Damn," he whispered, and then his mouth touched the very corner of hers.

She let out a helpless little murmur and strained even closer, wanting more, so much more, but he pulled back. Stared at her as the corner of her towel slipped entirely free from between her breasts.

The only thing holding it in place was James's body, and they both knew it. "Uncuff me," she whispered.

"Tell me that you don't want me anymore," he whispered back.

Damn it. If she said the words, they'd be a lie, and he'd know that, too. He always knew. But here she was, literally trapped, and a complete wreck from just one tiny kiss, ready to toss all pride to the wind and beg him for whatever scrap he had left to give her.

Six months ago, he'd told her all bets were off, that he couldn't love her as wildly and fully as he did and watch her destroy herself with the job. In her stubbornness, all she'd heard was the ultimatum, him or her dangerous job, and she'd reacted. Badly.

He'd left their L.A. condo and she'd hit rock bottom, or so she'd thought.

But she'd been wrong. *Today* was rock bottom. Being forced to admit still wanting him . . . it was too much. "I don't—" But the lie caught on her tongue.

"Tell me," he insisted in a rough whisper, his length bumping hers.

She had to close her eyes in an attempt to deny what he could make her feel with just that barely there touch of his hot, tough bod.

"Tell me."

God, it'd be so easy to do just that, but then they'd be back at square one, with her loving him ridiculously, and him wanting her to be someone she wasn't.

No.

She was stronger than this, and to prove it, she lifted her chin, staring at a spot just over his shoulder. "I don't want to be married anymore."

He studied her for a long beat, his gaze burning a hole in her heart.

Not for the first time, either . . .

"That's not what I asked you," he finally said.

"I want you to sign those papers at your office, James."

"And what about me, Ella?" He nudged even closer, slipping a muscled thigh between hers.

She nearly melted into a pool of longing on the floor.

"You don't want me?" he asked softly, silkily.

She closed her eyes, gathered her strength, then opened them again. *I don't want you*, she tried to say, but he shifted again, that thigh moving between hers, rubbing against her, and all that came out was a whimper.

Chapter Three

James waited for Ella's answer with an expectation that he didn't want to feel. He hadn't come to Baja hoping for anything but a few days without expectation, grief, or a page from the beeper he'd left at home. He certainly hadn't expected his estranged wife.

Who stood before him like a tempting, forbidden treat with her long, wild, blond curls playing peek-a-boo with her torso and shoulders, her clear blue eyes full of the wanting she wouldn't admit to, and then there was her mouth. God, that mouth, with the full, pouty lips that could give a grown man a wet dream, damp from her own nervous tongue.

His first response had been a resounding, *Yeah, baby.*

But then they'd gotten to the part of her story where he realized she hadn't come here for him at all. It'd been her work, *again*, the same work that had split them up. Thanks to the kind of characters she investigated—the scum of the earth, basically— she'd been manhandled into this helpless, compromising position, and that both terrified and infuriated him because one day she was going to get herself killed.

And he'd have to bury her.

His heart clenched good and hard over that. When they'd been together, she'd had him popping Tums like candy, and he couldn't handle it. Now, with a few months of distance beneath his belt, he figured he deserved a little revenge for his heart, which she'd broken.

Make that decimated.

Oh yeah, definitely he had a little payback coming his way, and he was nothing if not a man who made the best of his time. Well aware that the only thing protecting her modesty was his chest against hers, he shifted back an inch.

Her towel hit the floor.

"*James.*"

Probably not his smartest idea, letting the towel fall, because with her standing there wearing exactly nothing, virtually his captive, his every muscle shifted to full alert status.

She tried to turn away, which was not easy restrained as she was. She bumped into his fully clothed body, things shimmying and shaking, mostly her glorious breasts. She had tan lines, which dissolved his bones right then and there. Her breasts gleamed pale and beautiful, and between her legs she'd waxed or shaved, or whatever it was a woman did to drive men right out of their minds.

She let out an infuriated sound and fought with the cuffs. It was sick of him, he knew, but he was getting off on this.

"This is ridiculous," she spat out.

No, what was ridiculous was what the feel of her bare ass to the front of his crotch was doing to him. He spun her back around to face him. "Then you should be able to say the words. And when you do, I'll uncuff you and we'll go on our merry way. Our merry *single* way."

She went very still. "Is that what you want?"

Christ, no. "Just say it."

She lifted her free hand, presumably to cover some part of herself or another, or maybe to smack him, and he caught it, holding it out to her side. "Say it."

"*Fine.* I don't want y—" As before, the words tripped on her tongue and she closed her eyes.

He realized he'd been holding his breath, but something surged through him now. It felt like triumph, but also a bone-quivering relief.

His gut *had* told him the truth. She still wanted him. *Damn, Ella.* He didn't know whether to kiss them both stupid or shake the hell out of her and demand to know why she'd sent those divorce papers. "Finish it."

She licked her lips. "I . . ."

Looking into her huge baby blues, he momentarily couldn't see the body he wanted to drop to his knees and worship but that didn't matter. Her dazzling, lush curves had imprinted themselves on his brain years ago. Had he thought he was merely exacting a little revenge? Like hell. More like sinking his own ship here. But definitely, he liked her tied up. Liked it that she couldn't run, couldn't go off to her dangerous job, couldn't do anything but face him.

Which she hadn't had to do in too damn long.

"Okay, but you'd better listen," she warned him. "Because I'm only going to say this once." She stared at a spot just over his shoulder. "I. Don't. Want. You. Anymore." She shot him a shaky smile. "*There.*"

"Uh-huh." She was gorgeous and smart and funny, and everything he'd once upon a time wanted, but she was a horrible liar. And she *was* lying, he had no doubt, a particularly fascinating fact.

Also fascinating, against him her body was screaming the opposite. Her heart raced, her nipples bore two hard points into his chest, while her skin radiated a heat that had nothing to do with the warm evening. It caused a surge of excitement through his own body that he hadn't felt since . . . since he'd been with her.

"I said it," she whispered into his silence, lifting her head slowly, which had her out-of-control hair tickling his chin and throat in agonizing little butterfly kisses. "So now you have to undo me." Her nose just barely glanced along his throat, and all of it combined, slamming home memories of the times they'd been together, when he'd practically inhaled her every night.

They'd never been able to get enough of each other. "You lied."

"Did not," she said. Her eyes were still wide, dilated nearly black. Her breathing was shallow, and he knew damn well that wasn't fear.

"I have proof," he said, and slid his fingers along

her jaw until they sank into her hair. Her eyes drifted shut again, slowly. She'd always loved when he'd played with her hair.

"Don't," she whispered.

"You can't catch your breath." He dipped his mouth to the spot beneath her ear, which he knew was incredibly sensitive to his touch.

She shivered.

Now *he* was the one cheating and he didn't care. He danced his other hand down her free arm, then squeezed her hip before skimming up the bare skin along her ribs. He spread his fingers wide, so they rested just beneath her breast as he let his gaze once again fall over her. "God, El." His entire body clenched, hard and throbbing. "How could you have forgotten what it's like between us?"

She drew her bottom lip between her teeth, and he wanted to do the same. He wanted to gobble her up whole. "Your nipples are hard." He glided his thumb along her highest rib, just barely brushing the curve of her breast.

"Maybe I'm cold," she said in that same shuddery voice that told him she was having as much trouble controlling herself as he was.

"It's ninety degrees in here." He was sweating. She had a fine sheen to her skin, as well. He wanted to lap it up. Wanted to lap *her* up. His thumb slid over her nipple, catching on the very tip.

Both of them caught their breath.

Her head fell back and thunked against the wall. He leaned in, mouth open, to nibble at her throat, but that was instinctive, that was affection and heat, and he stopped a breath away because this wasn't supposed to be about any of that. Damn, he'd nearly forgotten. He was trying to prove a point here. "Maybe you are cold," he allowed with some disbelief. "But there's one reaction you always give me that has nothing to do with being chilled." With that, he glided his fingers down her belly, her muscles quivering at his touch.

"Don't even think about it," she whispered.

"Oh, I'm thinking about it, Super Girl."

"James," she choked out as he stroked a finger over her mound, then into her petal-soft folds.

"You're wet." His legs nearly buckled at the feel of her. "Is this for me, Ella?"

Letting out a half whimper, half sob, her free hand fisted in his shirt. Definitely not a sound of distress, he noted, but of arousal, and he groaned as he sank into that creamy heat.

She squeezed her eyes shut. "So I lied. So I want you. It's only because I haven't had sex in too long and I ran out of batteries, so don't flatter yourself."

His gaze met hers as his thumb found her clit and lightly stroked.

Her eyes went opaque. Her fingers dug further into his chest, pulling out more than a few hairs, which made him wince, but he kept up the torment. It was the least of what she deserved.

"I'm going to go off like a rocket," she gasped.

Yeah. And he wanted to see it, feel it. Cause it. Wanted to remind her exactly what she was missing out on. Pride and brainless ego on his part? Maybe. He didn't care. He kept stroking her.

"James." A few more chest hairs were lost. "*Stop.*"

Damn, the magic word. He stopped but left his hands on her.

She dropped her head to his chest and gulped

for air. "I told you," she said tightly, head still down on his chest. "I told you what you wanted to hear. Now please, James, get me free."

He didn't want to, but there was something in her voice that stopped him cold, and he was deathly afraid it was tears. "Okay," he said quietly, and stroked a hand over her long, wild hair. She was trembling, and his heart wrenched. Christ, he was an ass. "Okay," he murmured again softly. "I'll free you." He just wished she meant only the handcuffs, and not their marriage.

Or that he'd been the one bound, because one thing was damn sure, he didn't want to be free.

Chapter Four

Ella turned from James and set her hot face to the wall. She felt him move away, even out of the room, and she told herself she didn't care.

Then, though he didn't make a sound, she knew he was back. She didn't look at him.

Couldn't.

She still wanted him. She'd never stopped wanting him.

Neither was a crime, but thanks to his torturing of her for his own amusement, she had so many emotions battering her, she didn't know which one to start with. Furious, aroused, and embarrassingly close to tears for reasons she didn't understand, she shifted to hug herself.

Only to discover she could use both arms.

James had released her.

Still facing the wall, she rubbed her wrist, gave herself a bolstering pep talk along the lines of, *You can do this, you can face him and not let him see how much he's destroyed you,* and slowly turned back.

She was alone.

Bending, she grabbed the towel and wrapped it around her torso. With her armor back in place, she stared at herself in the mirror. Yikes. She needed an entire tube of no-frizz and an hour with her makeup bag.

But first things first. She stepped out of the bathroom. The cottage was cozy but small. Single bedroom, living room, and kitchen open to each other. It'd come casually painted in beachy, muted colors of light blue and earth tones, and the little bit of furniture they'd put in matched. They'd bought the place as a fantasy escape, but their harsh reality had been that they'd rarely had the time to come.

Or Ella hadn't. In the past two years her job had cut into her personal time considerably, something else James had hated.

But for the first time she'd had a career, not just a job, and Ella had loved feeling needed.

With perfect twenty-twenty hindsight, she could admit she'd given her job more than she'd given her marriage, and that shamed her to the core.

But James had never needed her. He'd loved her, passionately, of that she had no doubt, but he'd never needed her. Not like she'd needed him.

Still, their relationship had deserved more. James had deserved more.

In one sweeping glance she could tell she was entirely alone. The west-facing wall was all windows, open to the ocean. The sun had gone down, leaving the sky flaming in purples and blues, and there, at the water's edge, stood the shadow of a man.

James.

As she watched, he stripped out of his shirt and

pants in economical movements, his tanned, sleek, hard flesh nothing but a blur in the night as he lifted his arms and dove into an oncoming wave. She lost sight of him after that.

It wasn't the first time. She'd lost sight of him when he'd walked his damn fine ass out of their house six months ago, which had nearly killed her.

But thoughts like that one only made her sad, and she didn't have time for sad. She needed to get home. Needed to get back home to Los Angeles, and then up to Santa Barbara to get onto the *Valeska*.

And yet she stood staring out at the ocean, at the occasional flash of James, swimming as if the devil himself was on his heels. It used to be she'd go to him . . .

But his problems were no longer hers. *He* was no longer hers, and to prove it she turned away to grab her duffel, still on the couch. She'd grab some clothes, get dressed, and go.

Any minute now.

With a sigh, she dropped her towel and grabbed the bikini off the floor, the one she'd stripped out of a couple of hours ago, before hopping into her fated shower. She slipped back into the wet scrap of material thinking the modesty was silly, considering James had just seen her stretched out and captive for his perusal, but she figured it might put them on more even ground.

Even ground was good, and she was a master of finding it. After living with well-meaning but hard-to-please parents all her life, then a string of boyfriends who'd lasted for less time than her string of meaningless jobs, she'd learned what she wanted.

And that was to be appreciated for being who she was. Whoever *that* woman turned out to be. She'd thought James had been the man to do it, but she'd learned things didn't always turn out how she wanted. That was life.

She stepped outside into the warm night. There were no city lights, no highway noises, nothing marring the still, humid air but the sound of the waves pounding the shore and the small sliver of the moon lighting her way. She walked the sand until the water lapped at her toes. Every few seconds or so, as the waves shifted and moved, she could still see James bodysurfing, working his long, lean muscles for all he was worth, swimming out some nameless demon that she had a feeling might have a name after all.

Hers.

He took a four-foot swell, diving into the arc of water with skill and precision. He'd always swum like a fish, and standing there watching him, Ella was hit with a wave of her own, filled not with water but yearning and memories that made her want to sink to her knees and pound the sand in frustration.

She'd missed him, so damn much.

They'd met three years ago when she'd still been just a clerk at the insurance company. Big surprise, she'd butted into a case that had gone bad, and had been mugged coming out of her parking garage late one night.

James had been the responding officer.

And the rest was a sweet, sexy, shivery, heavenly blur as he'd insinuated himself into her life until she couldn't remember what she'd done without him.

She'd been forced to remember that very thing these past six months.

The water was nearly the same temperature as the air, and as she waded out, the black, swirling depths and the dark night sky above her blended into one, like a comforting blanket. When she could no longer touch the bottom, she began to swim.

As if sensing her coming, James turned. She couldn't see his features but felt his eyes search hers as he waited for her. "Still here?" he asked.

"I wanted to talk to you before I left."

"Why?"

Why? She blinked at that, but he took the next swell, giving her time to think about her answer. When he came close again, tossing back his wet hair, his face and shoulders gleaming in the moon's reflection, she tried a smile. "Maybe to thank you?"

Treading water, Ella remembered in vivid Technicolor how they used to thank each other for things. *With sexual favors.* She'd always wanted the same one, his talented mouth on her body. He, however, had been forever inventive with his own owed favors, and she'd never known what to expect—maybe to find herself bent over the arm of the couch for him to take her from behind, or on her knees before him . . . and then there'd been the time he'd requested a raunchy striptease on their brand-new kitchen table, culminating in dinner, which, in fact, had turned out to be her.

"You'd have been fine if I hadn't shown up," he

said now, his eyes dark and glimmering with the same memories. If that was so, she marveled at his ability to keep his cool, because even in the water, she was beginning to sweat.

"Yeah, maybe." She managed to smile at him. "But I'm glad I didn't have to find out."

He treaded water effortlessly beside her, saying nothing. His manner bespoke quiet, rock-solid confidence. It always had.

She, however, had to work at feeling confident on the best of days. "I know I was unwise today," she admitted, getting a little breathless from keeping herself afloat. "Letting my guard down like I did."

"Wasn't the first time," he said, not at all breathless.

"No, it wasn't. But at least I didn't get myself mugged in the parking lot, and then splashed across the human interest section of the paper."

One black eyebrow shot up. "Or locked in the meat freezer of a packing plant, and then on the *front* page."

That had been last year, and after his fury had worn off, he'd had the nerve to laugh at her. "Or locked in a trunk," she said softly.

Another episode, from eight months back, and he let out a sound that might have been frustration or dark humor as he shook his head. "Good thing you had your Nextel on you that time."

"It's a good thing I had *you* on the other end of my Nextel," she corrected. "Come on, admit it, some of my more colorful cases might have brought me trouble and grief, but you eventually always found the humor in the situation. You think I'm cute."

He shot her a baleful look and caught another wave.

She watched him vanish beneath the black, swirling water, then caught sight of his strong, lean body riding the crest. When he came back, she reached out for him, setting her hand on his rock-solid shoulder to hold herself up.

"Tired?" he asked.

"Nah. Just wanted to make sure you weren't too cold."

He snorted and slid his hands to her hips, still treading without effort, now supporting both of them. "Still stubborn, I see."

"And you still have to be right all the time."

"Yeah." He toyed with the bathing suit string low on her hips. He'd always loved this particular suit, and as he tangled his fingers in the ties on either side, her brain tangled with memories of what exactly those fingers could and had done to her. "I'm thinking of switching departments," she heard herself say. "Back to investigating worker's comp cases instead of fraud."

Once again she felt his assessing stare, though he said nothing as he kept running his fingers in and around and under the string on her hips in a way that seriously hampered her thinking ability.

"Did you hear me?" Her breath was soughing in and out of her lungs now, and since he was holding her, it wasn't from the effort of remaining above water.

"I heard you." He towed her closer to shore so she could stand. "Before you drown. So did your own personal insurance company beg you to change jobs, or what?"

That sounded like amusement in his voice now, and she set her jaw in annoyance. "I just thought you'd like to know."

"What you do for a living is no longer my concern, as proven by the papers you sent to me."

She'd sent the divorce papers out of hurt, not that she'd tell him so. "I figured you might be in a hurry to get rid of me."

"Why would you figure that?"

"Because your brother told me you were dating again." Just the thought left her cold. Terrified. "He said you needed a date for some charity event."

He sighed. "Cooper has a big mouth."

"No, he doesn't. He's protecting you. And anyway, what you do is your own concern now, right?" she asked, tossing his words back at him.

"Ella—"

"It's okay, James." She shrugged in the water, the motion bringing her breasts in direct contact with his broad, wet chest. Because that hit her with a jolt like an electric shock, she began to turn away, wanting to hide the madness that overtook her whenever she thought about him touching someone else, kissing someone else, loving someone else.

It haunted her. He was a sexual man, demanding, earthy, rawly sensual, and she couldn't imagine he'd really gone six months without—

"Oh no, you don't." Grabbing her arms in his big hands, he whipped her around in the water, frustration written all over his face. "I hate this," he ground out. "Hate the doubts, the anger, the fear—"

"James—"

"You're standing there picturing me with someone else. I know it because I'm doing the same thing and it's killing me. Killing me, Ella."

"I haven't—"

"I haven't, either, damn it. God, I hate this, hate all of it, especially the missing you." He gave her a little shake, then hauled her up against him. "So you know what? The hell with that part, at least."

And he covered her mouth with his.

She had exactly one coherent thought: *Yum.* Then her every brain cell checked out, replaced by pleasure cells, of which he hit them all.

It amazed her. One second they were standing there in the ocean, the water pummeling them, staring at each other with all the pent-up emotion and exhilaration that was never far from the surface with them, and the next his mouth opened on hers, making her whimper with a carnal need so powerful it shook her to the core, taking away all rhyme and reason.

Then he pulled back and stared at her, water dripping into his face, eyes dark and hot.

Her own heart was drumming so hard and heavy she could hear nothing but the blood roaring through her ears.

"I can't do this again, El," he said. "But I can't not, either." And he came at her again.

Chapter Five

*H*e tasted the same, Ella thought dazedly, like heaven on earth, and in the water as they were, their bodies being gently battered by the rise and fall of the swelling waves, she pressed closer.

At her movement, James groaned, low and throaty, and then he was inside, his tongue tangling with hers, his taste hot and sweet and so right she felt her eyes sting as she opened to him with a low murmur of acquiescence.

He shifted in the water so that she was flush to him, her breasts mashed to his chest, her soft, giving belly pressed to his hard, ridged one, her legs entangled with his. She'd always loved the way she felt so small and protected in his embrace, and that hadn't changed. Neither had the fact that he could still thoroughly ravish her mouth with a skill that rendered her completely witless.

And only when he'd accomplished that did he rip his mouth from hers. "God, El. You feel so good." This was punctuated by hot, little, biting kisses along her jaw to her ear, which he nibbled while breathing with thrilling unevenness, all of which combined to make her eyes cross with stabbing lust.

"I can't stand anymore," she gasped.

"Here." He lifted her up. "Wrap your legs around me. There. Oh yeah, like that. I can't get enough of you," he muttered as a wave washed around them, lifting them up and then down on the endless tide. "Just can't." Holding her head still with one hand fisted in her hair, his other slid down her spine and into her bikini bottoms, squeezing, molding, pressing her against his shorts, thin and wet now, hiding nothing, especially not the hot, pulsing erection nudging between her thighs.

"More," he growled, palming one butt cheek and then the other before dipping his fingers between and exploring there.

"*James—*"

He cut her off with his lips and teeth and tongue, coming at her hard and fierce, still holding her head in place as if afraid she'd pull away.

Fat chance. She couldn't get enough, either. Slippery strands of her hair caught in the stubble on his jaw, stabbed into her eyes, clung to their shoulders, releasing the scent of her shampoo in the air along with the tangy salt from the ocean spray.

Inhaling her as if he wanted to gobble her up whole, James sank his teeth into her earlobe and pulled lightly as he exhaled slowly, raising a delicious set of goose bumps along her flesh. Lifting his head, still holding hers, he stared down into her eyes, then at her lips. When she licked them to get the last taste of him, he groaned.

All while his fingers gripped her bottom hard, grinding her against him, his hips moving, moving, moving, in a slow, snug, rocking motion that had her whimpering in helpless delight, gasping, sobbing for breath as she squirmed to get even closer. Her skin felt too tight, her heart too full as he drove her toward climax with nothing more than those maddening, increasing oscillations of his hips.

When he pulled back for air, breathing fast and shallow, Ella nearly died. No stopping! She moaned low, a protest deep in her throat, and slid her fingers into his hair, trying to bring his mouth back to hers. Her hips were still rocking, her heart still pumping, her nipples had shrunk to painful, tight little ball bearings that ached, *ached* for his attention. Between her legs she felt hot and desperate, and with him holding her open, spread to his rocking hips, his erection within easy access of every critical nerve ending she owned, she couldn't stop, just couldn't stop.

"James." The word was a mere whimper, dark and disturbingly needy, and in another time and place she might have spared the time to be horrified to hear herself begging, but not now. Now she needed him, hard and pulsing, needed him to tear away her bikini bottoms and his shorts, needed him thrusting into her, taking her over the edge, now, now, now. "*Please . . .*"

"Yeah, I'll please." He rasped a thumb back and forth over her nipple, then drew his hand down her belly to do the same over her bikini-covered sex, outlining her in slow precision.

"Ohmigod."

"Here, Ella? Now?"

"Here," she panted. "*Now.*"

He dragged her out of the ocean. She thought maybe he intended to take her inside the cottage, but apparently it was too far away because the moment their calves were free of the water, he sank to his knees and brought her down with him.

Their hands fumbled for purchase, hers skimming over his glorious body, touching his shoulders, his flat belly, his thighs . . . between them.

His were no less desperate, his fingers spread wide as if to touch all that he could with every sweep of his hands.

She tugged down his wet, clinging shorts.

He bit her shoulder.

She licked his Adam's apple.

He growled and tumbled her all the way down to the sand, spreading her legs and making himself at home between them, cupping her bottom and pulling her forward in a quick, hard movement that settled her more completely against his straining erection before he covered her body with his and kissed her, hard and wet and deep. She tried to get her hands between them, to draw him inside her, but he manacled her hands in one of his and drew them up over her head. Towering over her, he stared down at her. "You're not going to rush me. Not after six months of this, getting hard at the mere thought of you beneath me like this."

Then he sank his fingers into her hair, drawing her head back, forcing her to arch beneath him so that he could drag his mouth down her throat toward the curve of a breast. His handling of her was presumptuous and aggressive and she didn't care. She knew what he could offer her, knew how far he could take her, which was further than anyone had ever taken her before. And she wanted to go there, *now.*

Water and sand swirled around them in the dark, dark night as he tugged her bikini top off and tossed it aside before dipping his head and capturing her nipple in his mouth, lashing the tender tip with his tongue.

Stars burst in her vision, but she had no idea if they were the real ones hanging in the sky above them or only manufactured in her head from what he was doing to her as she cupped his head in her hands and held him to her.

Water lapped at their feet with each wave. She loved the weight of him, thrilled to the way he thrust a thigh between hers, spreading her, holding her open as he lifted his head and blew hot breath over her wet nipple. "I missed the taste of you here," he said.

"Keep tasting, then."

Curling the fingers of one hand around the bikini tie on her hip, he tugged until the wet, stretchy material popped free. Then he was scraping the bikini bottoms off her. "I missed the taste of you everywhere." His knuckles brushed her trimmed pubic hair, the very tips of his fingers just barely skimming over her folds as he kissed his way past her belly button. "But I especially missed the taste of you right"—he nipped at her inner thigh, brushed his nose over the center of her and then kissed her—"*here.*"

Ella gasped and tightened her grip on his hair.

"Mmm." He kissed her again, using his tongue this time to circle her clit, and her entire body bowed, tightened. She was going to come, thank God, but then he pulled back a fraction of an inch, and she dug her fingers into his shoulders. "*James.*"

"Still here. God, El." He nipped at her other inner thigh again, then a little higher, moving tantalizingly close to where she throbbed for him, for release—

Yes.

But the man only danced his tongue over her, moving half an inch to the right. Frustrated beyond speech, she gripped his hair tight and tried to direct his head.

"Easy," he murmured as a wave teased just past their knees.

Easy? She'd give him easy! Again she gripped his hair and shifted his head and felt a puff of air in the right spot.

He was chuckling. Bastard. *Rat bastard.* "Goddammit, James, do me!"

"I intend to. My way." He took her with his mouth then, by turns soft and gentle, demanding and aggressive, and yet when she was a quivering, desperate mass—which took all of two minutes—he pulled back again. "Anyone else ever make you feel this way?" he murmured, nudging her legs even wider with his shoulders, cupping her bottom in his big hands, making himself at home while she let out urgently needy, panting sobs. "Ella?"

"No one," she admitted in a strangled voice, crying out when he finally sucked her into his mouth, his own uneven pants against her captive flesh sending her even further onto the edge. "No one," she managed to say. "But you."

He rewarded her by moving to the preciously

correct spot, unerringly laving at her with his tongue in the rhythm he knew she needed. Each heartbeat, each breath, shoved her closer to the unrelenting, building heat threatening to consume her, and she went willingly. Her fingers slid out of his hair and went to his shoulders, roped with lean muscle as he bent to his task. Her skin tightened, her muscles began to shake.

"Mmmm," he murmured, lapping her up like cream, sliding two fingers deep inside her, stroking her both inside and out now, in a way she couldn't have resisted if she'd tried.

"Don't stop, don't stop," she panted as water lapped at their lower bodies.

"I won't," he promised, and then she was coming, bursting apart at the seams really, with the water hitting her at mid-leg now, the dark night sky drifting over them, and James doing as he promised, not stopping, licking her more softly now as he held her frantic hips, slowly bringing her back to earth.

Her hands fell to the wet sand at her sides as she fought to catch her breath. "My God. What was that, a hurricane?"

His hair brushed over her as he turned his head and kissed her inner thigh. "Hurricane James."

She laughed breathlessly. "F-5 strength. I think I have sand in all my parts," she said, but then the laughter caught in her throat because James surged up to his knees, gripped her hips in his hands, and stared down at her with burning eyes.

"I have something else to fill you with," he said, and in one smooth, controlled thrust, buried himself to the hilt.

Her pleasure-filled cry comingled with his. Wrapping both her arms and legs around him, she tipped her mouth up for his crushing kiss as he began to move. Water continued to lap at their feet and calves, the sand warm and giving beneath them. The light hair on James's chest teased her nipples as he stroked her smooth and sure, then harder, grazing her already sensitized, wet flesh with each flex of his hips.

Then he tore his mouth from hers and lifted her hips higher for the thrusts she couldn't get enough of. The breath plowing in and out of her lungs, she felt her body tighten again, but she struggled to hold back, to wait for him.

"No, you don't," he growled, and spread the fingers of the hand on her hip so that he could glide his thumb over her clit.

She exploded again, from an even deeper, darker place than she had before, and even as she let go and cried out his name, she knew. God, she knew.

She was still hopelessly, helplessly in love with him.

When she came back to herself she realized he was still hard as iron inside her, holding himself rigid. He hadn't come. She ran her hands down the taut, damp, quivering muscles of his back.

"Don't," he choked out. "Don't move, don't touch."

"But—"

"Don't talk, either." He buried his face in her hair and took several long, gulping, deep breaths before speaking in a tight, guttural voice. "I don't have a condom."

He was barely clinging to control, and a burst of warmth and affection for him nearly overcame her, so much so she could hardly breathe. "But I do."

He lifted his head, his eyes black and glittering.

"In my purse," she said.

They both craned their necks and stared at the little beach cottage, a good hundred yards away.

"Fuck," he said tightly.

"We can do that," she said coyly.

He met her gaze, his unwavering and no-holds-barred dark and hungry. And *not* playful, not at the moment. "One condom isn't going to cut it," he growled. "Not tonight."

Good thing she was flat on her back because her knees went rubbery at his thrillingly rough tone. "Then we'll have to get creative, won't we?"

With a groan, he rolled off her to his back and tossed his arm over his eyes. "You're going to kill me. Give me a second." His chest rose and fell rapidly as she watched him fight for control. A fascinating sport.

And arousing. His chest, defined and delineated with lean, hard muscles, heaved with each breath, his flat, ridged belly quivering. She straddled him, murmured "Shh" at his low, tortured groan, and slid down that delicious body. "Let me get started on that creativity," she murmured, and ran her tongue up the length of his rock-hard penis, swirling it over the tip.

James groaned raggedly, struggling with that control she always admired but wanted no part of at the moment. She *wanted* him to lose it. *Wanted* to watch. Just as he'd watched her. And she had the advantage of knowing that *this* act was one of his favorites, guaranteed to take him over the edge. She licked him again, then raised her head and surveyed him, sprawled out before her, back bowed, body drawn tight as an arrow, his face a mask of both pleasure and pain. "Want me to stop?" she asked softly.

"No." His head thunked back on the sand as his fingers tunneled into her hair, clutching her head. "God, no."

Chapter Six

Afterward, they staggered through the dark, balmy night toward the small cottage like a pair of drunks. *Drunk on lust,* James thought, grabbing Ella's hand before she could fall over as she tripped over her own feet yet again.

She collapsed against his chest with a muffled snort of laughter, and just like that, with her hair up his nose and her naked, warm, damp body sliding against his, his heart melted.

Maybe not just lust.

She curled into him and somehow he found the strength to hoist her up.

"Mmm," she murmured, burying her face in his throat and inhaling deeply as if she loved the smell of him. "I love it when you do the he-man thing."

"No, you don't." He looked down at her in his arms and laughed. "You hate it when I try to protect you."

Her eyes were clear of amusement now, gleaming

in the night and full of things that made him reel. "Maybe I've changed."

He wasn't sure how to take that as he nudged open the front door with his shoulder and dropped her down on the couch, lit only by the slant of moonbeams coming through the blinds. Nor was he sure what she wanted when she reached up and tugged him down over the top of her.

Her kisses, as she rained them over whatever part of him she could reach, were greedy, her hands demanding, and she urged him close, touching everything she could.

Not understanding how it was that they could ravish each other like they just had and still want more, he gave into it, into her, gathering her close with a confusing mix of heat and tenderness. He'd only been half kidding earlier when he'd said she was going to kill him—she was. Death by broken heart.

"Love me," she murmured, holding his head to her breast.

He kissed her there, curling his tongue around her nipple until it beaded hard for him. "I am. I do."

She bucked, and together they toppled to the floor, mouths and fingers frantic as they rolled, jockeying for position. She crawled to her bag, dug through it, and came up with a condom.

He grabbed it, and her, tucking her beneath him, kissing her, smiling when she rolled them again. They bumped into a lamp, nearly upending it over the top of them, then bashed into the coffee table. Beneath him, Ella laughed breathlessly and dug her fingers into his butt. "What's taking you so long to get inside me?"

"I have no idea."

"Make it up to me."

"Done." He tore open the condom and protected them both with fingers that actually trembled, then grabbed her bare thighs, opening her to him. They were bathed only in the meager moonlight from the window, but it was enough to have him moaning at the sight of her spread for him, vulnerable and fragile, pink and glistening. "Mine," he said in primal instinct. "All mine." He sank into her, a movement that had them both going still, flummoxed by pleasure.

Slow down, he told himself but he was tense and quivering, his every muscle straining with the need to posses and take.

Then Ella surged up and sank her teeth into his shoulder, and any good intentions flew out the window. "Take me, James." She soothed the bite with a lick of her tongue. "Hard. Fast. Now."

He opened his mouth to quip "Yes, ma'am," but he couldn't speak. He slid his hands beneath her thighs and rocked his hips, going even deeper now.

Tossing back her head, she gasped his name, and just like that he was a goner in the control department. He drove himself into her again and again. She was wet and mewling for him, hips pistoning to meet him thrust for thrust. Hot and wild. Hard and rough.

Out of control.

Outside, the ocean crashed into the shore with the same uncivilized force of them pounding into each other, damp flesh slapping against damp flesh, hearts thundering, wordless murmurs and cries, breath ragged as lungs fought for air . . .

James forced his eyes open as he felt the inevitable tightening between his legs.

Ella opened hers, too, and hit him with a one-two punch of those two baby blues, drenched and brilliant and glazed over. In them was everything he'd ever wanted, and his heart tightened with the rest of him as he barreled toward a freight train of an orgasm he couldn't stop to save his life. "I'm too close—"

"You're perfect," she panted, and wrapped her legs around his waist. "God. Right *there*—"

"El, I can't hold on—"

"I know, me either—oh God, James . . ." Her body constricted, then was wracked with a shudder as she let go, milking him with each contraction, throwing him right off the edge with her.

For those few moments being held by James, being touched and kissed, hearing his low, husky voice murmur things in her ear that made shivers rise on her spine, Ella felt like her old self.

Not lonely.

Not worried that her heart might never feel full again.

Not struggling just to make it through her next breath.

But happy. Full of hope.

It'd scare her if she could muster the energy for it, but at the moment she lay facedown and sprawled across the bed, sated and exhausted in a way that completely excluded thinking. That was good because she didn't want to think, didn't want anything to pierce this lovely protective layer he'd given her, or she might have to remember that being with him was a sheer accident of fate.

And temporary.

A warm, callused hand smoothed up the back of her thigh and her exhaustion vanished. "Careful," she murmured into the pillow. "My husband is home."

The hand came down on her butt in a light smack that made her laugh. She tried to roll over but James held her still, nipping lightly at the back of a thigh, then higher, and a rush of excitement surged through her. "Again?" she whispered, fisting her hands in the sheet at her sides.

He yanked her hips up so that she was on her knees. "Yeah, again. I can't get enough. Christ, I still can't get enough of you." One hand smoothed up her belly to cup her breast, his other slid between her legs, testing the way, which was already wet enough to make him groan. Leaning over her, he put his open mouth on her neck and drove into her, and just like that they moved from the eye of the storm back into the frenzy. With his fingers stroking on the outside, his erection filling her to bursting on the inside, he began to move within her, until with a sobbing cry, she came. From a long way away, she heard her name ripped from his throat and realized he'd had to pull out of her to come, and that he trembled around her.

Her entire heart caved, just opened up and let him in. Stupid, she knew, but she couldn't help it, or hold back, not with him.

"James—"

"Shh." He gathered her close as he took them both back down to the mattress. Stroking the hair from her face, he pressed his lips to her temple and breathed her name. Breathed it again as she drifted off in his arms.

James woke as Ella carefully slid out of the bed. With dawn nothing more than a purple tinge in the far eastern sky, he propped up his head with his hand, watching as she tried to pull the corner of the sheet from beneath him. She had the rest wrapped around her already. "Where are you going?"

She went still, and he knew. Damn it, he knew because his heart gave one bruising kick to his ribs. "You're running," he said flatly.

"Actually, no. I'm walking." She tugged on the sheet.

He just looked at her.

She tugged again. "Let go."

He could have let go of the sheet, if he wanted. But he found he couldn't let go of her. He'd been wrong to think he ever could.

"Damn it, James."

He fisted his hand on the sheet and gave a yank, and the thing came off her entirely. "There," he said, deliberately misunderstanding her. "You're free."

Nude, she let out a sound of pure exasperation and shot him a look that said, Grow up. Her sweet little ass sashayed across the room, where she bent for her clothing. He could see the bite mark he'd left in the crease where her thigh met her buttocks, and smiled grimly. He could leave all the marks on her he wanted, she still wouldn't be bound to him. Not by hook or heart.

His own heart suddenly aching like a son of a bitch, he plopped to his back and stared at the ceiling. "Hell if I'll watch you walk away."

"I watched *you* walk away."

At that, he swore again, more creatively. Then he got off the bed and moved to her.

She stood before him in a pair of panties, holding a camisole tank top in front of her breasts. He took it out of her hands and tossed it over his head. "I didn't *want* to walk away."

"I was driving you crazy, I know." She went back for the top, then stepped into it and yanked it up, fussing with her straps. "I tend to do that to a person."

He lifted her chin with a finger. "It wasn't you, Super Girl, it was your job."

"Really?" Her huge eyes searched his. "I think it was more than that."

His heart caught at the look of pain on her face. "What do you mean?"

"I loved you. *You*, James. I loved every single part; your loud rock music, your silly big oaf of a dog, the way you sneak sips out of the milk container when you think I'm not looking, how you snore when you're tired—"

"I do not."

"I loved every part," she said again in that terrifyingly soft and final voice. "But what kills me is that you can't say the same about me."

And on that shocking statement, she walked out of the bedroom.

He followed her to the living room, where she

was digging through her duffel bag. She pulled out a khaki cargo skirt and shimmied into it. She was putting on her sandals when he found his voice.

"It's your job," he said quietly. "It scared me. You scared me. Still do, damn it. I want you as my wife, Ella. I want that more than I want my next breath, but I want you alive and well and *safe*."

She gave him a long, considering look as she zipped up her bag and prepared to walk out of his life the way he'd once walked out of hers. "That's funny coming from you."

"What? *Why?*"

"You're a cop. *Your* job terrifies me but I don't tell you to change."

"I'm not the one who's been shot at, kidnapped, stuffed in a trunk *and* a freezer, and nearly killed at every turn!"

Slowly she shook her head. "I'm not going to do this, James, not again. I . . . can't."

His heart began to thud hard and fast. "You said you were thinking about making a change. Was that just what you thought I wanted to hear?"

"No, I meant it. But I'm not a quitter. I'm going to finish this case first. They made it personal now, and that pisses me off."

"See, that's exactly what makes this so danger-ous," he said, feeling desperate. "You've got to get it through your head, El. With these guys, it's not per-sonal. It's drugs. It's drug money. It's you getting in their way—"

"They handcuffed me in my own home."

"Because you wouldn't stay out of their way! Christ, El, just stay out of their way."

"And let the police handle it?"

"Yes!"

"And I just bet I know which cop wants to handle this for me."

"You've got that right."

They stared at each other, and right then, he knew. He'd blown it. She was going to go, and he couldn't stop her.

Sure enough, she grabbed her keys and stalked to the door.

He snagged her wrist, pulled until she looked at him. "Don't go," he said quietly. *Begging*.

But she tore free. "I have to. I have to do this for me." She shut the door quietly, with a finality that frightened him more than anything else had.

Chapter Seven

Ella knew what she had to do, but just in case, she made a list on the long, bumpy flight back to Los Angeles. She committed it to memory on the two-hour drive from Los Angeles to Santa Barbara:

1. Get onto the *Valeska* and find *something* to nail my suspects.
2. Switch departments to a safer investigative job that doesn't involve being stuffed into any Dumpsters or getting handcuffed to towel racks, and as a result, live happily ever after.
3. Without James.

That last made her throat tight as she navigated the windy Highway 1, the summer-browned California hills on her right, the sparkling, whitecapped, azure Pacific Ocean on her left. She'd had months to get used to the idea of being without him, and in that time she'd learned to spend whole minutes without dwelling on it, but her heart just couldn't wrap itself around the idea of this being permanent.

Angrily, she swiped at a tear and told herself it'd been caused by the sun in her eyes. No more of this. She was her own woman, and didn't need nor want a man who didn't love her for all her little pieces and neuroses. It was all or nothing, damn it.

And in any case, she didn't have any tissues with her, so she sucked it up, parked in the marina, and slipped her binoculars out of her purse. She checked out the long rows of boats harbored. There were many, certainly more than a hundred, and they ran the gamut from small dinghies that hardly seemed seaworthy to party-sized catamarans and sailboats, to the multimillion-dollar yachts such as the ones she'd been investigating.

She sought out the *Valeska*. She sat in her car and watched the boat carefully for ten minutes, and saw nothing. No maintenance, no guests, no movement at all. Hoping her luck had finally turned, Ella twisted into the backseat and grabbed her disguise: a white cap with a bobbling plastic pizza on it, and the pizza delivery box, which didn't hold pizza but her Mace, tape recorder, and ID, just in case. Once, she'd been arrested snooping around in a shipping yard because she hadn't stowed her ID and couldn't prove who she was. James hadn't enjoyed bailing her out, or the crap he'd taken for it from his station, but he'd enjoyed teasing her about it later.

Not this time.

Taking a deep breath, she shoved him out of her mind, exited the car, and made her way down the wooden planks of the docks with purpose. As a pizza delivery girl, she'd want a tip. As Ella, she just wanted a damn break. She was due for one. This sort of thing used to excite the hell out of her but she felt no rush of adrenaline now, nothing but a confusing mix of duty and dread. She had no idea what was the matter with her. Catching bad guys had always been so thrilling.

But actually, in truth, she did know what was wrong. It wasn't the job that amped her life up and gave her a buzz.

It'd been having love. Having James.

Hell of a time to realize that, since she'd left him a thousand miles away, with a finality she didn't want to think about right now.

Couldn't think about.

She came upon the *Valeska*. Sleek, shiny, posh, and so expensive she couldn't imagine planning to destroy it, insurance money or not. She shielded her eyes from the sun and called out from the deck. "Hello? Anyone home?"

No response.

It wasn't too difficult to get on board; she simply hopped the waiting plank and walked on. She figured if she could just get belowdecks, she could check out the place, look around, and . . .

And she had no idea. She just hoped to God some sort of evidence leapt out at her. She ducked beneath the bowline and walked along the bulkhead, heading astern, marveling at all the glass and flashy gold trim, at the lushness and sophistication.

At the back, on a vast white deck, she came across two wet suits and a pile of diving gear.

Still wet.

Roped to the back just below the deck was a small motorboat that hadn't been there last week. She stared at the diving equipment at her feet and understood. The drugs had been held on the second yacht, the one that had been purposely sunk, and they'd just gone back to retrieve the drugs, thinking they were safe because she, with her questions and interest, was locked up in Mexico.

Now that they had their insurance money from the first boat, and the drugs from the second boat, they thought they had it all.

She was about to change that perception.

The brass door heading belowdecks wasn't locked. A strange oversight with a boat as expensive as this one.

Or, and much more likely, the divers were still on board. As she stepped over the threshold, she heard the telltale muted voices. Heart kicking into high gear, she flattened herself against the inside bulkhead, between two large gold-framed paintings that she recognized as museum quality, but because she'd skipped more art history classes than she'd actually attended at UCLA, she had no idea what they were other than pretentious renderings of some fancy gardens.

The voices came from below. Ella kept moving and found herself in the galley, surrounded by a luxurious crystal and china lunch spread that had been ravished. Leftover lobster, shrimp, and fancy pasta salads lay around with three empty bottles of champagne.

Seemed someone—several someones—had been celebrating.

Ella reached into the pizza delivery box and flipped on the small tape recorder. No one in their right mind was going to believe she really was delivering a pizza to this ship, but it was too late to change her disguise now. And she wanted to hear what was going on.

What would they do to her if they found her snooping?

Didn't bear thinking about, she decided. Tiptoeing through the galley, she came out into a stateroom with plush seating, state-of-the-art entertainment center, and—

Her husband coming in the opposite door, dressed in black jeans, black running shoes, and a black T-shirt draped over the bulge of his gun, looking fiercely intense as he met her gaze.

"What are you doing here?" she hissed across the thirty-foot room.

He took in the pizza delivery hat and shook his head. "You're kidding me, right?"

"This is *my* case. Get out."

"Can't do that, sweetheart. You need backup. Jesus, tell me you're at least armed with something more than pepperoni."

"I'm fine solo."

"Sure you are, but wouldn't it be nice to know someone had your back?"

She let out a soft breath and felt her stomach twist. "More than anything in the world," she admitted. "But it's more than that, James. You want to change me. Dominate me. Run my life."

"*What?*" He looked around them and then hissed back, "I don't want to change you, damn it. I don't want to dominate you, or tell you how to run your life."

"So you're saying you love all my parts?"

"Every goddamn one," he said fervently. "And

trust me, I need all those parts, El. So let's get out of here—"

"Even this one?" she asked, gesturing around her. "The part where this is my job? You love that?"

"Look, all I want is for you to live long enough to love me back—" His head came up at some sound that she didn't hear, or maybe it was just his sharp instincts.

"What?" she whispered.

"We're going to have to discuss this somewhere else, say far away from the three guys downstairs divvying up their drugs, armed to the teeth."

"There's drugs?" *Her proof!* "Where—" But she broke off because someone was coming into the galley behind them.

She froze.

James drew his gun and jerked his head toward the door from which he came. He wanted her to get out, and she knew he'd stand there in the open, covering her, until she did.

But no way was he going to risk himself for her. She shook her head and dropped down behind one of the couches.

James didn't make a sound as he shot her a look filled with sick dread and fear, *for her*, then backed out the door from which he'd come just as someone opened the door from the galley.

She ducked low, her heart going high. James loved her. He'd never stopped loving her. And he needed her. *Her.* The woman she was. God, she'd been so stupid, chasing after all this adrenaline within her job when everything she'd ever wanted had been right there in front of her.

From her perch behind the couch she couldn't see him, couldn't do anything but wait and hope and pray she hadn't just given them both a death sentence.

A man entered the room, and another behind him, both in nothing but swim trunks, their hair still wet. Ella recognized the voices as the men who'd been speaking belowdecks.

The divers.

"We should get a move on," the first one said. He was in his thirties, built like a heavyweight boxer, with tattoos covering most of his upper body. "Our flight's in a few hours."

"No rush now that our resident insurance investigator slash pain in the ass is detained." This guy was thin and lanky, with no tattoos, just plenty of scars, and a chuckle that gave Ella a shiver. "Lou and Raul said they handcuffed her nosy, naked ass to her towel rack. I can't believe they didn't take pictures of her, man. She's still there, you know. Maybe we should go see her for ourselves."

Ella fisted her hands. James had in all likelihood saved her life.

"Raul said she squirmed a lot." Tattoo Guy let out a lecherous grin of his own. "He kept getting handfuls. Damn, we should have been the ones to catch her."

Fully creeped out, Ella huddled behind the couch, her finger on the Mace trigger.

"Got the shit?" Tattoo Guy asked.

"Oh, yeah, and it's pure, baby."

Ella felt the couch shift as both men sat on it. It was a low back, thick-cushioned leather number, and though she flattened herself to the floor, if either one so much as craned his head an inch to either side, he'd see her.

Her eyes searched frantically for a way out. There was an end table to her right, a glass and chrome deal that had some fancy steel sculpture displayed. The sculpture was about a foot high and looked like a wire cage, though she knew better and figured it was another ridiculously priced piece of art.

The thin thug opened a baggie, and Tattoo Guy stuck his pinkie finger into it, then brought it to his mouth to taste. He nodded and smiled. "Nice."

"Our cut's going to set us up for life."

"Then let's go get started on that life."

No. No one was leaving. But just as Ella went to make her move, a big, hot, sweaty hand settled on the back of her neck and hauled her up.

Bad guy number three. Heck of a time to remember the *three* bottles of champagne.

Tattoo Guy and his partner whipped around, jaws dropped. "What the—"

Ella hung from the third man's grip, feet swinging a few inches off the ground. Bringing her hand up, she nailed her attacker in the face with her Mace.

He screamed like a baby and let go of her. She hit the ground hard, scrambling to crawl away, but he fell on her, all three hundred pounds of him, a full dead weight.

Tattoo Guy let out a howl and dove over the back of the couch, landing on top of both of them.

Ella took the weight, her mouth opening and closing like a fish, her poor lungs uselessly attempting to drag in some air. Her one last thought was that she'd screwed up again.

Then there was rapid gunfire and suddenly she was free of the weight pinning her down. Sitting up, she saw Tattoo Guy rolling in agony, hands to the bullet hole in his thigh. Scrawny guy and James stood face-to-face, each holding a gun on the other.

"Drop it," James demanded, but the scrawny guy just shook his head.

Ella glanced to her right just as the third guy sat up and glowered at her.

She'd dropped her Mace. Bad.

Without thinking, she grabbed the steel sculpture, which was heavier than she thought. She chucked it at his big, meaty head. By some miracle, it actually beaned him between the eyes, and with a sigh he toppled back over.

"Drop the gun," James said to the skinny thug.

He just leered and pivoted, abruptly changing from pointing his gun at James to pointing it at Ella.

Uh-oh.

She dove to the floor as gunshots pinged and ricocheted around her, crawling beneath the coffee table. Before she could even attempt to peek out to see James—*God, please don't let him be hit*—she was hauled up against a warm, hard chest.

"Are you hit?" a rough voice asked as gentle hands ran over her body. "Ella, Christ, *say something.*"

She could hear Tattoo Guy squalling about his leg. There were sirens in the distance, and she realized James must have called it in on his cell before he burst back into the room and saved the day. Her hero, she thought dreamily, and grinned. "You still smell good."

He stared at her for one beat and then yanked

her closer, burying his face in her hair. His arms were banded so tightly around her she couldn't breathe, but that was okay because breathing was entirely overrated. She could feel his heart thundering steadily beneath her ear, could hear his not quite steady breathing as he nuzzled close. The feel of him warm and hard with strength surrounding her had always worked like an aphrodisiac, and now was no exception, except it was deeper than mere physical wanting. "You were scared for me," she murmured.

"I think I had a coronary."

"You didn't."

"Then I definitely got gray hair."

Throat tight, she ruffled his jet black hair, completely free of gray, and burrowed in closer.

"You know I love you, right?" he demanded. "I need you, too. So much, Ella."

And because she did know it now, she smiled through her tears. "Don't let go, okay?"

His arms tightened. "I won't."

"No, I mean don't ever let go."

"Never." He lifted his head and cupped her jaw. "Let's go home, Ella."

"Yeah, leave." Tattoo Guy pulled himself to a sitting position, sweating and gritting his teeth in pain, but lifted his hands in surrender when James pointed the gun his way. "Look, I'm not stupid. I'm staying right here."

James looked at Ella again, and everything within her quivered with hope. She'd wanted this, had ached for so long. "Really? You want to go home with me?"

"Yes. I want both of our shoes in the closet and both cars in the garage."

"Just one bed, right?"

"One bed, and you in it," he murmured, dipping his head to rub her jaw with his. "Beneath me. Wrapped around me." He lifted his face again and held her gaze with his dark one. "And I don't mean just for tonight."

"Good, because I'm free tomorrow night, too," she quipped, her stomach jangling with hope and what she was deathly afraid was nerves. She'd faced three crazed drug runners without blinking and now she was going to fall apart. It didn't make sense, and yet it did.

Because this, with James, was the most important thing she had going on in her life. She had to get it right. *They* had to get it right. "And the night after?" she whispered.

"All of them," he said gently, and kissed her. "It's okay, El. We're going to be okay. We're going to have the forever after we promised to give each other."

She meant to laugh confidently but ended up letting out a gulping sob instead. "I want that, too. I want that so much. In fact, maybe you could take me home right now and we could get working on that forever part, with your pager in the freezer and my cell phone turned off. And without any clothes on."

Tattoo Guy rolled his eyes. "Hey, felon in the room."

James smiled and kissed her, and everything was in that kiss—his promise, his hope, his love. All she ever needed.

SEDUCING
TABBY

Lucy Monroe

Chapter One

"*Secret Service? Really?*"

"Jane said her dad said he heard it from Tom Crane, the Realtor."

"Well, Patty Lane said her mother heard from her hairdresser that he's nobility, like an earl or something."

"Maybe he's *both*."

Tabby's friends spoke in low undertones laced with breathless curiosity. Wearing identical expressions of titillated speculation, the only two women in Port Diamond shyer than she was turned to face Tabby.

"Do you know anything?" asked one.

"He's got a boat docked here at the marina," the other added. "A luxury cruiser."

"My dad runs the marina, not me," Tabby reminded them.

"But you've got to have heard *something*."

Tabby had spent most of her adult life being pumped for information about her gorgeous, *thin* sister, Helene. So, this was nothing new. She was adept at sidestepping answers she did not want to give, but at least when it came to Helene, she *could* answer the inquiries when she wanted to.

However, Tabby knew nothing more than the other women about the mysterious Englishman who had so recently moved to Port Diamond.

Nothing except that, despite the fact she'd never said more than ten words to Calder Maxwell, he sparked a desire in her that fried her nerve endings and froze her vocal chords. She'd woken up pulsing from a dream-induced climax for the first time in her life the night she'd met him.

"I can tell you he's not Secret Service. He's from England, not Washington."

"Well, you know what I mean. He looks like he could give James Bond a run for his money."

Tabby looked across the room at the gorgeous man standing with her dad and Helene, and had to agree. A cross between Timothy Dalton and Cary Grant, he was every fantasy she'd ever had rolled into one perfect package—the only flaw being his obvious interest in Helene.

Just like every other male who came into contact with the Payton sisters, he found Helene's sweet nature and gorgeous looks irresistible. Tabby had seen them talking on the pier near his boathouse a couple of times, but hadn't been able to nerve herself up enough to join them. Helene wouldn't have minded. She was always happy to see her sister.

Tabby doubted Calder would have been as appreciative, which is why she'd stayed away—no matter how much she'd longed to simply stand close enough to hear his voice.

Noticing her gaze still fixed on Calder, Tabby's friend gave a theatrical sigh. "He's yummy, isn't he?"

"Yes."

At that moment, the object of their speculation turned and caught the trio of women gawking at him. One corner of his mouth tilted, but it couldn't quite be called a smile, and his dark gaze assessed them with cool regard.

"Oh, my gosh, he's looking this way. Quick, turn around and pretend to be getting food at the buffet."

Tabby rolled her eyes. "He's already seen us. I don't think he'll be fooled." And she didn't particularly want him thinking she was interested in the buffet.

A throwback to her paternal great-grandmother, she didn't have the willowy figure of her mom and sister, or anything approaching her dad's athletic build. Nope, she was a little too round, a lot too curved, and slightly too short for that.

"He's headed this way!"

And suddenly she was alone, deserted by her gossiping friends.

He stopped in front of her, his tall frame towering over her own five feet, five inches. He would fit in with the rest of her family just fine. *In fact, he and Helene make a striking couple,* she thought with an inner twinge.

"Good evening, Miss Payton."

Her heart fluttered at the smooth English accent and her lungs refused to issue forth enough air to power words of greeting. It had felt like this the first time they met in her bookstore, too. He'd come in looking for a book on home improvement, of all things, and she'd barely said six words to him between recommending a title and ringing up his purchase.

Feeling crowded by his proximity, although he wasn't standing all that close, she took an involuntary step backward and ran into one of the buffet tables. She grabbed for the edge to steady herself and got a handful of crab salad instead.

Turning to look, she stared in horrified stupefaction at the mess covering her hand. Mom was going to have a hissy fit. The salad required a two-day prep and was her most recent culinary pride and joy. Now an entire buffet-size bowl of it was good only for the garbage disposal.

"I can't believe I just did that," she muttered.

"Can I help you?"

She looked up at him then, too upset by her predicament to be her usual tongue-tied self around him. "Do you have any suggestions for hiding the evidence?"

"Perhaps we could take the bowl to the kitchen?"

"And leave a gap on the table?"

He took hold of her wrist and lifted her hand away from the bowl, careful not to let the crab salad anywhere near his dinner suit or her dress. "Go clean up and I will take care of our small disaster."

In spite of her embarrassed chagrin, the feel of his fingers curled around her wrist was surprisingly nice.

"It's not your disaster." She sighed in self-deprecation. "It's mine and I can't leave it to you." Even if she wished she could.

"Of course, I'm at fault. I startled you." She

opened her mouth to argue, but he shook his head. "Don't let it concern you. I have some experience in this sort of thing."

"Rescuing women from the wrath of their temperamental chef mothers?"

He smiled, even white teeth flashing all too briefly. "Hiding the evidence."

Her eyes widened in mock horror. "Oh, my gosh, you're a member of the British mafia and here everyone was thinking you were some sort of displaced nobleman or spy or something."

That made him laugh, and she felt the sound all the way to her toes.

"You have a nice laugh." She couldn't believe she'd said that. Trust her to go from mute to uttering inanities. What an improvement.

"And you have a charming sense of humor, but you also have a hand that is about to drip crab salad on your lovely dress."

She extended her arm farther from her body, having no desire to ruin the dress it had taken four hours of shopping in San Diego to find. "I'll just go wash this off."

She took as long as she could in the ladies' room, washing her hands, tidying her appearance, and wishing she could fall through a hole in the floor rather than go back out and face Calder Maxwell.

She got a moment alone with the focus of her fantasies and what did she do?

Go diving in a buffet bowl.

She never had been all that handy in the kitchen.

* * *

When she came out of the softly lit alcove, Calder was waiting for her. He gave her a look that made her go tight in some really interesting places. "Are you all right, Miss Payton?"

"Fine. Uh . . . call me Tabby. Everyone else does."

"Tabby, then." He drew her name out as if he were savoring it on his tongue.

What a ridiculous thought.

She peeked around him at the buffet table and saw that the bowl was gone and things had been re-arranged so no one could tell it had been there to begin with. "Thank you for hiding the evidence, although she's going to know something happened when she finds the salad in the kitchen."

"I emptied it into a trash bag and tossed it in the Dumpster outside. Unless she's watching closely, she'll assume it all got eaten."

"You really are good at this sort of thing."

"Thank you."

"You're fast, too."

"So I've been told." The chill in his voice, despite the humor in his eyes, made her wonder by whom.

"Enjoying the party?" she asked by rote.

Technically, the Port Diamond Yacht Club hosted the annual summer gala, but her parents owned the marina and restaurant where it was held, making them the unofficial hosts of the evening and her their not-so-willing accomplice.

She wasn't overly fond of large crowds.

"Everyone has been quite nice."

Which wasn't an answer to her question. In fact, it sounded like one of her own sidestepping comments, the kind that got her out of trouble with her mother for not trying hard enough to be social without having to lie. She found herself smiling.

"Obsessively interested, you mean."

His smile short-circuited her brain receptors. "There does seem to be a great deal of speculation about me."

"Well, as I said, rumor has it you're former secret government something, or maybe a member of the English nobility, but you've shown your true colors to me," she said in a teasing tone usually reserved for close friends and family. People she trusted.

His willingness to shoulder responsibility for something that had been entirely her fault, and then rescue her from the consequences, had gone a long way toward relaxing her with him.

"Is that your subtle way of fishing for the truth?"

"Not if you don't want to tell me." So far, so good. Her tongue wasn't tied in knots yet and she hadn't made an inane comment in five minutes.

"The truth would no doubt bore you," he said dismissively.

"You're very good at that."

"What?"

"Sidestepping."

"And you are more observant than most."

She shrugged. She'd had a lot of practice.

Just then her sister walked by on her way to the deck with one of her many boyfriends and waved at Tabby.

Tabby waved back and smiled.

"She's quite effervescent, isn't she?"

With a sinking heart, Tabby nodded. The inquest had begun. Would he be as good at seeking out information as he was at avoiding giving it?

For once, she really wished one of her sister's admirers had gone to someone else for insights into Helene.

"She's very bubbly," Tabby said, answering his question. "One of the nicest people I know."

"Your family is very close, aren't they?"

"Yes, we are."

His gaze was focused on the dancers on the deck, probably watching Helene charm her partner. "You are lucky."

"Blessed. My parents are both good people and they raised Helene and me to value the bonds of family."

He turned to face her again. "Would you care to dance?"

The question hit her like a brick upside the head. No. Not that. The pumping was bad enough, but to have to dance with him, being held in close proximity to a body that made hers go haywire while he did it? That would be cruel and unusual punishment. Besides, he didn't want to dance with her. Not really. She'd had this ploy played many times before.

A man asked her to dance and then made some excuse for her to switch partners with Helene. Calder was just the type of man to handle that sort of thing with aplomb, but she didn't want to be handled. Not that way, anyway.

"I'm not much of a dancer," she lied, and hated herself for doing so. She put a lot of stock in honesty and even white lies bugged her.

"Your father said differently."

Darn it, Dad had ratted her out. "Did he?"

"Yes."

She barely refrained from rolling her eyes. He'd probably told Calder all about the lessons she'd taken as a kid. She'd danced in competitions until she was thirteen and sprouted breasts and hips overnight. "Um . . ."

"Don't you want to dance with me?" he asked, sounding amused.

And well he should be. He had to know that half the women present tonight were panting for a chance to be held by the gorgeous Englishman. She should be thrilled he'd picked her to partner, even if it was with ulterior motives. What woman wouldn't be, knowing they got to dance with their idea of male perfection?

One smart enough to realize it would be pure torture, she thought. However, he was looking at her expectantly and she let out a huff of frustration.

Better to get this over with and then go back to lusting after him from afar.

"Sure, I'll dance with you." She grimaced inside at her lack of savoir faire.

Charm, thy name is not Tabitha Payton.

He put his hand out and she took it, pretending for this short space in time that it was her he was interested in, and knowing as she did so how dangerous such inner pretence could be.

Chapter Two

He led her to an outdoor dance floor lit by nothing more than several strands of twinkling lights and the full moon. He drew her to him as a bluesy ballad filled the night air. The atmosphere surrounding the dancers was one of romantic intimacy, something she could do without if she wanted to keep her mental faculties together.

He pulled her into shocking full body contact before she realized his intention. Okay, maybe there was an inch or so between them, but she'd seen him dance earlier with Helene and he had held *her* at arm's length. Tabby had expected the same.

She'd been wrong, so utterly, beautifully wrong.

A riot of sensations exploded through her and it was all she could do to stay vertical and breathing as her body reacted to his nearness. He started them swaying to the soft beat and her hands went of their own volition around his neck. His skin was warm and his black hair silky against her fingers.

And he smelled delectable. His expensive after-shave was subtle and did not mask his personal scent, which teased her senses.

"You're a good dancer."

"I'm not exactly doing anything," she said, no hope of tact anywhere on the horizon. She was too busy trying to focus on not jumping his bones.

But, *man*, how she wanted to. She *ached* to rub certain body parts against his hard, masculine form, and her mouth watered at the thought of tasting the smooth jawline so temptingly close.

"You're doing enough." His voice sounded funny, but she couldn't concentrate on what that meant, not with her brain on meltdown.

Suddenly, it occurred to her that while it might feel more incredible than anything she'd ever known, if she didn't get out of his arms very soon, she was going to do something that would lead to her utter humiliation. Like grab his face and kiss him stupid, or close the inch of distance between them and press hardened nipples against his sculpted pecs.

Oh, yeah, that would feel good. Too good.

"She looks eighteen, but she's twenty-four. She teaches kindergarten because she loves children, but she hasn't gotten married because she's never been in love." The words came tumbling out in a torrent of jittery need to get this over with. "She's not dating anyone special at the moment, but she does date. A lot," she couldn't help inserting. Tabby was a much better relationship bet, not that Calder would see it that way, of course.

No more than she wanted to date the guy who came in every Wednesday to ask if she had any new Earl Stanley Gardner books in the shop. Even if he didn't have that little quirk, she wasn't attracted to the mystery fan. Couldn't help it. Neither could Calder wanting Helene.

"Her favorite color is yellow, her favorite candy is peanut butter fudge. There's a place up the beach that makes some she cannot resist. She looks great in evening wear, but her preferred date is a trip to the San Diego Zoo, or even Sea World. She's a sucker for cotton candy and despite the fact we were raised on the beach, she's not all that enamored of the ocean and hates getting sand in her shoes."

"What?" He stared down at her, but she ducked her head so he couldn't see her eyes. "If I might be so bold as to ask, who the bloody hell are you talking about, Tabby?"

"As if you don't know. Who else would I be yammering on about while dancing with the sexiest man in the room?" she mumbled at his chest. "My sister, Helene."

She didn't mind the information seeking, but she hated the protestations of innocence, which was why she rarely let on she knew what was happening. She hated being lied to more than she hated lying. Only, she couldn't believe what her frustration had led her into saying this time. *The sexiest man in the room?*

Oh, man.

"And you've shared this wealth of information with me because why?" he asked, his precise English accent laced with inexplicable amusement.

Not appreciating being laughed at on top of everything else, she tipped her head back and glared up at him. "You want to know. I don't want to spend all evening fencing with you verbally so I can feed the information in such a way as to preserve your illusions or my pride."

"You believe I am dancing with you because I want information from you about your sister?" he asked in a voice that implied he doubted her sanity.

"Are you trying to tell me you aren't?"

"Why do you believe this?" he asked instead of giving her a direct answer again.

"You really are a master at conversational misdirection."

He smiled, the latent amusement still there in his dark eyes, but a surprising determination was evident, as well. "I am also quite adept at procuring the information I require. Why do you believe I am dancing with you in order to draw particulars about your sister from you?"

"That's what men do. Since I was eighteen and she was a precocious, gorgeous fourteen-year-old with more friendliness and native grace than I will have when I'm ninety."

"You believe men approach you only to get closer to your sister?"

"Yes."

"You are wrong."

"I made the mistake of believing that a few times, but after ten years I'm no longer that naive." She took a deep breath, wishing things could be different. Knowing they weren't. "It's always about Helene. Always."

"Yet you two are very close."

"I adore her as much as everyone else does."

His fingers locked at the small of her back, while one thumb caressed a lazy pattern against her spine. "You aren't jealous at all."

"No. Why should I be? I don't want to be her. I'm a lot more private. I'd hate a gaggle of boyfriends following my every move."

"Your father said you were shy."

"I don't like meeting new people. It makes me nervous."

"You do not appear nervous right now."

That's because she was too busy trying not to drool or rub against him like a cat in heat. "No," was all she said.

"She is twenty-eight and rather shy. She is not overly fond of candy, but she adores ice cream, especially coconut macadamia."

All the air whooshed out of Tabby and she stopped dancing in shock.

Calder didn't seem to mind. In fact, now that she realized it, he'd danced her off the deck and into a secluded spot away from the other party guests. She could hear the ocean, and the sound of wind on the waves stirred her already stimulated senses.

"I'm the one who likes coconut macadamia ice cream."

"Yes. You also love the beach and will spend hours walking in your bare feet right at the tide line."

"I don't understand."

"You are not dating anyone special and you haven't in a long time. You own a small bookshop on the pier, which you bought with a trust fund left you by a great-aunt. You quit university after getting a two-year degree instead of a bachelor of arts like your parents wanted you to."

"They've gotten over that."

"No, they have not, but they respect your right to make your own choices."

"Oh."

"Shall I go on?"

"About what?"

The sound he made was one hundred percent masculine irritation, all of his humor seemingly having taken a vacation.

"Very well. You are quite blunt with people you know, kind to strangers even if they intimidate you, and your favorite color is sea green. Oh, yes, and you love the opera and theater. You adore yellow roses, but I personally think you should consider the beauty of the scarlet blooms."

"Red is for passion, yellow is for everlasting love," she said in a dazed voice.

"Ahh . . . that explains it. You are a romantic."

"I'm . . ." She had no idea what to say. It sounded as if he'd been pumping someone else for information on her.

"Your father is very proud of you, if a bit exasperated at times, and is more than willing to wax poetic on the subject of his eldest daughter."

"You asked him . . . about me?"

"Yes. I have also discussed you at length with Helene, who thinks as highly of you as you do of her."

"Why?" she asked, stupidly maybe, but with a genuine need to know.

"I should think that was obvious. I want you, Tabitha Payton, and I intend to have you." His Cary Grant eyes glittered down at her, the words coming out in his precise English accent, somehow making them even more sexy.

She shook her head, trying to clear it, convinced she couldn't have heard him say what she'd thought he'd said.

"Oh, yes . . . and I think you want me, too, in spite of your rather blatant attempt to toss your sister in my path."

Calder watched in fascination as multiple emotions chased across Tabby's expressive features.

Shock. Disbelief. Hope. Pleasure. Desire.

It was the desire he reacted to.

He pulled her into his body, pressing her soft curves against flesh hungry for the feel of her. He had wanted the little darling since the first time he saw her walking along the beach close to sunset. He'd been sitting on the deck of his recently inherited house, trying to determine what he wanted his future to hold, when she came into his line of vision.

His first thought had been the foolishness of a woman walking alone on an almost deserted beach; his second thought had been both carnal and imaginative.

The red glow from the fading sun had outlined her luscious form while a gentle wind stirred her dark blond hair around her shoulders and face. She had looked both ethereal and incredibly sensual. Simply watching her had made him hard.

Although her body had called to him like a siren, it had been the sense of solitude surrounding her that did not smack of loneliness, which had cemented his ache to possess her. Her words tonight had only fueled that fiery need.

She'd spent her adult life fending off her sister's boyfriends and yet did not resent the other woman.

Tabitha Payton was a very special woman.

However, she was oblivious to her uniqueness and appeal. While he found that refreshing, it was also frustrating. Seducing her body would be quite easy. It was something he was very good at. However, making her believe she was the woman he wanted above all others might turn out to be bloody difficult.

"I want you." He brushed her lips with his, a mere whisper of touching, nothing too passionate. Not yet. "Tell me you want me, too."

She quivered against him, her lips full and soft in preparation for the kiss her feminine instincts knew was coming even if her mind did not. "I . . ."

"I do not want Helene."

She licked her lips and stared at him, big green eyes begging reassurance while her mouth remained stubbornly mute.

"Believe me."

"But everyone wants her," she said, sounding bemused and disbelieving.

"Not everyone. I want *you*. Now tell me you want me."

She'd pulled her hair up in a sleek French twist and it framed a heart-shaped face creased in doubt. "If I tell you I want you, you could hurt me."

"Never."

"Not physically, I know that . . . but if I say it, you'll know . . . and then you could turn away and say you never meant me to take you seriously."

He didn't think she knew what she was saying. She sounded dazed and her words came out in disjointed bursts.

"Has that happened before?"

"Yes."

Bloody idiotic men she'd known. "I mean what I say. There is no mistake. I am quite serious when I say you are the one woman I want."

"The *one* woman?" She laughed like it was a joke.

With a suddenness that shocked him, his patience gave out and he kissed her, claiming her mouth with hot passion and a lot less finesse than a man of his talents should exercise. However, there was no room for refinement in this kiss. She belonged to him in a way he neither understood nor would deny, and he felt a remarkably savage need to imprint that truth on her body.

The only option available to him at the moment was a kiss, and so he took it.

Her mouth remained impassive in surprise for several seconds, and then she kissed him back so hard his teeth ground against his inner lip. He opened his mouth and licked the seam of her ardent mouth with his tongue. She jerked in his arms and went completely still, like a fawn drinking from a stream for the first time.

Only he was the one doing the sipping.

The kiss changed as he revered sweetly compliant lips that assured him of the desire she had been incapable of voicing. Deliciously female, her mouth was unconsciously sensuous in its startled immobility, and yet temptingly pliable.

Perfect.

But not nearly enough.

He needed more than her lips. He wanted all of her, and he would have her soon or he would go mad.

He undid her hair, pulling out pins and fingering through the silken strands because he needed to touch her this way. He massaged her head and she moaned against his lips, pressing her body intimately to his. That small sound, coupled with background noise that had suddenly grown louder, brought him back to his senses.

They could not do what he wanted to do with her out here, and regardless of how much his body craved hers, it was too soon. He did not want to spook her.

He pulled away, gently removing her hold on him. She stood there looking shell-shocked, her lips swollen from his kisses. He wanted nothing more than to pull her back into his arms, but he forced himself to refrain. Now was not the time.

The music had been turned up. Playing at a much faster tempo than it had been, it filled the silence between them.

She bit her lip and then looked at him as if he were a species alien to her experience. "Why did you do that?"

Chapter Three

O f all the questions he might have anticipated at that moment, why he'd kissed her was not one of them.

"Because I wanted to, though I can appreciate now might not have been the best time."

"You wanted to kiss me?" She needn't sound so surprised.

"I did say I meant to have you. Kissing is the normal prelude to what is to come."

"Is there something wrong with you? I mean, maybe your family sent you over here because you're their big embarrassment. Do you howl at the moon during lunar eclipses, or get so drunk on your birthday you dance on tabletops?"

"I assure you, I am no one's big embarrassment." He would have been offended by her suppositions if she weren't so charmingly confused by his attentions. "You really are used to men trying to get to Helene through you."

"Well, um, duh . . . yes. I did say so, didn't I?"

He laughed. He couldn't help himself. He couldn't remember the last time a woman reacted to him with such refreshing honesty.

"I suppose it's going to take some getting used to you having me around."

"You're going to be around?"

"Love, you're not exactly tracking tonight, are you?"

"I hear what your mouth is saying, but the words don't make any sense in my world."

"I guess it's a good thing I'm in your world now because they make perfect sense to me."

"You want to date me?" she asked, as if she were trying to get it absolutely straight.

"Yes." And more, but he'd already told her that.

"You don't want to date Helene?"

"No."

"Why not?" she asked, her tone just the tiniest bit aggrieved.

"Because I am not attracted to her."

"And you are attracted to me?" She peered at him through her lashes, this time as if she were trying to see into his head.

"Yes. Very," he added for good measure.

"You did notice I'm the one with a figure from a bygone era? The shy one . . . not a tinkling laugh in my repertoire?"

"I noticed everything about you and I find it quite a potent package, if you must know."

"You're not over here de-stressing from some over-the-top job, are you? I mean, that would explain your aberrant behavior."

"There is nothing aberrant in my behavior." Well, not much. Or at least not what she was thinking.

He had never had a relationship of the type he wanted to have with her. Purely personal, possibly permanent, and definitely passionate.

"Right."

He couldn't decide if he wanted to laugh again or shake her. The woman was annoyingly stubborn and fixated. "I'm thirty years old. I know my own mind."

"What size was your last girlfriend?"

"What?"

"Dress size. What did she wear?"

"I don't know the American equivalent."

Her lips twisted. "Uh-huh. Just show me with your hands how big around her waist was."

He did.

Tabby nodded, her expression gleaming with triumph. "Exactly. Probably a size six."

"What the hell does that have to do with us?"

"You normally date women like my sister. Men like you do."

"According to you, all men prefer women like your sister."

She bit her lip. "They do."

"I don't, and do not start yammering about dress sizes again. You are perfect as you are." In fact, she was luscious. "I don't want you to be any different."

"This is really weird for me."

"Let's spend the rest of the evening together and see if we can't get you used to it."

"All right." She said it grudgingly, but he could have sworn her green eyes reflected the same yearning that made it so impossible for him to leave her alone.

* * *

The next morning, Tabby awoke to the strident ring of the telephone. She fumbled for the receiver from underneath the light comforter on her bed.

"Hello?"

"Did I wake you, dear?"

"Hi, Mom. Yes, you woke me."

"Sorry, you're usually up early on Sunday, but I couldn't help noticing you missed church."

"I slept through my alarm."

"Up late?"

"You know I was."

"Later than I think?"

Tabby sat up and fluffed the pillows behind her as a backrest. "I did not bring him home with me!"

Not that she would have turned him down—she didn't think—but he hadn't asked, which made her protestation sort of overdone.

"I see. So, is he nobility, former spy, what?"

"What do you *see?*"

"Nothing in particular. It's a phrase we mothers use. I'm sure you'll find yourself saying it someday, too. It means we're thinking over what our child just told us. Now answer my question."

"The answer is: I don't know. We didn't talk about his past." He'd managed to neatly sidestep any conversational byways in that direction.

"You spent the whole evening so wrapped up in each other's company, you barely noticed when everyone else had left and you didn't talk about his past? What *did* you talk about?"

"Everything. It was wonderful, Mom."

It had been like talking to a really good friend,

one she'd known forever . . . which had been as worrisome as his strange fixation on her instead of Helene. She could really fall for this guy. That would leave her open to major pain when he figured out that James Bond was supposed to date Octopussy, not Anne of Green Gables.

"Everything including why he's in Port Diamond?" her mother probed.

"He inherited his house from an uncle on his mother's side. She was American."

"Is she dead?"

"No, but she's got her British citizenship now."

Silence. Then, "So is he sticking around or what?"

"I don't know."

"Does he have a job?" her mother asked suspiciously.

Tabby grinned. Overprotective, but lovable. "I suppose. He certainly seems to have money, but the truth is we spent a lot of time talking about me. It was weird."

Her mom laughed. "If you dated more, that kind of thing wouldn't be so strange. He's been pumping your dad and sister about you for a couple of weeks now."

Tabby smoothed the sheet and blanket over her legs. "Why do you suppose he waited to approach me?"

"Helene said you avoided them whenever he was with her. Maybe he thought you weren't interested."

"I didn't want to intrude."

"I don't think he would have seen it as an intrusion."

"No, I guess not." But how was she supposed to

know? This whole thing of being the sole recipient of a man's interest was new to her, and she couldn't help feeling it wasn't fated to last very long.

"My crab salad went over very well last night. I knew it would."

It was all Tabby could do not to blurt out the truth. "It's a wonderful recipe."

"Yes."

They chatted for a few more minutes and then her mother rang off.

Tabby was in the shower when her doorbell rang. She grabbed a towel, did a quick dry-off, and then wrapped it around herself sarong-style to answer the door.

Expecting her sister or someone equally innocuous—like *anyone else*—she reared back in shock when she saw Calder standing on the other side.

"Good morning, love." His dark eyes made a meal of her, and the oversized bath sheet felt like the most revealing piece of lingerie she owned.

"I wasn't expecting you this morning." He'd said he would call, not come calling.

His dark brows rose. "Then who were you expecting?"

"No one in particular."

"But definitely not me?"

"Honestly? No."

He frowned. "Do you frequently answer the door wearing nothing more than a towel when you don't know who is on the other side?"

"Of course not. How often do you think I'm in the shower when someone stops by?"

"I can only hope the occurrence is rare." He sounded annoyed. He certainly looked it.

Which was interesting, if confusing.

"Getting a visitor at my door is pretty rare. People usually stop by the store to see me."

"If you didn't think it was someone you knew, then you thought you were opening the door to a perfect stranger?" he asked as if carefully putting a puzzle together and not liking the way it was turning out.

"Nobody's perfect," she quipped, but his stiff expression said he didn't appreciate the joke. She sighed. "I don't know why it matters so much, but I thought it might be a book delivery made to my home address by accident. It's happened before, though never on Sunday. It could have been someone looking for directions, too."

Suddenly, he was a stranger. No longer the charismatic man of the night before, this guy emanated menace and made James Bond seem like a pussycat.

"If I understand you correctly, you are telling me you opened your door dressed like that"—he pointed to her towel-clad self with a precise movement—"believing a stranger was on the other side?" His tone could have frozen underground lava.

"That bothers you?" Okay, so it was hard to interpret his reaction any other way, but the concept was so foreign to her, she felt like she needed a translation guide to deal with it.

"You have to ask?" He looked pointedly at the swell of her breasts revealed above the towel. "Do you mind stepping back inside to continue this discussion?"

"Uh . . . no problem." She moved back a couple of paces.

He followed, shutting the door behind him, and

then reached for her. "In answer to your rather obtuse question, yes, I am more than mildly irritated that you would answer your door wearing nothing but a towel if you were expecting someone besides me . . . or maybe your mother."

"That sounds awfully territorial." And the fingers wrapped around her upper arms certainly felt like it.

"It is."

"Oh." She licked her lips nervously, and then bit them when his expression turned from disapproving to heated. "Um, I don't think we have that kind of relationship yet."

"I beg to differ. I made my intentions clear last night, Tabby, and I won't share." His voice was like razed steel. His hands moved to cup her face, his touch gentle even if his tone was not. "I don't want anyone else seeing you like this."

"No one else wants to."

He shook his head. "You cannot be that naive. You are a beautiful, desirable woman and even if you were a wrinkle-ridden hag, it wouldn't be safe to answer your door practically naked."

"But Port Diamond—"

"Is on a major highway, and small towns have crazy, nasty people, too, love." He sounded so serious, so concerned.

And she realized he was probably right. It was just that living her whole life in a small town, she sometimes forgot the world was bigger than her own backyard. "I won't do it again," she promised softly, still not sure if this whole territorial attitude of his was good or not.

"Thank you." And then he kissed her—as if he

couldn't wait one more second to connect with her lips.

She went under immediately, just as she had the night before, but when she tried to get close, he pulled back.

"Don't, love. I came by to see if you wanted to spend the day with me, not to seduce you in your living room." He looked down at her precariously wrapped towel, his gaze glittering with unmistakable desire. "Though it's a bloody tempting prospect."

"I'm glad."

He closed his eyes, as if the sight of her was too much for his self-control. "If you don't get some clothes on immediately, all of my good intentions are going to disappear."

"Maybe I don't want you to be governed by good intentions." The kiss they'd shared last night had been incredible. She wanted more.

At some point, he was going to realize she was not his type and move on. Was it wrong to want to experience all the passion he had to offer before that happened?

She'd been practical and cautious her whole life, and that had gotten her exactly nowhere in the relationship department. One thing she knew, this man wanted her, not some other woman and not her sister.

That meant their connection had more going for it than any of the others she'd had in her life.

His jaw tightened, as if he was trying to gather inner strength. When he opened his eyes, they were hard with resolve. "We're going to the San Diego Museum of Art."

"This is the last week of their special El Greco exhibit. I've been wanting to see it."

"I know."

Whoosh—the air rushed from her lungs as shock reverberated through her.

It was unbelievable that a man so incredible would go to such lengths to please her. Every bit as overwhelming was the reality that she wanted to stay home and continue their kiss more than she wanted to go to the exhibition. She'd never been this physically stunned by a man's nearness.

"We don't have to go anywhere for me to enjoy being with you," she admitted.

He smiled, that Cary Grant charm on display again. "I am delighted to hear that."

"But you still want to go?" she guessed.

"Yes. I want to see if your expression is the same looking at one of your favorite painter's masterpieces as it is when you look out over the ocean from the front window of your shop. I want to enjoy your company in the car and at the exhibit. I'm hoping you will give your whole day to me."

He'd watched her watching the ocean from her bookshop? Wow. "Um . . . I can't think of anything I would enjoy more."

He smiled, and then looked down at her body encased in the towel and his eyes burned with something besides a desire to go to the museum.

She blushed for no reason she could discern. "I guess I'd better get dressed."

He took a deep breath and turned away as if she, Tabitha Payton, was so irresistible, to look at her one second longer would be to take her. "That would be a good idea, yes."

* * *

Calder breathed a sigh of relief when Tabby left the room to get dressed. He'd bedded women with a lot more sophistication, definitely women with more confidence in their innate sexual appeal, but not one of them had made him feel like a panting, hormone-driven teenager—not even when he'd been one.

He didn't know what was so different about the sexy little bookworm, but he was bloody well going to figure it out.

Chapter Four

The El Greco exhibition was everything Tabby had hoped it would be. Unlike other companions she'd dragged along to art museums, Calder seemed perfectly content to let her sit and contemplate whenever a painting struck her in a special way. He didn't hurry her, didn't talk incessantly, and yet she felt his presence as deeply as she felt the spirit of the artist reaching out to her.

She'd never been so aware of another person while indulging her love of art. Usually, even chatterboxes like her sister could melt into the background like ghosts that made noise, but couldn't impinge on her consciousness.

Not Calder. He remained a solid, tantalizing presence throughout their tour of the museum.

It was only as he led her from the building, though, that she realized he had his arm curved proprietarily around her waist and had done every time they walked anywhere.

"Would you like to stop for an early dinner before we head back?"

"I can't believe you let me stay in the museum so long."

"I enjoyed watching you as much as I thought I would."

She tilted her head sideways to see his face. "You're a strange man, Calder."

"No. Merely an intrigued one."

She shook her head, but didn't demur when he pulled her body closer to his. "Dinner sounds great."

"Good. There's a gallery showing we can attend afterward if you are not tired of looking at paintings."

"I never get tired of it, but I'm surprised you're not climbing the walls at the prospect of more stopping and staring." Which was what her mom had labeled her tendency to become engrossed in a visual image. It didn't only happen at museums; she reacted the same way to a creative window display when she was out shopping.

"The artist has a hint of the master in his style, but his work is definitely no copycat."

"You mean El Greco's?"

"Yes."

She sighed in bliss at the thought. Maybe she would be able to buy one of the paintings. The walls of her home were still bare for the most part because of her pickiness regarding the type of artwork she wanted to hang.

But after a dinner where it was all she could do not to leap across the table and plant her lips in close contact with Calder's—did the man have a clue how irresistible he was?—she discovered the artist Calder thought she would like was already selling way out of her price range.

She sighed over several gorgeous paintings, but one stopped her and held her in its thrall for so long, Calder finally asked if she was all right. Similar to El Greco's *Laocoon*, the painting was not easy to interpret, but it stirred so much latent emotion and pricked at her view of her own sexuality to such an extent that she reached out to touch it.

Only Calder's gentle hold on her wrist stopped her from the major faux pas. She smiled at him with gratitude, even as her heart was caught by the image of him beside the painting. Both were doing serious damage to her ability to control her physical impulses.

"If you don't stop looking at me like that, I'm going to kiss you."

The hushed voices of other visitors to the gallery faded to a whisper against her consciousness. "I wouldn't stop you."

He shook his head. "I'm not sure I could stop at a kiss."

"Oh . . ."

He quickly led her from the gallery. When they reached his car, he put her inside, his face set, his body vibrating a message of sexual hunger even she couldn't mistake. He drove with quick, jerky movements until they reached an overlook and then he parked the car.

He turned to her. "Come here, Tabby."

"You couldn't wait until we got home?" she teased, her own voice betraying how much she wanted this.

"If I had, I would end up making love to you and I'm not ready for that step yet."

She stared at him in shock. "You aren't ready? I thought it was the woman who was supposed to want to wait." And her body was clamoring for what she knew his would provide.

Pleasure. Acceptance. A sense of closeness she craved. Even if it was temporary, it would be good.

"Once you take me into your body, Tabby, you'll be mine." He sounded so serious, as if his sexy charm was just a front for the deep and somewhat primitive man under the surface. "You have to be absolutely sure I'm what you want before we take that step."

"You're so serious. You make it sound like making love would be a permanent, irrevocable decision for long-term commitment." Which was how she had always seen it—until now, when she'd decided to take what she could get and live with the consequences later.

He was saying those consequences were different than the ones her heart told her were waiting on the other side of sharing her body with him.

"That is precisely what I mean."

The idea that he shared her solemn, but atypical, view of intimacy made her dizzy. It also confused her. "You're not a virgin."

He frowned, an unreadable expression in his dark eyes. "No. I am not."

"So, you couldn't have always felt that way."

"I have never before felt this way."

"You mean, this isn't a general principle?" That made a lot more sense in some ways and was totally beyond her comprehension in others.

"No . . . it is a Tabitha Payton principle."

What in the world was she supposed to say to that? He couldn't be serious and yet his tone of voice said he was—deadly so.

But he didn't expect her to say anything. Didn't so much as give her the chance.

He kissed her instead, and from the first contact, she knew just how easy it would be to make love with this man.

He tasted like he had the night before, but now she recognized the flavor. He tasted like he belonged to her. She didn't care how ludicrous the thought was, she couldn't dismiss it. They connected on a level not governed by what made sense. It was too elemental for that.

When he dropped her off later that night, her lips were still tingling from his kisses and her body was throbbing from unsatisfied needs. From the pained expression on his face, she guessed he was experiencing the same thing.

She didn't ask him inside, though.

He'd made it clear he wanted to wait and she liked what that said about his feelings for her.

After the first night of torture, Calder was careful not to allow the passion between him and Tabby to flare out of control. He kept the kissing light and their time alone together minimal, which was why he hadn't taken her to his home yet. Even his well-honed self-control wasn't up to the temptation.

The only time they'd come close to making love again was when he'd presented her with the gift of the painting that had so enamored her from the

gallery. She'd gotten all teary-eyed and kissed him.
They were half naked and panting before he'd
been able to rein in his libido.

She'd gotten testy about it, but he could see she
liked knowing she had such a strong impact on
him.

The unwitting temptress was going to be his
soon, or he was going to go stark staring mad.

She seemed to love everything they did together,
but when he invited her to the opera, her eyes lit up
like stars on a perfectly clear night. When he arrived to pick her up, it was all he could do to take
her out to the car and not ravish her right there.
She'd donned a silk dress the color of coral flame
that accentuated her voluptuous curves. Her green
eyes sparkled in contrast and she'd left her hair
down in an alluring curtain around her shoulders.

He was painfully hard the entire drive into Los
Angeles. By the time intermission came, his erection was past painful. It was a pulsing ache that demanded satisfaction. He'd listened to her sighs,
watched her sensual reaction to the performance,
and been tormented by her scent, which revealed
an arousal he wasn't sure she was even conscious of.

He led her into the pavilion's reception area, the
teeming mass of fellow attendees doing nothing to
curb the primal need roaring through him.

Without considering whether she wanted to go
or not, he led her upstairs and into a small hall that
was blessedly quiet. He stopped at the first door to
his left. He tried the handle. It was locked. Using
techniques he'd learned early in his career, he
picked the lock and pushed the door open. It was a
meeting room.

He tugged her inside, took a quick look around, but saw no signs it would be, or had been, occupied tonight. He shut the door and locked it again.

Other than the illumination from the streetlights outside, filtering in through the almost closed blinds, it was dark. It was private. And that was all he needed.

"What are you doing? What's the matter?" she demanded, her voice soft in the darkness around them.

He didn't answer, but took her lips with an animalistic growl that should have shocked him. This was not his normal technique, but she brought out things in him no other woman ever had.

She kissed him back, her mouth eager and pliant against his, her breathing erratic.

Cupping her sumptuously curved bottom through the slick fabric of her dress, he lifted her against him until he no longer had to bend his head to kiss her. She liked that, and wrapped her arms around his head as if wanting to hold onto him for dear life. Did she think there was any chance he would pull away?

Not bloody likely.

He nipped at her lower lip. She whimpered and opened her mouth, inviting him inside. He accepted, sweeping her mouth with his tongue and savoring the flavor that was hers alone. Candy sweet and addictive.

Her small feet brushed against him, trying to find purchase. She made a frustrated sound when they couldn't and almost kneed him in the groin, but her lips never stopped devouring his.

When her knee came perilously close to his sex

again, he broke his mouth away. "Wrap your legs around me."

She was trying to resume the kiss, oblivious to his demand.

He avoided her seeking lips and spoke directly into her ear, as he was already pulling the skirt of her dress up. "Your legs, love . . . put them around me."

"Oh . . . okay." She obeyed, moaning with sexy abandon when her panty-covered mound rubbed against his abdomen.

He exulted in her unrestrained passion and kneaded the round cheeks filling his hands with fingers that actually trembled. It had been so long since sex had been this important or this uncomplicated . . . perhaps it never had been. But she didn't want anything from him, wasn't trying to manipulate him in any way, and he wasn't using her attraction against her, either.

They were just a man and a woman making love because they wanted each other and that felt incredibly good.

He kissed her again, and to his delight she started moving her pelvis, pressing the hot apex of her thighs against his torso. He sucked on her tongue and she increased the bucking movements of her lower body. He growled, primal desire coursing through him in a hot rush.

She matched him perfectly.

He could smell her arousal, could taste her passion, and he could no more stop himself from sliding his hands under the silk covering her ass than he could stop kissing the glorious creature in his arms. Her skin was softer than the silk that covered it.

"You're perfect," he bit off against her lips.

She moaned something inarticulate in response.

When his fingertip delved between her cheeks, she went still again. He adjusted his hold on her so that he could reach farther and then slid one questing finger down to the heated moisture of her core.

She was slick and swollen—everything a woman should be in her lover's arms—and he shuddered convulsively with the need to be inside her.

She whimpered again, the sound so hot and sexy, his dick bobbed against the tightened muscles of his abdomen. Pushing against his finger, she forced him to penetrate her to the first knuckle . . . and then the second. Wet, silken tissues clamped his finger like a vice, and he ate at her lips, caressing her even more deeply with his finger.

She made a high-pitched, desperate sound and he knew she was close. He wanted her to go over.

Her legs were locked around him so tightly, breathing was a challenge, but he wouldn't ask her to relax her hold for anything. He needed her unbridled passion. He would settle for nothing less than the pure honesty of her response, so different than the world he had left behind.

He moved his hand so his finger slipped out of her silken heat and searched out her swollen clitoris. He swirled and rubbed, then pressed . . . then swirled . . . then pressed again.

And she came, arching her body, convulsing in pleasure.

He muffled her cry of completion with his mouth, swallowing it as appreciatively as the finest wine or most decadent dessert known to man.

Unable to stop, needing as much as she would

willingly give, he played her straining body. After only seconds, she convulsed again, throwing her head back, her throat locked on a silent scream and her legs going so tight they threatened to crack his ribs.

Then the tension in her body snapped and her head fell forward onto his shoulder, her torso resting against his. Sighing breaths shuddered in and out of her body as he cradled her close.

He kissed her temple, licking the salty sweat there, the silver path of tears from her eyes. "You are amazing, Tabby."

"You're the amazing one, Calder."

He didn't argue. He was still hard as a rock and it was taking everything he had not to throw her down on the tabletop and thrust inside her silky, swollen heat.

After a few minutes of utter bliss and sheer torture, she unhooked her legs from behind his back. "Let me go."

He did as she asked, gently lowering her to the ground and releasing her. She dropped to her knees. At first, he didn't know if it was because her legs were too weak to hold her, but then she touched the buckle on his belt and he knew what she wanted.

"I don't think that's a good idea, Tabby."

"Oh, yes, it is. I want to taste you." For an introverted bookseller, she could sound bossy when she wanted to.

And he couldn't begin to pretend he didn't want to feel her luscious mouth on him. He moved a few feet backward so he could lean against the wall. "I'm all yours."

She giggled and the sound entranced him.

But all thought fled when she undid his pants and pulled his throbbing member free. He thought he was going to come from that simple touch, but he managed to hold on.

Chapter Five

She explored him with her fingertips and her tongue, making sexy sounds of pleasure when she licked moisture from his tip.

She engulfed his head in the heat of her mouth and curled both hands around him. Her movements weren't practiced, but they were passionate and he bit back the shout of his release in an embarrassingly short time.

She didn't seem to mind. In fact, she acted rather proud of herself.

He couldn't help smiling. "They rang the second bell for taking your seats." He had acute hearing, a benefit in his profession. "If we hurry, we'll be able to watch the second half of the performance."

"I'd like that."

Later, when he dropped her off at home, she snuggled into him for a good-night kiss.

"Did you enjoy the opera?" he asked as he pulled away, wanting nothing more than to stay, but there were things they needed to talk about before they took what would be an irrevocable step for him.

She smiled saucily. "I liked the intermission best."

"I did, too, love. Will you come by my house for lunch tomorrow?"

It was Sunday, the only day her bookshop was closed.

Her smile fell away from her lips, leaving them looking kissed and vulnerable. "Yes, I think it's time."

Tabby showed up for lunch fifteen minutes early. Calder opened the door on her first knock.

She didn't even get a greeting out before he pulled her to him for a passionate kiss.

He swept her inside and then stepped away from her. "This is every bit as difficult as I thought it would be. Lunch and conversation first. All right, love?"

She nodded, unable to make her still yearning lips form words.

They were eating on the deck overlooking his private beach when he broached the subject of his past. "Your friends' speculation about my past wasn't far off."

"You're an earl hiding out in America because you don't want the title?" she quipped.

"Actually, I am MI6."

"Are as in you're still a spy?" Oh, great. She had fallen in love with a man whose life couldn't be more different and less likely to meld with her own.

"At the moment."

She swallowed, wishing she could cling to the implication it was a temporary condition. "I see."

"I doubt it."

She frowned, not liking the amusement lurking in his brown gaze while her heart felt like it was going through the shredder. "Even a small-town bookstore owner knows that trying to make a lasting relationship with a spy is asking for trouble."

"So, you finally acknowledge I want more from you than an entrée into your sister's life or a quick coupling we both forget about soon after the fact?"

She rolled her eyes. A lot of good that did. "Yes, but I don't see how that can work. My life is here . . . your life is there." She waved her hand toward the east. "What are the chances? Unless you want me to move to England?"

He shook his head and her bleeding heart plummeted. So much for sacrificing her comfortable existence for love.

"Your life is here. Your bookshop. Your family."

"Yes, I know. I'm the one who lives in my skin," she said with more acerbity than she wanted, but he didn't need to rub it in.

"Tabby, I don't know if I can explain this very well, but I'm not MI6 because I want to be more than anything else in the world."

Hope stirred beneath her battered emotions. "Then why are you? It's not exactly an easy job to come by."

"You'd be surprised, or at least I was. I wanted adventure, wanted a career that used both my brain and my brawn, as it were."

"And . . ."

"And I got hired by the organization right out of

university. I made agent very quickly and have enjoyed my job, though I'm not necessarily proud of all I've done to achieve success."

"Like what?" Had he killed people?

"I seduced women with the intention of procuring information. I developed friendships for the same thing." He sighed. "I've never actually killed anyone, but I have shot two agents from opposing governments."

"Does all that bother you?"

"A little, but I have to be honest . . . not much. I did what I had to do to protect my country."

"And now?"

"Now I've met a woman I want more than an adrenaline-pumping career."

"Me?"

"You. Haven't you figured out yet that you generate more excitement in my life than ferreting out dangerous national secrets?"

"Oh." It wasn't the brightest response, but she was reeling inside from an emotional overload.

"I've been considering settling here in Port Diamond, but whether or not I stay depends on you."

She didn't know what he wanted, what he was asking exactly, but she did know one thing. "I love you, Calder. I want you to stay."

There was a blur of movement and then she was being lifted from her chair against a hard, masculine chest. The desperate intensity of his kiss stunned her, and at first she was too taken aback to respond.

He pulled away, his gaze probing hers. "Tabby?"

"Calder . . ."

"You said you loved me?"

"Oh, yes, I do . . ."

"You want me. I know you do."

She smiled at his arrogance. "Yes."

"Now?"

"As you English blokes are wont to say, not beforetime."

He grinned at her mock cockney accent and then frowned. "But you hesitated."

She looked coyly up at him, when she'd never looked coy in her life. "I think starting somewhere less than mach speed might help."

Incredibly, his sculpted cheekbones streaked a dusky red. Nevertheless, the smile he gave her was all confident, sensual male. "I think I can handle that."

And then he kissed her again, but it was nothing like that first kiss, so desperate and urgent.

His lips brushed hers as softly as butterfly wings. Barely there and then they were gone, only to come back again and again, and each time she tried to cling. Only he kept the touches light, making her hunger for the deep kisses of the night before.

She moaned with the urgency of her need.

When he'd teased her lips into swollen sensitivity, he moved his mouth onto her cheek and she discovered that her lips were not the only sensitive skin on her face. He blew softly in her ear and then bit down gently on the lobe. She arched toward him and shivered convulsively.

She held onto his shoulders, knowing to let go would mean sinking into a puddle of aching feminine desire.

His lips moved onto the column of her neck, and the sensual shivers wracked her body as each kiss heightened her sensitivity to his touch.

She'd worn a tank top, giving him free access to her bare skin all the way to the upper swell of her breasts. He took advantage, pressing small, nibbling kisses all over and tasting her with the very tip of his tongue until he reached her neckline. He stopped there, with his mouth hovering just above her skin.

She made a small, animal-like sound of need, unable to stand his teasing anymore, and he laughed softly, his breath hot against her.

Then he tugged her top up from the hem until her bra-encased breasts were revealed. "You're beautiful, Tabby."

She couldn't respond; she was too busy experiencing the way he laved her cleavage with his tongue. It felt like she could come right then, without any further preliminaries. Unbelievably, she was more excited than she had been the night before.

He flicked the front clasp of her bra open and peeled it back to reveal her already hard nipples to the air.

Her breathing fractured. "Suck them, Calder, please."

He did, taking one into his mouth and tugging on it with just enough pressure to send her body convulsing in a miniclimax.

She gasped, her body rigid with pleasure. "Oh, man, Calder, you're good at this."

Husky laughter vibrated against her breasts. "I've had a lot of practice." He licked her nipple, swirling his tongue around the aureole, but not taking it into his mouth again, as if he was building her toward another climax.

He probably was.

She sucked in air.

Then he stopped moving and she whimpered.

"I shouldn't have said that." He sounded embarrassed, irritated with himself. "I'm sorry, love."

It was her turn to laugh, but the sound was breathless because she could barely force her lungs to take in air over her skyrocketing excitement. "I don't mind. If your, um . . . enhanced experience is what makes you such an amazing lover and capable of giving me this kind of pleasure, I'm certainly not going to complain about it."

His mouth moved back to hers with lightning speed and he spoke against her lips. "Tabby, you're so bloody perfect. I love you."

"Are you sure?" she asked, despite a wealth of evidence in favor of his words.

Years of living in her sister's shadow had taken a toll she hadn't fully appreciated until this moment, when the man she loved spoke his own love to her.

He cupped her face and looked her square in the eye. He didn't say anything, but it was all there for her to see in the intensity of his dark gaze: knowledge of who and what she was because he'd taken the time to find out. Not only did he know her on a level she would have thought impossible, he approved of what he knew.

Her shyness did not bother him. He wanted her. Only her.

She had no words to react to such a thing and simply pressed her lips against his, offering her body and her trust.

He accepted with a care that brought tears to her eyes. Knowledgeable fingers brushed down her bare back, drawing small circles against her skin, doing things at the base of her spine that turned the muscles in her legs to water. He caught her around the waist and held her up, pressing her against him for balance.

There was something incredibly erotic about having her naked breasts against his shirt-clad torso.

She wanted to touch him, too, and tunneled her hands under the dark T-shirt. His skin was so warm, but he shivered at the touch of her hands on his back.

As sexy as it felt to be half naked while he was fully clothed, she wanted his shirt off. She wanted to see and feel him without restrictions. She yanked at the hem and he broke the kiss to help her peel it off him.

"Oh my . . ." she breathed.

He stood there, letting her look her fill, somehow knowing that as simple as it was, this permitted voyeurism was the sexiest kind of foreplay to her. Last night, it had been almost dark. His body had been nothing but a shadow, but now she could see him clearly and what she saw entranced her.

He had a light smattering of dark hair covering his chiseled abs and well-defined chest muscles. She reached out and brushed her fingers down his torso. The silky texture of his hair against her fingertips excited her unbearably and she smoothed her hands all over his hot skin, excitement melting the core of her.

She whispered, "You're incredible," and then blushed. "I mean—"

Once again, he pressed his finger over her lips. "It's okay. I'm glad you find my body as pleasing as I find yours."

It was then she realized that while she'd been enjoying the display of his body, he had been looking at her bare breasts because her shirt was still pushed up under her armpits. She went to cover them in a reflexive action, but he forestalled her with a quick movement that pulled her into his body.

Her nipples pinched tight, rubbing against him, and then pulsed with indescribable pleasure.

He kissed her, his tongue coming out to master her mouth, but he did it with such tenderness that her heart squeezed.

Was it possible to fall in love this quickly . . . to know you needed another person to complete the other half of your soul? She had to believe yes.

She wasn't sure how it happened, but they were completely naked, standing skin to skin, heartbeat to heartbeat, at the end of a bed in a bedroom she had no recollection of moving to.

She'd daydreamed so many times of her perfect lover taking her, sharing his body with her as she shared hers with him. Only daydreams could not begin to compete with this reality. Calder was so in tune to her every response, he seemed to know her body better than she did.

He touched and caressed and tasted, while encouraging her to do the same. She touched him in ways and places she'd never wanted to touch another man, but with Calder, she wanted to know him completely, intimately, and forever.

Her whole body trembled with the need to be joined to him. "Calder, please . . . I want you inside of me."

"Yes, Tabby, damn it . . . yes!" He swung her up in his arms and then carried her down to the soft bed.

The down comforter was soft and cushiony, but then he was lying down and pulling her over him, and she forgot about her surroundings. "Ride me, sweetheart. Ride me hard."

She'd never seen herself as the passionate type, but with those words, he unleashed the primitive, sensual woman within. She lowered herself over his hardness, realizing only as she did so that he'd managed to get a condom on sometime in the last few minutes. Probably the same time he'd managed to get her clothes off . . . during that kiss that had taken her under in a haze of passion.

She'd been too busy kissing and touching to notice anything else.

She pushed down on his hard penis, but she gained only partial penetration. He was big and she was tight. It had been so long for her, and it had not been all that many times to begin with.

"I know we're supposed to fit, but I can't . . . please, help me, Calder."

He gripped her inner thighs from the front so that his thumbs played across the swollen wet flesh of her clitoris. He caressed her, teasing her into movement in order to increase the friction on her sweet spot. He surged upward, his hold on her thighs keeping her in place. It was a pleasure this side of pain, but so intense she would die if he stopped.

He didn't stop. And though he had told her to ride him, he was the one doing the thrusting. But the wild woman inside her didn't want it to be all him. She matched his rhythm, adding a variation of her own that had him gasping under her.

She leaned down and offered her breast to him.

He took her nipple into his mouth and started to suck, then nipped her with his teeth.

They came together in a paroxysm of surging limbs and hoarse, elemental cries.

Afterward, she collapsed on top of him, her whole body limp with pleasure.

"Marry me, Tabby."

Her heart stopped and then started again at a gallop. It was more than she'd ever hoped for or dreamed of. "I . . ."

"Please, Tabby, say you will. Don't make me spend the rest of my life alone."

Tears washed into her eyes and she hugged him tight, unable to voice the maelstrom of emotions going through her. She understood exactly what he meant. If it wasn't Calder, it wouldn't be anyone. She guessed some people were just so perfectly matched that once they clicked, breaking open the lock would damage them both.

Finally, she choked out, "I want children."

"Yes."

"And a house on the beach."

"What a coincidence, I've got one."

"And a fish."

"A fish?"

"I'm allergic to cats and dogs, but our kids have to have pets."

"I'll buy you a fifty-gallon aquarium for our first anniversary."

"Why do I have to wait?"

"I want to make sure you have staying power. It's an incentive."

She sat up in outrage and started laughing at the expression on his face.

"I was having you on, love. I'll buy you interest in Sea World if it will get you to marry me."

"I only need you. I love you, Calder."

"You'll marry me?"

"Oh, yes."

"Thank you." He kissed her until they were making love again.

When they were once again sated and lying together, this time under the soft, fluffy comforter, he whispered against her lips, "I love you, Tabby, and I always will."

"I love you, Calder."

And a year later, when she told him she was pregnant with their first child and he bought the fifty-gallon aquarium complete with fish and live coral, she knew she would love this man into eternity.

No Shirt,
No Shoes,
No Service

Kate Angell

Chapter One

"Cup of coffee and a piece of apple pie."
Violet Cates gave a start at the sound of the deep voice behind her. There hadn't been a customer in Molly Malone's two minutes ago when she began counting her tips at the narrow waitress station between the soda machines and shelves of condiments. Apparently, someone had snuck in.

She sighed as she folded the one-dollar bills and pocketed the change. No fortune was made from the noon rush, she realized, disappointed. Her regular customers were generous, but the surfers and skimboarders who'd jammed the diner earlier could barely cover the cost of their meals. Most of them paid in change.

They sat at her tables, talking waves and swells, and Gulf temperature for the entire lunch hour. They seldom left her a tip. She'd chased out several guys for not wearing shirts or shoes. Barefoot William, Florida, was a beach community. Still, it was diner policy that customers must wear a T-shirt and flip-flops. No exceptions.

Violet glanced at her watch. Three P.M. She worked the dining room alone during the middle of the day, when it was usually quiet. The dinner shift started at five. Two other waitresses would be on the floor with her then.

The customer who'd called out his order had one of those smooth, sexy male voices that sifted into a woman and made her sin. She shivered. She'd only known one man who sounded that hot. She hadn't heard his voice in five years.

She was curious to see what this guy looked like.

Removing her order pad from the pocket of her short khaki skirt, she turned, put a smile on her face, only to have her heart nearly stop when she rounded the corner. There on the counter stool sat *Brad Davis.* She was sure of it.

The memory of him nearly knocked her off her feet. She'd never forgotten the boy with the black hair, smoke-blue eyes, and lean body. His teenage good looks had sharpened as an adult. High cheekbones. Sexy lips. Solid jaw.

"Brad?" she asked, curious, crossing to the counter.

"Hello, Vi," he said easily. One corner of his mouth tipped up, just enough to flash the single dimple in his unshaven cheek.

He rose, stepped over his duffel bag, and gave her a hug. He tucked her so close she could barely breathe. Not that she was complaining. She loved his touch. His shoulders were wide; his chest was thick. The muscles in his body flexed and rippled against her.

She inhaled against his neck. His cologne was subtle. He still wore Fierce, she realized, a blend of citrus, musk, and masculinity. The scent hinted of lust-darkened eyes and unzipped jeans. Of low moans, flushed skin, and twined limbs. Of rumpled sheets and orgasms.

"It's good to see you, babe," he said near her ear. His words tickled warm against her skin.

"You look great," she managed. Sensations from their past stirred her present. Her skin prickled. Her nipples hardened as his dick brushed against her belly. She had the crazy urge to nip his jaw and lick the pulse at the base of his throat. Then get naked and kiss her way down his body.

She'd missed him. Terribly. Even after all this time. She wanted to curl her fingers in his shirt and make a fist so he couldn't leave her again. Her sigh was heavy, reflective, as his body pressed hers.

A subtle shift in his stance and his knee eased between her legs. Her already short skirt hiked up an inch. The intimate rub of denim against her bare inner thighs gave her goose bumps. What was she thinking? Although the diner was quiet, a customer could walk through the door at any moment. Violet stepped back.

Brad was slow to release her. His hands slid intimately down her back and over her hips. His thumbs stroked her belly, dented her navel, then creased the top of her thighs. His touch was sexual and familiar. Her heart was racing by the time he let her go.

"Pie," she repeated to clear her head. "Apple." Her voice sounded raspy. She moved down the counter to the revolving pie case. Molly baked twice a day, offering a variety of homemade desserts.

There was one slice of deep-dish apple left. Sure enough, it had Brad's name on it. The pie had a crisscross crust and was sprinkled with cinnamon. Just the way he liked it. She scooped the last piece onto a small plate.

Déjà vu, she thought. How many desserts had she served him when they were together? Too many to count.

Memories took hold and time suddenly receded. She was drawn back to her senior year in high school.

It was late October. She'd been taking notes on *The Great Gatsby* in English Literature class when the gossip reached her. Brad Davis's parents had kicked him out of the house on his eighteenth birthday. His family was large, his father was out of work, and there'd been too many mouths to feed.

He'd shown up at Barefoot William High with an athletic bag in hand. He went through the day surrounded by friends and their support. After the last bell of the school day, he went looking for work.

Molly Malone's was a popular locale on the boardwalk. The diner had a steady stream of traffic. Molly was the kindest person Violet knew. She offered the outcast a sandwich and a soda, then hired Brad before he finished filling out his application. He would help Vi bus tables.

Molly also put a roof over his head, Violet recalled. Her aunt offered him the storeroom with its fold-out cot and small bathroom. She fed him two meals a day and gave him a chance to finish his education.

Violet remembered sneaking peeks at him while they worked, asking herself how she'd gotten stuck with this jock. No clear answer ever presented itself since she and Brad ran with different crowds. She wrote for the high school newspaper and yearbook, while he played baseball and wrestled.

They hadn't known each other well until they'd started working together. She was all legs and wild, curly, blond hair. He was cocky and too good-looking.

She spent her free time studying.

He went on dates.

Violet had gritted her teeth when groups of girls followed Brad to the diner after school. They'd sit at the counter, sipping sodas and watching him clear tables. Their heads going up and down like bobble-heads.

She'd barely tolerated Brad, but that changed when she turned eighteen the following February. Molly threw her a small party at the diner after closing. The guests drifted out by ten P.M., leaving Brad and Vi alone with the last two corner slices of yellow cake with whipped cream confetti frosting.

She could still sense their quiet intimacy. She shivered even now. They'd sat side by side in a booth. The window shades were drawn and a single vanilla votive candle flickered on the tabletop.

She'd taken a final bite of cake, only to have the whipped icing smudge one corner of her mouth. She reached for a napkin just as Brad leaned in and licked her lips clean. She'd stared at him, stunned and wide-eyed.

There'd been challenge in his eyes. Heat, too.

She'd felt uncertain, yet curious.

Her heart fluttered with the memory of that life-altering moment when she flicked her tongue back at him, touching his lower lip. He was quick to bite the tip. She'd felt the jolt in her nipples, her belly, her crotch, and all the way to her toes. Her entire body blushed.

He went on to angle his head and kiss her fully. It had been an unforgettable kiss, one that was long and deep and tasted of sugar and candied dots of confetti.

She fell in love with the way he kissed.

They'd made out until their lips were numb.

From that night on, awareness hovered between them. They began to look at each other in a new light. Their heated stares led to stolen caresses behind the soda machine. Kisses in the last booth after closing. Before long they couldn't keep their hands off each other.

They were daring, sneaking into the back storeroom with the fold-out cot. They did more than sleep. The brooms, buckets, and cleaning supplies kept their sexy little secrets.

That first summer after high school, Molly promoted Brad to short-order cook and Violet started waiting tables. They went on to work together for six years. They shared great sex and their dreams for the future. They were both ambitious, though there wasn't much room for advancement at Molly Malone's. Still, they both hoped to open their own restaurants someday.

Violet's heart broke the day Brad left Barefoot William. He'd grown restless. A man could only flip so many pancakes. Scramble so many eggs. Butter so many slices of toast.

She'd understood, but that hadn't lessened her pain.

He promised Vi he'd return someday. Once he'd made something of himself. Was today that day?

As she looked at him now, he appeared much as he had before he'd left town. A man still down on his luck with long hair, wrinkled blue T-shirt, and faded jeans. His tennis shoes appeared to have walked a million miles.

Right back to Barefoot William. And to her.

Violet cast him a glance as she reached for the coffeepot. Her heart quickened. There was something appealing about a man with rough edges and a raw attitude. Brad had both. She found she was as drawn to him now as she'd been at twenty-four. His male heat touched her across the counter.

He caught her eyeing him and his grin spread, knowing, lazy, unsettling. His single dimple was so damn sexy. It softened his sharp cheekbones and firm jaw.

Violet collected herself. She served his pie, poured his coffee, and located a set of napkin-wrapped silverware. He took two big bites, leaned back on the stool, and patted his stomach. She noticed the stretch of the cotton over his abdomen. He was definitely cut. His belly was flat. The bulge behind his jeans zipper stood out significantly. His legs were long, his thighs muscled.

"The pie is as good as I remember," he told her.

She met his gaze. "Molly hasn't lost her touch."

He cut a look over his shoulder. "She's redecorated, too." He noticed.

"Twice now, since you left," she said.

The present color scheme reflected the beach,

aqua and sand tones. There were blue leather booths and light brown tiles. One wall was decorated with restored vintage photographs, each one depicting the growth of the town.

Barefoot William valued its history. The photos showed the fishing pier under construction and the boardwalk with only three shops. The largest of the photographs depicted ten big boats scattered off-shore. Commercial fishing had supported the town for fifty years.

Brad took a sip of coffee, then said, "I've missed you, Vi. How've you been?" He seemed genuinely interested. "Still planning to go into business for yourself?"

So he remembered her dream. Her heart warmed. "I'm two thousand dollars closer," she said honestly. She didn't mention her crisis stash, an additional five hundred that she kept hidden in an empty shampoo bottle beneath the sink at her cottage.

Sadly, she'd saved very little money over the years and hated to admit her failure. "I love mom-and-pop corner diners. Nothing beats home-cooked meals. I'm not interested in buying a franchise, but I'd like to have a small diner someday."

He nodded. "You'll make it happen, Vi."

"I hope so." She swallowed her pride, said, "Unexpected emergencies cut into my savings."

"Your sister?" he was quick to guess.

She nodded. He'd met Lydia, her sister with three kids and no job. "She's a single mom and needed my help more than once," Vi said, holding back her sigh. Lydia could be exhausting.

Whenever her younger sister held out her hand, Violet was there, paying a bill, buying clothes for Lydia's kids, or filling the refrigerator with groceries. Last week, Vi had bought two retread tires for her sister's dented, rusted, and outdated Datsun. The bucket of bolts was falling apart and had no trade-in value.

Violet was the only person she could turn to. Their parents no longer loaned Lydia money. She never paid them back. She was in debt not only to family but to countless friends. Lydia lived off people. She used her kids to gain sympathy, but people were tired of her ploys.

It seemed for every two dollars Violet got ahead, she fell back five. Her credit cards were maxed out. She wasn't making enough money at the diner to qualify for a bank loan. Life was as life was. She refused to throw herself a pity party. She'd make it. Somehow.

"I'm in a rut." She smiled thinly. "I'm still waiting tables."

"You look good doing it," he complimented her, giving her the once-over. His gaze lingered on her breasts and the bare length of leg below her short skirt. "Don't give up, Violet. You never know when your luck will change."

"Have you been lucky?" she asked, and instantly regretted her question. He appeared the worse for wear. Brad needed a shower, shave, and change of clothes.

He shrugged. "I've had a few things go my way," he slowly said, only to pause when Molly pushed through the swinging kitchen door.

She wore a plain brown dress, white Keds, and carried a bank bag. She crossed to the counter. "Brad Davis!" Her excitement was genuine.

"Sweet Molly." Brad hugged the older woman. He was as tall and lean as she was short and plump. Molly was a testament to her home-style cooking. She sampled every dish and dessert before it was served to her customers.

"Have you come back to me?" Molly asked, hopeful.

"Did I ever leave you?" he asked.

Molly patted him on the arm. "Stick around," she said as she filled the bank bag from the cash register. "You couldn't have arrived at a more opportune time. My cook is going on vacation for two weeks. I'd hate to hire someone for such a short time. You know the ropes, son. Care to help out, unless you have other commitments?"

"Nothing much going on in my life at the moment," Brad said. He released her and returned to his stool. "Let me think about your offer over a second cup of coffee."

Violet gave him a refill. She listened as Molly and Brad spoke a moment longer. Her aunt had always been fond of him. She saw him as a good guy and a hard worker.

Molly had no idea he used to jump Vi's bones whenever she left to make a bank deposit in the middle of the afternoon. Fifteen minutes was the perfect window for a quickie in the storeroom. Their nightly sex stretched for hours. Brad had been insatiable.

The bank bag in her hand, Molly was headed for

the door that very minute. Violet's pulse picked up and her stomach fluttered. Memories of his mouth, hands, and cock stroked her like foreplay. Her face flushed and her nipples hardened. Her bikini panties felt too tight.

She was afraid to look at Brad; afraid he'd notice how mere thoughts of him still turned her on. Her body was heated and humming. She could barely catch her breath.

"I'm off," Molly finally said, clutching the bank bag to her ample bosom. "It should be fairly quiet while I'm gone. The local coffee crowd will be trickling in around four, and a few will order pie. I have two peach pies and one apple baking in the oven. Listen for the timer, Violet. It should go off in ten or eleven minutes." Then she left.

The click of the door sounded loud in the silence. But not as loud as Violet's heart thumping in her chest. It wasn't often the diner stood empty and sexual opportunity knocked. She practiced self-control. Biting down on her bottom lip, she glanced through the wide set of windows that faced the southwest Florida beach.

Her hometown had once been divided by a century-old feud, but the conflict between its two founding families had recently been resolved. Still, there were considerable differences in the two sides of the boardwalk, separated by Center Street.

The Cates northern cement boardwalk linked to a wooden pier that catered to fishermen, sun worshippers, water sports enthusiasts, and tourists who didn't wear a watch on vacation.

Amusement arcades and carnival rides drew large

crowds. The specialty shops sold everything from Florida T-shirts, ice cream, and sunglasses, to sharks' teeth, shells, and hula hoops.

A vintage carousel whirled within a weatherproof enclosure. Its wall of windows overlooked the Gulf. The whirr of the Ferris wheel was soothing, while the swing ride that whipped out and over the waves sent pulses racing.

Barefoot William was as honky-tonk as Saunders Shores was high-end. Couture, gourmet dining, and a five-star hotel claimed the southern boundaries. Yachts the size of cruise ships lined the waterways. Private airstrips replaced commercial travel. The wealthy were a community unto themselves. The Saunders boardwalk was too rich for Violet's blood.

She preferred the warmth and wholesomeness of Barefoot William. She wished there was a career opportunity for her here. However, all the storefronts were rented. The Cateses owned and operated each one. The shops were handed down over generations.

Violet's parents had chosen to work at city hall instead of the boardwalk. Her mother was the mayor's secretary and her father did maintenance. They budgeted, took a yearly vacation, and lived a frugal lifestyle.

Vi had started working for her aunt when she was sixteen, but over the years, she'd slowly outgrown the diner. She desperately wanted to be her own boss.

Her stomach sank at the thought of how long it would take her to achieve her goal. Someday, she promised herself. Someday . . .

"Vi?" Brad nudged into her thoughts. "You look sad, babe. Want to talk about it? I'm a good listener."

She shook her head. "Thanks, but there's nothing you can do."

"I can check on the pies," he offered. He grabbed his duffel bag and pushed off the stool. "Molly would kill us both if the crusts burned."

"That she would," she agreed, grateful for his concern.

He held the kitchen door for her. As she walked past him, her shoulder brushed his chest and her hip bumped his thigh. He flattened his palm on her lower back. His fingers tipped the upper curve of her bottom.

That did it. Apprehension marked her steps as their history surrounded her now, drawing her back to what they'd once had together. The storeroom stood off to the right. The door was closed to the orgasmic moans of her past.

Were Brad's memories as vivid as her own? Violet felt suddenly shy. And very nervous. Her confidence failed her. She'd always wanted to see Brad again, yet five years stretched between them. Could they pick up where they'd once left off? She wished she were twenty-four again.

She watched as he tossed his bag in the corner by the dishwasher, then checked out the kitchen. "Lots of updates," he noted, nodding his approval. "The grill I used to cook on had a slant. This one's brand-new."

"Repairs were eating up Molly's profits," Vi said. "She decided new equipment was the best investment."

"Smart lady." The timer buzzed. "Oven mitts?" he asked her, moving toward the commercial stove.

She pointed to the second shelf. "Between the colander and tongs."

He removed the pies and set them on a metal cooling rack. The scents of warm peaches and apples crooked like a beckoning finger. Removing the mitts, he located a knife and spatula and snuck a thin slice of peach. He motioned to Vi to take a bite.

She blew to cool it, then pinched off a piece with her fingers. There was nothing better than warm, out-of-the-oven peach pie.

Brad eyed her mouth. "Crumbs at the corner," he said.

Time stilled, along with her heart. She waited a second too long for him to kiss them away or brush them off. He made no move to do so. She was embarrassed by her need to have him touch her, even lightly.

She turned toward the polished stainless steel of the refrigerator. Staring at her reflection, she swiped at the specks with her palm. Brad came to stand behind her. He was a man of dark good looks and impressive height. They stood in silence, anticipating, evaluating, and thoughtful.

"Relax, babe," he finally said. He wrapped his arms about her waist and drew her to him, gently at first, until she pressed against him. He rested his chin on the top of her head. "I remember the old days, too. I can still see us in the storeroom, naked and so close. I can hear your breathing against my neck, feel you bite my shoulder."

She remembered the arch of his back and the

rock of his hips. The way he slid inside her. She leaned back then, closing what little space remained between them. Her spine curved fully against his chest. Her round bottom pushed against his thighs. He tightened his hold as if he planned to never let her go.

"Your body's talking to mine, Violet," he said. "You're getting hot and going soft. You just sighed for me."

That she had. There was familiarity in his touch, in the steadiness of his breathing. In the male power of his stance. In the swell of his sex. Desire rekindled their past. She let go and lived their present. She tilted her head and raised her chin, seeking his mouth with her own.

Chapter Two

The diner wasn't the ideal place for his home-coming kiss, Brad Davis thought, but he could never deny Violet anything. Sex was waiting to happen. Yet all he could give her at that moment was a kiss. He hated to start what he wouldn't be able to finish.

His pulse picked up as he looked down on her face. Damn, she was beautiful. Her eyelids were shuttered, her light brown lashes long. Her blond ponytail shadowed one cheek. Her lips were inviting, full and generous. The flick of her tongue aroused him.

He put his forefinger and thumb under her chin and tilted her head back farther. Their past emerged with a hungry need and embraced them both. His mind shut down as his body turned on. The light brush of her lips made him instantly stiff. Her mouth was sweet and yielding. What started as a short kiss lasted a good long while.

Never breaking their kiss, he slowly turned her to

face him. She wound her arms about his neck and went smooth against him. The softness of her breasts pushed into his chest. His erection settled between the V of her thighs. His hands slid up her sides to cup her full breasts. His thumbs rubbed across her nipples, drawing them to points.

He kept going, in spite of himself.

He scrolled his knuckles down her ribs, then circled her navel. He went on to caress her lower spine, her bottom, the crease of her ass through her short cotton skirt. The skirt bunched high on her thighs. He stroked the smooth, tan backs of her bare legs.

His libido was hyped, and he had the wild urge to walk her backward toward the storeroom, to open the door and slip inside. To take her with the passion of a man long without his woman.

It was not to be. Reality soon separated them. He drew back and exhaled his frustration. Violet looked dazed, confused. Flushed. He wanted to go on, reconnect with her sexually, but their timing was off. Molly could return at any minute. Locals would soon cluster for their daily chat and slice of afternoon pie. The last thing he wanted was for Molly to catch them in the act. He held great respect for both Violet and her aunt.

That didn't make the situation any easier. He had to face the facts. He and Vi were older now. Lives changed in five years. The days of their slipping into the back room for sex had passed. The next time they went horizontal it would be on a big, comfortable bed. He wondered if she had her own home or if she still lived with her parents.

He thought back to the day he'd left town. He'd packed their goals and dreams in his heart and driven off in his Chevy. Now, returning on a summer day in mid-July, he looked much the same as when he'd left, scruffy and broke. He wore clothes from his laundry basket and his high school sneakers. He'd saved the Nikes. They reminded him of his roots. Something he vowed never to forget.

He hoped with all his heart that Violet would accept him as he was. He hadn't changed all that much.

The back door suddenly slammed and a burly man in a white T-shirt, camouflage pants, and black army boots walked into the kitchen. He nodded to Violet and raised an eyebrow at Brad.

"Joe, this is Brad," Vi said, introducing the two men. "Brad was the short-order cook before you."

Joe ran one hand over his buzz cut and frowned. "The same Brad who broke your heart?" His tone was blunt, rough, and protective. Brad wasn't jealous. The man was old enough to be her father.

Color rose in Violet's cheeks. "One and the same."

Brad's chest clenched. He'd thought Vi understood the importance of his leaving town, his need to make something of himself. To hear how much he'd hurt her from a stranger was a punch to his gut.

"I'm back," he finally said.

"Staying or passing through?" asked Joe. He widened his stance, crossed his arms over his chest. A *Fry It* tattoo was revealed beneath the sleeve of his shirt.

"I'm here to cover your two-week vacation," Brad decided on the spot. He couldn't help noticing that Violet appeared relieved. "Afterward, we'll see." He and Vi had a lot of catching up to do. He refused to disclose his future plans to a man he'd just met.

"Don't commit to more than two weeks," Joe stated, cracking his knuckles. "I like working here."

"Brad's a placeholder until you return from Las Vegas," Molly clarified as she swung through the kitchen doors. "The menu hasn't changed much. Brad knows the ropes and can pick up where he left off."

Joe gave Brad a man-to-man look, one that openly asked if Brad would be starting up with Violet as well. Brad had no reason to respond to the older man, yet something inside him wanted to reassure Joe that he wasn't out to hurt Violet a second time. "Barefoot William is my home," he said firmly.

Joe gave him a brief nod before heading to the storeroom. He cracked the door, took two fresh aprons off a hook, and tossed one to Brad. "Suit up," he said. "We'll work the dinner rush together, if that's okay with Molly."

"Fine by me," Molly agreed, smiling.

"The coffee crowd's coming through the door," Joe said. "I'll start setting up for the dinner rush."

Brad watched as Violet adjusted her ponytail and straightened her shirt. She bent to retie the lace on her tennis shoe, giving him a view he couldn't resist. He admired the curve of her slender shoulders and sweet ass. She had great legs.

Vi glanced at him on her way to the dining room. Her green eyes warmed and a sexy smile tipped her lips. She wanted him. Brad's balls tightened. Tonight couldn't come soon enough.

The dinner hour passed in a flourish of orders.

The waiting line grew so long it stretched half a block. No one seemed to mind. The boardwalk entertainers were out in full force. The unicycle troupe, stilt walkers, and mimes left the customers laughing and applauding.

Polka music from the carousel danced in with each opening and closing of the front door. Families with kids and lone surfers crowded the counter, tables, and booths. The customers brought their smiles and high spirits to dinner.

Service ran until eight P.M. That's when Molly turned the sign on the door from OPEN to CLOSED. The shift wrapped up with a clearing of tables and thorough cleaning of the kitchen.

Joe shook Brad's hand on his way out. "You're a hard worker. I'm leaving the diner in good hands." He was gone.

"What's his story?" Brad asked Violet when she passed through the swinging doors.

She untied her short apron and tossed it into the laundry bag. "He's retired army. He worked in the mess hall. He's divorced, but never talks about his ex. No kids. He showed up one morning when we were short of help. Molly had burned her hand on the stove after our cook Kevin went home sick. Joe walked into the kitchen and started filling orders. He saved the day and stayed on. He lives in a trailer south of town."

Vi glanced toward the office, where Molly counted the receipts. "I think Joe's got a soft spot for Molly," she whispered. "He brings her flowers every Friday."

"Your aunt doesn't have much of a social life," said Brad. "She's married to the diner."

"I'll be committed to my restaurant, too," said Violet, chin up, "once the stars align and fortune falls in my lap."

He believed her, too. He could see it in her eyes; she was determined and filled with faith in her ability. All she needed was start-up capital. Life was all about timing. Her success was inevitable. "What now?" he asked.

"I walk home, take a shower, and change clothes," she said. "What's your situation? Do you have a car, a place to stay?"

"I rode in on the bus," he told her.

"Care to come home with me?" she invited.

He nodded. "Let me grab my duffel bag."

"I'll get my purse."

Molly stuck her head out of the office door. "Have a good day off tomorrow," she called to them. "See you bright and early on Thursday."

"Is bright and early still five A.M.?" Brad asked Vi as they stepped out onto the sidewalk.

"We'll be serving breakfast before the sun rises."

He didn't shun hard work. He was looking forward to renewing old customer acquaintances. He was damn glad to be home.

Brad curved his arm over Violet's shoulders as they strolled along Center Street. He liked walking beside her. The soft outer swell of her breast brushed his chest. They bumped hips and thighs. The scent of food traveled with them.

He drew in a breath, then said, "You smell like coffee and blueberry pie."

"I'm sniffing French fries on you, big guy."

He hugged her even closer. "Do you have a car?" he asked.

She stiffened. "Cars cost money," she said. "I only live four blocks from the diner. I don't mind walking. Molly picks me up on rainy days."

Brad's jaw set. She didn't have a car. He bet her sister had one, even if it was a junker. He couldn't fault Vi for being a giver, but Lydia would take and take until Violet had no more to lend.

He would buy Violet a vehicle of her choice someday when she stepped back and made Lydia stand on her own two feet. He was a patient man.

Looking around him now, he noted that they'd crossed into Olde Barefoot William, where the majority of the Cateses lived. The streets were quiet and the old Florida-style cottages were quaint. The homes were shingled and shuttered with wide porches. They'd withstood hurricanes and time. The homes were handed down through generations. Here lay the inner circle.

Enormous evergreens lined the narrow two-lane road. The late-afternoon sun winked between the branches. Ancient moss hung from the boughs. The scents of hibiscus and plumeria were heavy on the air. Sprinklers whirred as homeowners watered their lawns.

"South on Seashell," Violet directed, pointing left.

They turned the corner and stopped midblock. Her cottage was the smallest on the street. Painted green with white shutters and narrow window boxes, her house blended with the flowers and the foliage. Magnificent Queen Palms formed crescent arcs on both sides of the house. Red rosebushes lined the brick path that led to her front porch.

Brad followed her to the door. "How long have you lived here?" he asked.

"Three years," she said, fitting the key into the lock. "It was a Cates family hand-me-down from my great-uncle Thomas. He retired from the post office, bought a camper, and took off for Colorado. He prefers the mountains to the beach."

Vi bumped the door with her hip and he came in behind her. She sidestepped a small pink tricycle. He nearly tripped over a plastic water gun that had leaked onto the floor.

"Lydia and her kids stopped by while I was at work," she said. Her voice was flat.

They'd left one hell of a mess, Brad noted. "They came, they played, they didn't clean up."

Violet sighed. "They never do."

"Where does your sister live?" he asked. Vi's cottage wasn't very big. He figured two bedrooms at the most. There wasn't enough room for four more people. They'd be walking into walls.

"She lives boyfriend to boyfriend," she told him. "Lydia's staying with her latest, as far as I know. His name is Mark. He's a mechanic and a decent guy. She gets bored during the day and often drops by. My cottage is her day care center."

He caught her eye and she read his look. "Vi . . ."

"I know, I know," she said, making excuses. "Changes are coming soon."

They walked into the living room and Brad swore a tornado had hit the place. Hundreds of Legos were strewn across the blue and beige diamond-patterned carpet. Board games sat upended. The playing cards from Candyland lay amid a rifled deck of Uno. The plastic body parts of Operation were mixed with the Hungry Hungry Hippos. A dollhouse had fallen over. The roof was cracked.

A Teddy bear held a toy camera in the corner. A dozen wooden soldiers surrounded the stuffed animal, as if holding him hostage. The TV had been left on, and Big Bird waved from *Sesame Street.*

A glass of orange juice had tipped over on a side table and the juice dripped onto the couch, sticky and staining a cushion. The remains of a peanut butter sandwich smeared the glass coffee table. Graham cracker crumbs were as thick as sand.

"Sorry about this," Violet apologized. "Why don't you take a shower while I clean up?"

He had a better suggestion. "How about we both straighten the place and shower together?" He tossed his duffel bag back into the hallway. "Where can I find garbage bags, paper towels, and a sponge?"

She set down her purse on top of the television and came to him, her expression soft. "Thank you."

He drew her to him, held her close. "I'd do anything for you, Violet, even vacuum."

"I'm in your debt. I'll repay you in the shower." She smiled suggestively.

His body stirred at the thought. He set her gently from him. They had a mess to clean up. The faster they scrubbed and straightened, the sooner they'd have sex.

He worked like Mr. Clean. Thirty minutes later, the living room was spotless. There was a minor mess in the kitchen; together they loaded the dishwasher and wiped down the counters.

"All done," he said, drying his hands on a dish towel.

"That's what you think," said Vi as she turned on the dishwasher and crossed to him. "We're just getting started."

His gaze was hot. "I haven't even put my mouth on you, and I'm betting you're wet."

"I'm betting you're hard."

His dimple flashed. "See for yourself."

She tucked her fingers into the waistband of his jeans, flicked the snap with her thumb. She lowered his zipper and reached inside the Y-front fly of his navy Jockeys. Her tender touch set him on fire. He came alive for her. She led him to the shower, and not by the hand.

Chapter Three

Brad's cock swelled in her grasp. She loved the feel of him, all taut, hot, and satisfying inches. She gently rubbed her thumb over the head of his penis, then down the underside of his shaft. Sensitive to her touch, he groaned.

"Easy, Vi." His voice was tight, almost choked. "You're killing me."

"Death by my hands?" she asked as she slowly stroked and squeezed him. She loved doing this for him.

"Better than by my own."

"You've been flying solo?" she had to ask. That both surprised and pleased her.

"For too long," he admitted.

She liked the fact that during his absence he hadn't had a lot of sexual partners. But then, neither had she. Her vibrators had done their job just fine.

"Condoms are in my duffel," he said.

Violet lifted his bag. It was light for a man returning from his travels. Apparently, he didn't have many clothes. She'd buy him a new shirt and pair of jeans tomorrow. The ones he wore now had seen better days.

She led him into her bathroom. The space was small, narrow, and it was a tight squeeze for the two of them. She loved having him so close that their bodies touched. Tingly sensations ran up and down her spine when she pressed up against his broad chest, making her nipples harden. She ran her fingers from the base of his shaft to the tip, then gently released him. His sex stood at attention at the opening of his Jockeys.

She set his duffel bag down on her clothes hamper, then faced him. She slipped her arms around his neck and stood on her tiptoes, just looking at him. Wondering where he'd been, if he'd thought about her as much as she dreamed about him. And now he was back. They'd been separated too long. She felt a hot, immediate ache for this man. Her panties were already damp.

She licked her lips.

His nostrils flared.

They were all over each other in two heartbeats. Their bodies slammed together with a force that should've flattened them both. Grabbing on to every second they'd lost with such passion it made Violet's head spin.

She banged her hip on the sink. He hit his elbow against the wall. It became a race to see who could get the other person naked first. Who would beg for mercy.

Violet wasted no time. She shoved his white T-shirt up his chest and stared. How could she ever have been satisfied with a vibrator? Look at the man. He was all solid muscle and six-pack cut. Her fingers played over his ribs. She brushed his male nipples. His breathing deepened. She felt the race of his heart beneath her palms, appreciated the twitch of his dick against her belly. Her whole body softened when he widened his stance and drew her between his thighs.

She tugged off his shirt, let it fall and crumple on the tile floor. She stood back a moment, admiring his deeply tanned chest, wondering if he'd been doing hard labor under the hot sun all these years. She didn't care. She wanted him, *whatever* his past. Taking advantage of his bare shoulders, she nipped him, leaving her mark. She flicked her tongue to the pulse point at the base of his throat. Blew her breath where she laved.

She kissed her way to his jawline. His evening stubble was dark and rough against her lips. Her kiss to the soft spot beneath his ear made him moan. He lost it when she bit his lobe. He grew sexually impatient.

He cupped her face, looked deeply into her eyes, before raking his hands through her hair. His intimate touch spiked her need for him. He took her mouth with passion, arousal, and pure male urgency.

She blinked when her polo crowned her head and Brad tossed it aside. He pulled the scrunchie from her ponytail and her hair went wild. A cool shiver slid over her when he unsnapped her bra and let it slip off her shoulders. Her breasts spilled onto his palms. She threw her head back and gasped softly when his thumbs pressed her nipples and his fingers curled around her breasts. He teased the tips to tight points.

They kicked off their sneakers.

As he hurriedly undid the side buttons on her khaki skirt, two popped off. The skirt shimmied over her hips.

She jerked down his jeans. Her fingers caught in a front pocket, tore the seam. She definitely owed him a new pair now.

He freed her of her panties.

She took off his Jockeys.

They stood naked, and the air around them seemed to explode. Her face flushed and her lips parted. They kissed again. His warm tongue thrust into her mouth and tangled with her own. The man could kiss. She grew light-headed.

She dug her fingers into the corded curve of his biceps and clung to him.

She angled her hips toward him unconsciously.

He clutched her bottom.

"The shower." Violet could barely catch her breath. The words couldn't come fast enough. "The water's slow to heat."

Brad wasn't about to be deterred. "The vanity will have to do."

The countertop was old, a swirl of gold and pink marble. He boosted her up until her ass was braced on the edge. The marble was cool against her bottom, the back of her thighs.

She inhaled his scent and soaked up the warmth of his body. The plump swell of her naked breasts pressed his hard chest. She wrapped her legs about his hips and drew him close. His sex fit her V-zone.

His duffel was at arm's length. He upended the bag. Locating a condom, he stripped the wrapper, and sheathed himself. It was pure pleasure watching him, his eyes warming when he caught her. His fingers then moved between her thighs. He stroked her deeply. Her nerves tingled and her spine strained. Her fingernails traced the crease of his thigh and his muscles twitched in response. She tilted her hips and he entered her. He began to move.

She responded to the rock of his hips, to the tense heat of his body. She burned. She moaned. And he claimed her.

She made love with her heart.

He bared his soul.

Blood thrummed. Desire throbbed.

He pushed her to the edge.

She made him pant. Gasp. Groan.

Sensations built to wild currents.

Her climax shook her.

A hard shudder convulsed him.

A sated, sensual ease brought them back to reality. He rested his forehead against hers. He kissed the curve of her cheek, the tip of her nose. "You're amazing," he said, his voice husky.

"I could say the same for you." She sighed.

"We're good together." He leaned in, kissed her brow. His gaze remained warm and steady after their lovemaking.

He made her feel special.

Easing back, he got rid of his condom. He moved to the shower/bath combination, turned the hot water valve.

"It's been a long day," he said, his body sleek with the sweat of their lovemaking. "Tub soak or shower?"

She smiled, remembering their sensual bubble baths before he'd left town. Eucalyptus and almond had filled the air. Somehow Brad managed to look even more masculine immersed in bubbles. "A bath would be nice."

"I'll give you a foot massage," he offered.

Which she desperately needed. She'd worked a double shift today. Her feet ached and her calves were tight. He would take care of her, and then she'd relax him, too. "I bought a new Stimulite bath glove." Her lips twitched. "I want you slick and soapy and reaching for a second condom."

"You smell like almond," Violet said when they stepped from the bathtub, following their hour-long soak, sex play, and shower.

Brad wrapped her in a towel, securing the ends over her right breast. She liked nothing more than feeling snug and comfy in a big towel. Brad turned up the heat when he skimmed his thumb along the terry cloth edge, dipped a finger in her cleavage, and stroked the inner swells. "So soft," he murmured.

He continued to touch her. Vi found it difficult to breathe. The man was insatiable. She welcomed each brush of his fingers and press of his palm. He turned her on. Again and again. They both wanted to make up for lost time.

She loved his body. Always had. He was a man of strength and sensitivity. And charm. He'd always treated her well.

He stood in his own towel, secured at the blade of one hip. His shoulders were wide, the expanse of his chest mesmerizing. She was about to walk her fingers down his happy trail when the sound of the front door opening and closing announced they had a visitor.

Brad raised one eyebrow, then asked, "Who?"

She could think of only one person who would enter without knocking. "Lydia," she said on a sigh.

His jaw worked as he grabbed a fresh gray T-shirt and athletic shorts from his upended duffel bag. He was dressed in seconds.

Violet's clothes were in her bedroom. She didn't want to put on her dirty polo and skirt. Not when she felt so clean and refreshed.

She looked around the bathroom. Her only option was a long nightgown, hanging on a hook on the back of the door. The blue cotton gown covered her fully. She wore it for both lounging and sleeping. She slipped it on now.

Brad was the first out the door. She followed him into the hallway. The pad of their feet warned the visitor of their arrival. None too soon, either.

Vi had been right—they found Lydia in the living room, her head bent as she went through Violet's wallet, which was sitting atop the TV. She didn't look up, didn't immediately react to being caught in the act.

"You're as broke as me," her sister snorted. She returned the wallet to Vi's purse, then scavenged the bottom of the bag for loose change. She came up empty-handed. She straightened then, revealing highlighted blond hair and a determined expression. Her tank top was a size too small, her skinny jeans were too snug, and the heels on her pumps were too high.

"Shit," she muttered as she moved to the couch and flipped up the cushions. There were no coins, only a sticky piece of hard candy and a broken plastic spoon. "Still stashing cash in the empty coffee can in the kitchen?" Lydia guessed.

Violet shook her head. "Finances are tight," she said, which was the truth. Fortunately, the tips she'd made at the diner remained in the pocket of her khaki skirt, crumpled on the bathroom floor. She had plans for the money. She owed Brad a pair of jeans. "Sorry, I'm tapped out."

Lydia slapped her palms against her thighs. "I've bills to pay. We're out of groceries."

"Get a job," Brad said evenly.

"Brad Davis." Lydia eyed him now. "Back in town, I see, and already gettin' busy with my sister." Her gaze came back to Violet. "Granny jammies?" Her smile was snide. "No wonder you're not married."

Embarrassed, Violet glanced at Brad. He wasn't uncomfortable with Lydia's careless remark, only annoyed. His gaze had narrowed and his jaw was set. His frown deepened. His biceps flexed. He looked ready to punch a wall.

She stopped him with her hand to his forearm, silently requesting that he let her deal with Lydia. He understood and gave her a brief nod. Then he crossed his arms over his chest and waited. She found his concern comforting, but that didn't help the situation.

Vi loved her sister, but Lydia took advantage of her more often than not. Borrowing what few clothes she had, using her as a babysitting service, then begging for a handout. Lydia expected the world to revolve around her and pay her way.

It was time Violet took a stand and set down some rules. She was grateful for Brad's support. She drew a fortifying breath, then said, "Brad is home and he'll be living with me while he's here. I'd appreciate you knocking next time."

"Brad is staying here? Now who's the mooch?" Lydia mocked.

"I invited him," Vi said evenly. She held out her hand. "I'll need your key."

"*My* key for *him?*" Her sister's eyes rounded. She looked so hurt, Violet almost felt sorry for her. *Almost.*

"The key, Lydia," she requested, waiting.

Grumbling, Lydia reached into the front pocket of her skinny jeans and produced the house key. "Not a nice way to treat family, Violet," she whined, trying to make her feel bad. "What about my kids? All their toys are here at your house."

"That's an easy fix," Brad said, taking the initiative. He walked into the hallway, lifted the tricycle by the handlebars, and said, "I'll help you pack and load your car." He opened the front door, peered out. "Is that your Datsun parked at the curb?"

Lydia hissed, and Brad carried out the trike. Violet glanced through the front window and watched as he loaded it into the trunk. A rusted trunk that popped open without a key.

"You'll regret this, Vi," Lydia said sharply from the corner of the couch. "Brad left you before and he'll do it again."

No regrets, Vi thought, shaking her head. If anything, she felt relieved. "I'll grab a garbage bag for the toys," she said without so much as a nod in Lydia's direction. "Brad can deal with the dollhouse."

"I feel ill," Lydia said, clutching her stomach. She

hurried down the hallway toward the bathroom, moaning all the way for effect.

"Will she be okay?" Brad asked, returning from his first trip to her car. He began dismantling the dollhouse next. It came apart in five pieces. Vi saw concern for her spoiled sister on his face in spite of Lydia's nastiness. She loved him for that.

"She plays the sick card whenever she doesn't get her own way." Violet was well acquainted with her sibling's role-playing. Lydia gagged, choked, feigned heart pains, anything to get sympathy. It hadn't worked today.

Violet went after a trash bag, returned with two. There were more toys in her living room than in a holiday display in the local discount store. Lydia's kids were cute, but not well behaved. Motherly discipline wasn't her sister's strong suit. Lydia needed to take charge of her life and stop depending on others. Including her.

The toys were bagged and in her car by the time Lydia returned from the bathroom. She didn't look sick, Vi noted, as she strolled down the hallway, a smirk on her face.

"See you, sweetie," she said, patting Violet on the cheek. She appeared far more carefree than when she'd arrived. Vi winced. Something was off.

Lydia had nearly reached the door when Brad caught her by the arm. She looked up, curled her lip. *"Now what?"* she demanded, ticked that he'd stopped her.

"You know what, Lydia," he accused her.

"I didn't take the last roll of toilet paper," she protested, "if that's what you're thinking."

His gaze lowered to her breasts. "The money," he

stated, a sharp edge to his voice. "You're not walking out with Violet's tips."

Color rose in Lydia's cheeks. "You're checking out my boobs?" Her tone was harsh. "Careful, Vi, Brad's got a wandering eye."

Violet now noticed what Brad had already seen. Her sister's breasts were lopsided, as if she'd padded her bra, one side with Kleenex, one side with a rolled-up sock.

Disappointment stung, sharp and bitter. Lydia's padding came from cold, hard cash. She'd pilfered the pockets of Violet's khaki skirt and stolen her tips. Vi wouldn't be surprised if Lydia had also located her crisis stash in the shampoo bottle under the sink.

"Hand it over, Lydia," Violet said, her voice soft, yet stern. "Right now."

Lydia swore a blue streak that left no doubt she was guilty. Stealing didn't seem to bother her, but getting caught did. She reached inside her tank top to the cup of her bra and removed a handful of bills. She slapped them on Vi's palm. "Happy now?" she growled.

"Not happy enough," came from Brad. "Take off your left high heel."

"What the hell?" Lydia's anger rose. "A strip search?"

Brad came back with, "I saw Benjamin Franklin's face peeking out the back of your shoe."

Begrudgingly, Lydia took off her left pump. Fifties and hundreds were stuffed inside. "You rob a bank?" she asked Brad, passing him the rest of the cash. "Your wallet was loaded. You've got more credit cards than God."

Violet blinked. *Where had Brad gotten so much money?* Surely her sister was mistaken. She looked his way, confused and at a loss for words. He avoided her gaze, but she didn't take that as anything to worry about. His life was his own. She had no right to question his finances.

Silence hung between them like a well-kept secret. Brad took a step back, then swung the door wide. Lydia tottered out, one shoe on, one shoe off. Halfway down the steps, she flipped them the bird. Vi rolled her eyes at her sister's brazenness.

Brad closed the door behind her. He leaned back against the frame. "Your sister is sneaky."

"It's who she is," Vi said on a sigh. "I'm glad you caught her."

"You'd better count your money," he said. "Make sure it's all there."

Vi fingered through the bills. Her tips and crisis stash were accounted for. "I'm good, how about you?"

He clutched his fifties and Franklins tightly. "I'm fine," he said without counting. "Lydia found my travel money. I was carrying enough cash to rent an apartment and get settled."

He didn't mention the credit cards, and Vi let it pass. Probably maxed out, just like her own. "I meant what I said, Brad," she offered. "You're welcome to stay here as long as you like."

He came toward her then, all hot eyes and flashing dimple. "I like a lot."

He drew her close, and showed her how much.

Chapter Four

Brad woke up with a sexual hangover.
He was wrung dry and needed hydration.

His night with Violet had been the best of his life.
He'd loved every minute. Sex had been a roll and
tumble, on the bed, on the floor, on the overstuffed
corner chair. They'd made up for lost time. He'd
had the energy of a wild-eyed, horny kid. Vi had let
herself go completely. She wasn't afraid to show her
feelings.

He had rug burns on his knees and he was certain Vi had her fair share of bruises. His stubble had
sandpapered her chin.

He sprawled on his back on her bed, naked, a
white cotton sheet drawn over his hips. Violet lay
beside him, her arms and legs all over him. She
reached for him in sleep, twining their bodies
tightly together. He couldn't believe he'd gone so
long without holding her. He'd burned for this day,
to have her sweet warmth all his again.

He gently brushed her bangs off her forehead

and pressed a light kiss to her brow. He couldn't stop looking at her. Her face was free of makeup; soft and vulnerable, beautiful. Her lips were slightly parted and her breath warmed his chest, right over his heart. Her knee was bent, a fraction from his balls. He shifted just enough that if she jerked awake, she wouldn't take out his boys.

He was a man who enjoyed morning sex with his woman. Today was no exception. He'd known five years ago that Violet belonged to him. They had yet to discuss love or their future, but that would happen soon enough. He was still working on *how* to tell her his whole story. There were truths to be told and surprises to unfold. He wanted the best for Violet Cates, but would she agree that his best was right for her?

She blinked awake now. Her smile was slow, lazy, and sexy as hell. Her body was soft and curvy, her silky hair crossing over one eye, giving a peekaboo look that promised more fun to come. She trailed her fingers down his chest, dipped them beneath the sheet, and stroked him lightly. "We have today off from work," she said on a sigh. "I'll cook you breakfast."

He circled her nipple with one finger. The tip beaded for him. "I'll have two legs over easy." He rolled her onto her back.

She grinned up at him. "I'm hungry for you, too."

She wanted him. Again. Arousal pulsed and heated the air. Sparks flew. He felt he was breathing steam. His erection thickened. He couldn't wait any longer. He snagged a condom off the bedside table, fit it in seconds.

He seduced her mouth with sensual kisses, soft,

yet deep, as if he had all the time in the world. Their hands strayed, drawing out each touch. An erotic mating dance, primal and seductive, their naked bodies touching, exploring. Passion glazed their eyes, and their need for each other became a power all its own.

He spread her thighs with his knee, and took her slow and easy. He didn't need long to find his rhythm, exciting her even more. Her fingers curled into his hair, stroked his scalp. Her lips nuzzled his neck. His shoulders bunched beneath her hands. She bit his bicep, marked him hers. Her gesture touched him, made him so ready for her, he was surprised he didn't come now.

Thinking of her pleasure and not his own, he gave great attention to her breasts. Sucking the tips and grazing each with his tongue.

She ran her hands down his back. Tautness strained his spine. He was dying, losing his mind.

He slid his hands under her buttocks, cupped and clasped her even closer. She felt so good.

She grew restless. Her ragged moans told him she wanted him in her deeper, harder. Her need braised his skin.

His hair was damp against his brow; his breathing labored. A muscle ticked in his jaw.

She lifted her hips, reaching for her climax.

He could hold back any longer.

His thrusts went from rhythmic and unhurried to a pulsing rush. His dick throbbed hotly inside her.

She braced against coming too soon, but it was no use. Her passion for him was strong and her climax overtook her. Pleasure and emotion surged, flooding her.

His chest heaved and his breathing caught. He lost control a moment after her. He growled her name, a lusty rumble that rose with his orgasm. It went on and on, and he knew he could never again be near her without wanting her in his arms, in his bed.

Spent, he hefted his weight off her.

She lay on her back, staring at the ceiling until she caught her breath. She looked stunned, but happy. He reached for her hand, tugged her to him. A satisfied grin curled over her lips, and then she rested her head on his shoulder. Her breasts and hips hugged his side.

He traced a finger down her nose, tapped her on the chin, and said, "You wore me out, babe."

"I feel boneless," she admitted, stretching lazily.

"Can you make it to the shower?" he asked.

She nodded. "Let's clean up and have breakfast."

She scrubbed his back and he worked his magic with the bath mitt. Soon, almond steam filled the bathroom. The mirror fogged. And their moans mingled with the shower spray.

Afterward, they toweled dry and dressed for the day. They cooked breakfast together. It was a simple meal: coffee, eggs, and toast. Violet didn't keep many groceries on hand since she took most meals at the diner.

Seated across from her at the kitchen table, Brad asked, "Plans for our day?"

She took a sip of her coffee, then said, "I want to take you shopping. I owe you a pair of jeans."

He raised a brow. "You want to replace the ones you ripped off me last night?"

Her cheeks heated. "I got carried away."

"It was only a pocket," he said, finishing off his slice of buttered toast.

"The denim's worn near your groin," she said in that cute way of hers that made his balls tighten. "I don't want people seeing too much of you with the pocket missing."

"I don't want you spending money on me, Vi," he insisted, knowing she lived from paycheck to paycheck. "I really don't need—"

"I insist." Her tone was firm.

He held up his hands, palms out, gave in to her. "How about a pair of board shorts instead of the jeans?" he asked. "I haven't swum in the Gulf for five years. It's time to skimboard again."

He loved the rush of standing on the shoreline, skimboard in hand while waiting for a wave. A good-size swell, and he'd run toward it, drop the board, and jump on. He'd glide out into the ocean toward the upcoming wave and bank off it, riding the swell back to the beach.

"You can skimboard and I'll sunbathe."

He stood, gathered their dishes, and set them in the sink. Vi came up behind him and put her hand over his. "Give me five minutes to load the dishwasher and we're off."

Perfect. He needed to make a quick phone call; one he should've made yesterday. He headed for the living room. There, he removed his BlackBerry from the pocket of his athletic shorts and scrolled for the number. He dialed, then spoke briefly with the man in charge. "Put the parking charge on my Visa," he finalized the transaction.

Disconnecting, he turned, and nearly bumped into Violet. She'd quietly approached, and was staring at him now. A hesitant smile tipped her lips and uncertainty darkened her green eyes. She was curious, but didn't pry. He wondered how much she'd heard.

She waited for him to say something, and when he didn't give an explanation, she didn't push him further. She allowed him his personal space. He loved and appreciated her all the more.

Shouldering a small beach bag, she moved toward the door. "Let's hit the boardwalk," she said.

He followed her out. He liked watching her walk. The lady had a great body. She was slender, fluid, and graceful. Her hair curled about her shoulders, free of its usual scrunchie. Her tank top was a faded blue, and her navy shorts fit loosely. The leather on her sandals appeared worn.

That bothered him. She had insisted on buying him a pair of board shorts when she was in need of new clothes herself. He hated her spending money on him. Her generosity was humbling. The moment would stay with him. Always.

He took her hand, and together they strolled down Seashell, then cut the corner at Center Street. They headed toward the beach and boardwalk. The day was young, yet the Gulf would be as warm as bathwater. Brad couldn't wait to hit the waves.

The Barefoot William boardwalk welcomed tourists with sunshine, specialty shops, and a promise of fun. All the stores had adjoining walls and multicolored doors. A crowd gathered at Brews Brothers as coffee drinkers waited in line for their favorite eye-opener. The scent of oven-fresh doughnuts wafted from the cracked door of The Bakehouse.

Seagulls swooped overhead. A few gulls seeking a handout tottered after tourists eating breakfast sandwiches. They squawked over crumbs, then scooted out of the way for the pedicab traffic. The covered, three-wheeled rickshaws carried summer visitors up and down the boardwalk. The friendly drivers pointed out landmarks and entertained tourists with local lore.

"Three Shirts to the Wind," Violet said, stopping before a bright tangerine door. "The best selection of tees and board shorts on the boardwalk."

He entered the shop behind her. Strange, him being here. He'd been in the store several times when he was younger, but only to browse. He'd never been able to afford a polo or designer shorts. The items were too pricey and out of his league. Yet this was where Violet chose to shop. For him. He looked around, hoping to find a pair of shorts on sale.

"Hello, Vi," said Jenna Cates-James, Violet's recently married cousin and owner of the shop. She stood beside a circular rack, hanging up tank tops. "Brad, welcome home. I heard you were in town."

Smiling, Brad acknowledged her greeting. No surprise actually. The Cateses were a grapevine for news. They were a close-knit family and kept each other apprised as to everything that happened on their boardwalk.

"We're here for a pair of board shorts," Violet told Jen.

"Feel free to look around," said Jenna. "Holler if you need help with size or color."

Brad spotted a SALE sign, and he headed toward the back of the store. Violet caught his arm before he reached the rack. She shook her head and gave him a small smile. "Let's check out Dune's designer line," she said. "There are lots of cool board shorts on the shelves over by the mirror."

Dune Cates was another of Vi's many cousins. He'd recently retired from professional beach volleyball, but continued in retail. The popularity of his signature beachwear collection was making him a very rich man.

"Vi, listen—" he began, but he was quickly silenced by the press of her fingertips to his lips.

"Let me do something nice for you," she said. Her eyes sparkled with delight. "You're home and my heart is happy."

He was damn happy, too. He drew her close and kissed her lightly. She sighed against his mouth.

No words needed to be said. They both knew what the other was thinking. Sweet kisses and roving hands would incite gossip. Best to cool their heat. For now.

Releasing her slowly, he led her between the round racks until they reached the far wall. "Trust me to pick something out for you?" she asked, skimming her fingers over the shelves.

"No metallic pink or yellow," he said, rubbing his jaw. "I don't want to shine like a fishing lure in the water."

She eyed him, bit her lip, then guessed, "Size large?"

He nodded, and she took her sweet time making a selection. She went through the whole rack, mumbling and shaking her head. The lady was picky. That made him feel good. She'd chosen him, hadn't she? Her final choice made him smile. She held up a pair of navy board shorts decorated with tan surf-boards.

"I like," he said.

"Me, too," she agreed, handing them to him to try on.

"Dressing rooms are open," Jenna called from the front counter.

He was in and out of the changing room in five minutes flat. He never looked in the mirror. Didn't have to. They fit, and that was all that mattered. Violet folded his athletic shorts and added them to her beach bag. They headed toward the register.

Scissors in hand, Jenna cut the price tag from Brad's board shorts. "Forty-six dollars with the Cates family discount." She rang up the sale.

Violet unzipped a side pocket on her beach bag and removed a stack of one-dollar bills. Her waitress tips, Brad thought. She counted out the exact amount.

"I'll toss in two towels and a bottle of suntan oil," Jenna said, collecting each one from under the counter. She put the items in a plastic bag with the Three Shirts logo. "No charge. Enjoy your day."

"Appreciated, Jen," Violet said. She hugged her cousin, turned, and took Brad's hand. "C'mon, we'll rent you a skimboard."

He grabbed the bag off the counter. "Thanks, Jenna," he said. The Cateses were a generous family. He felt a part of them today.

They cut across the boardwalk and walked down the wooden ramp to the beach. Footprints patterned the sugar sand. Beachgoers strolled the shoreline, collected shells, and sunbathed. It was summertime. Barefoot William lived easy.

The water sport shack was near the pier. Steve

Cates rented everything from surfboards to snorkel gear, air mattresses to paddleboats. Brad had sold his skimboard when he'd left town. He hoped to buy another one shortly. He was a man of motion; he liked to be active. However pleasurable, he couldn't have sex with Vi 24/7. He needed another outlet for physical activity. Skimboarding was his sport of choice. Surfing came in second.

"Fifteen dollars an hour or forty for a half day," Steve relayed the cost of the rental.

"One hour," Brad was quick to say. While he hadn't skimboarded for five years, he'd once been good at the sport. He hoped to regain his rhythm. More importantly, he didn't want to leave Violet on the beach alone sunbathing for too long.

Vi counted out fifteen ones. Brad noticed her stack of money was getting smaller. He shifted his weight from one foot to the other. He was used to paying his own way. While he appreciated Vi's gesture, it tied him up inside.

"Return the board when you're done," Steve said as he handed Brad a top-of-the-line skimboard, one polished a glossy black with a dark green stripe down the center.

They walked the shoreline until they found a secluded spot on the sand. She shook out their beach towels, and then removed her tank top, shorts, and sandals. She'd worn a turquoise bikini beneath her clothes. She was slender but curvy. Brad stared at her for a good long time. He could look at this woman for the rest of his life.

Vi settled on her towel, looked up at him. "You're frowning," she noted. "What's wrong?"

"You're too hot to leave here alone," he said.

"Guys will be all over you." Several surfers stood at the tide line, nudging each other and looking her way.

"I'm not interested in anyone but you." Her words stroked his ego. And his dick. As surely as if she'd taken him in her hand. She reached into the plastic shopping bag and held up the bottle of suntan oil. "Do my back before you leave?" she requested, stretching out on the towel.

He wouldn't mind doing her front, too, inside her swimsuit and out. A private beach for nude sunbathing appealed to him suddenly. Violet would look amazing with a full-body tan.

He poured the oil in his palm and rubbed it on her shoulders and down her back, along her legs. His fingers dipped between the shadows of her inner thighs. Touching her turned him on. He looked down to see a familiar bulge tenting his new board shorts. He capped the bottle and calmed himself before he stood.

He purposely left his size twelve Nikes sitting near the bottom border of her towel. Anyone approaching her would see she was with a man and do an about-face. After picking up his board, he jogged to the water's edge.

"Be careful," she called over her shoulder.

He signaled he'd heard her. He liked the fact that she looked out for him. Something he hadn't known often enough in his life. His mother always had a little one underfoot when he was growing up. She never had the time for him. He didn't blame her, but it sure felt good to have a woman care about him. Make that two. Violet and her aunt

Molly had shown him great kindness, which he would never forget.

With the first decent swell he tossed his board. He banked off the wave and rode it in to shore. His adrenaline pumped. It seemed he'd never left the sport. His body felt loose and fluid and up to the challenge. He spent what he assumed was an hour in the water. Then decided it was time to return to Violet.

He headed in, just as she swam out to him. She was a strong freestyle swimmer, sleek in her strokes.

"I missed you," she said when she reached him.

"I was on my way back," he told her.

He hooked his board under one arm and hugged her close. She snuggled up to him, letting him know with a sexy squeeze to his butt how much she'd missed him. The ocean splashed around them like a playful child. Tucked against him, her body was slick and slippery. Shimmering in the sunshine. Her hair had a life of its own. Her nose and the arc of her cheekbones were slightly pink. He didn't want her sunburned. It was time to seek shade.

"Let's set up under the pier," he suggested.

She agreed. They came ashore, collected their towels and clothes, and sought the shadowed canopy of a cement piling. "Popsicle?" she asked as they passed one of many refreshment stands. "Grape, banana, or cherry?"

"Grape, and I'll buy," he said, reaching for her beach bag. His wallet was in the pocket of his athletic shorts, folded inside.

She twisted away from him, shook her head

adamantly. "Today's all about you, Brad Davis. Save your money for another time."

She scooped out a handful of change from the side zipper enclosure, counted out two dollars. "Back in a flash."

He stared after her, admiring her walk across the sugar sand. Her steps were light; her energy was high. Her bikini rode up her bottom, revealing her tan lines and the tight curve of her ass. His hands itched to cup her. To draw her so close that he could trace the crease of her thighs with his thumbs. Then tease her beneath the elastic at her crotch until she was wet and wanting him.

Damn, he was about to have a heatstroke. And not from the sun. Violet Cates was one hot woman. It would take more than a frozen treat to cool him off.

She was quick to return. Her lips were already red and moist from her cherry Popsicle. Her tongue flicked the rounded tip before she sucked it into her mouth. Deep.

His dick twitched. "You're doing that on purpose," he accused, groaning.

"You think?" she teased.

"I know." He took the Popsicle she offered. Ate it in three bites. His mouth went from icy cold to dry as sand as he watched her finish off her treat. Her sensual licks, the erotic slide into her mouth, made him as stiff as his skimboard. He was thankful that his board shorts were baggy enough to hide his boner.

The sun spiked its zenith, and shade was minimal. They walked to the water sport shack and returned his rental, then captured a square of privacy beneath the wooden planks of the pier. They sat on their towels, their shoulders touching, as they held hands.

Brad looked out over the Gulf, letting their past return with the incoming tide. "In all the time I've known you, Vi," he said, "we've kissed three hundred and forty-eight times on this beach."

"You kept count?" She appeared surprised, yet pleased. Tilting her head, she took his mouth. "Three hundred forty-nine," she breathed against his lips.

"Three-fifty." He upped the count once more.

Her smile was soft. "Midnight was our make-out hour. We spent equal time between the storeroom at the diner and under the pier, The Gulf stole your shoes and socks and my scrunchies."

"I carried the beach home with me," said Brad. "There was always sand between my toes and in the crack of my ass."

"Your butt more than mine," Vi recalled. "You let me be on top."

"I was a gentleman," he said, tongue in cheek.

She laughed at him. "You were a bad boy with sex on your brain."

"My mind was always on you."

She rested her head on his shoulder. "Mine was on you, too."

He brushed her bangs off her forehead, grew serious. "Where are we at, Vi?" he asked. He needed to come to grips with where their relationship was headed and braced himself for her answer. Everything was happening so fast, but he wanted to get serious with her, have a life together. On the other hand, he'd just returned home. Maybe it was too soon for her to know where they stood.

She scooped up a handful of sand, let it filter through her fingers, like time slowing down. "Where do you want us to be?" She waited quietly for his answer, but he could see her hand was shaking. He imagined her heart was thumping in her chest. His was, for sure.

"In my perfect world, we'd work together and achieve our goals," he slowly said. That much was true. Here came the hard part. He reached for her hand, held it tight. He needed to know her true feelings. She believed he was the same man he'd been when he'd left town. He'd yet to tell her otherwise.

"I haven't changed much since the last time I saw you, Vi." He paused, then let go with the big question. "Are you willing to start where we left off?"

She sighed heavily, as if releasing the weight of the world. "I've struggled financially all my life," she said honestly. "It would be nice to have someone to support my dreams and believe in our future. You're the one, Brad. You always have been, always will be."

"Life partners, I like that." His chest warmed. He liked being *her one*. He had every plan to marry this woman.

He squeezed her hand, smiled. "How shall we celebrate our partnership in business and pleasure?"

"It's our day off from work, so no shop talk." She nuzzled his jaw, worked her way up to his ear. Flicked her tongue to his lobe. "How about talking dirty in bed?"

His agreement came with his erection.

The sun was hot on his back as they left the beach.

His groin burned even hotter.

Chapter Five

Life partners? Violet Cates hashed the words over and over again in her mind as she changed the sheets on her bed. Brad wanted to spend his life with her, they'd become business associates, but he had yet to mention marriage. That worried her, she realized. More than a little. She loved this man. She wanted commitment and a ring on her finger. She tried not to dwell on the matter.

Another issue weighed far more heavily in her heart.

Three weeks had passed. Joe had returned from his Las Vegas vacation, far richer than when he'd left. He'd hit big at the roulette table. He'd put his trailer up for sale and purchased a house several miles inland. Molly was his interior decorator. By the twinkle in her eye, Vi suspected Lady Luck had dealt the two of them a winning hand.

She figured her aunt was fixing up his home to fit her own specifications. She and Joe were often seen together after work, taking a walk on the boardwalk or at the movies. They'd been caught kissing under the pier, which made Violet smile. A person was never too old for a moonlight kiss. Molly had worked hard all her life. She and Joe needed to capture those special moments together and make their own memories.

Violet dropped down on the foot of her bed; her shoulders slumped. She dipped her head, clasped her hands on her lap. Joe had hinted to Molly that he'd like to travel, to see Europe and Asia before age crept up and kept them home.

Vi wondered what would happen to the diner if the two of them took off on their world tour. It was Cates policy to pass down the family businesses from generation to generation. Molly's father was a Malone who'd married a Cates. Molly had been their only child. Her dad had opened the corner diner when she was born. It had been named in her honor. Molly had never married. Chances were good one of her cousins would take over running the diner, or, Vi's worst fear, the boardwalk landmark would go on the market. Violet hoped that would never happen. Although she had a gut feeling it could.

The thought of Molly Malone's being sold chilled her to the bone. Tears pressed her eyelids. She wished with all her heart she had the money to invest in the diner. What if the new owner wanted to change things? The menu, the décor, even her uniform? She never considered for a moment that she and Brad could lose their jobs. That wasn't how things were done on the boardwalk.

A new owner might not see it that way, she realized. Then where would they be? Especially now when Brad was getting back on his feet. It wasn't fair, but what could she do?

Unfortunately, her finances were still tight. Even if she and Brad combined earnings and opened a joint savings account, it wouldn't be enough. Her debt and doubts seeped into their future. She hated feeling so vulnerable.

The sound of footsteps made her look up. She saw Brad leaning against the door frame. Tall and handsome and looking very much like a man happy to see his woman. "Everything okay?" he asked, concerned.

She shrugged, forced a smile. "Just thinking."

"Too hard, from what I see," he said, crossing to her. He lowered himself beside her. He was dressed casually in a navy shirt and khaki pants. "Share?" He curved his arm over her shoulders, offering to listen to whatever might be bothering her. She liked that about him. He didn't pass judgment, didn't pry, but he was there for her when she needed him.

She appreciated his strength and support, but she didn't want to lay her concerns on him. Why spoil everything? Brad was the best part of her day. They'd worked the early shift at the diner, come home, and picked up around the cottage. Then fooled around in bed. Cuddled up together afterward. Went on to take a shower. She breathed him in now. His skin still smelled of almond soap. His body was warm and wonderfully male.

"I was debating taking a walk," she said, wanting to clear her head. "Breathe some fresh air and catch the sunset."

"Want company or would you rather go alone?" he asked, offering her space.

His consideration warmed her heart. She kissed him on the cheek. "My life is better with you."

They rose from sitting on the bed; love and understanding stood with them. Their feelings only strengthened as they left the cottage holding hands and headed toward the boardwalk. Their silence held the familiarity of two people comfortable with each other.

They soon reached the corner where Center Street came to a dead end. Barefoot William stretched to the right, Saunders Shores to the left. Friday night and the Barefoot William boardwalk was alive with music and amusements. Sunburned tourists came off the beach and wandered into the shops, seeking souvenirs. Everyone wanted to take home a memory. T-shirts, sand globes, posters and postcards, tote bags, and bumper stickers were at the top of their lists.

Boxes of homemade fudge from Fudgin' It and bags of penny candy from Goody Gumdrops satisfied those with a sweet tooth. Florida Sunshine sold citrus. Old Tyme Portraits allowed customers to stand behind life-sized cardboard cutouts, their smiling faces showing above vintage swimwear. The framed black-and-white photographs were a popular keepsake.

"Which way?" Brad asked, allowing her to decide.

She was in the mood for peace and quiet. "The Shores," she said. "Let's window-shop with the rich and famous. Then sit on a bench and watch the sun set. Maybe stop at Lavender's for sorbet, if it's within our budget."

"Even if it wasn't, Vi, there are times we need to splurge," he said, squeezing her hand. "We can't stop living just because we're saving for our business."

She liked his way of thinking. Cool, honest, and practical.

He tucked her to his side, and they turned left. He gave her a sense of security. No matter what happened in her life, she and Brad were a team. They were business associates and partners in the bedroom, and, hopefully someday, they'd be husband and wife. *And* working together at Molly Malone's. Brad could work his way up to manager and she could learn to do the books.

Before them now, Saunders Shores bore the stamp of great wealth. It differed greatly from Barefoot William. The walkway shifted from cracked cement to cocoa-brown brick. Here, there were no in-line skaters, unicyclists, street singers, portrait painters, magicians, or vendors hawking hot dogs and churros.

There were no rickshaw pedicabs. No one wore swimsuits or walked around barefoot. The patrons shopping the main city blocks were dignified and well dressed. No one browsed; everyone bought. Customers carried designer boxes and bags. The boutique and café owners flourished.

Bronze-tinted storefront windows shone gold as twilight tugged down the sun. The sky became a spectacular finger painting of red, yellow, and orange. Purple smeared the horizon.

They stopped before a formal dress shop and admired the fancy dresses and proper tuxedos, then inhaled deeply as they passed an outdoor Italian bistro. A jewelry store caught her eye and Violet couldn't help staring through the window. Diamond rings of every cut, clarity, and carat were displayed on glass tiers. She sighed over a pink basket-set diamond on a platinum band. The ring radiated love.

Brad lifted her hand and gently kissed her palm. Her heart beat faster. Did he know what she was thinking? If so, he wasn't going to tell her. Without a word, he led her toward a polished wooden bench so lacquered it looked slippery.

They sat together, drawn into the darkness. Outside lights soon flickered on. The lantern-styled lampposts stretched the length of the boardwalk. Tall pole lighting lit the sugar sand for late-night walks. Cabana boys raked footprints from the sand at all hours, keeping the beach pristine. The ocean was as calm and glistening as a mirror.

Violet relaxed her body against Brad's. They seemed to sift together in a slow and easy rhythm. "Being superrich would be nice," she softly said, "but it would make me uncomfortable."

"How so?" he asked, interested in hearing what she had to say.

"I wouldn't know what to do with myself," she said. She had her own lifestyle. It would seem unnatural to her not to have bills to worry about or to buy retail and not off the sales racks.

"You could travel, or perhaps take part in charitable or philanthropic projects," he suggested, giving her alternatives.

"That's not me, Brad," she said, being open and honest with him. "The diner is my life, the customers are my family. I wish Molly and Joe well, but I'm afraid of change. Afraid of what it could mean for us."

"We don't know that she will sell," he said, his voice taking on a serious tone.

"We don't know that she won't." Her heart sank. "Has Molly said anything to you, one way or the other?"

He was slow to answer her. She took that as a bad sign. "I overheard her tell Joe that a potential investor would be stopping by tomorrow afternoon. Someone with a background in food service."

Violet could barely breathe. "I'd hate to see the diner turned into a restaurant chain. Molly Malone's has been the cornerstone diner on the boardwalk for eighty years. The thought of a new owner makes my stomach hurt."

"Speculation is pointless, Vi, until we have the facts," he said, attempting to allay her fears. "Whatever happens, we'll get through it."

"I'm glad you're here with me." She was trembling inside, but she tried not to show it. She felt better talking it out with him.

"So am I." He pushed off the bench and pulled her up beside him. "Sorbet?" he invited.

"Dessert is good," she agreed, "although one scoop of sorbet here costs more than a tub of ice cream at our local grocery store."

"You're worth it, babe." He kissed her then, a kiss as light as a breath of air. Violet sighed against his mouth.

They entered Lavender's through frameless glass doors etched with the letter *L*. The gourmet shop catered to the discriminating palate. The specialty flavors included coconut-caramel, burnt-sugar plum, cranberry pear, and raspberry truffle.

Violet noticed that each dessert came in a frosted

cut-glass bowl. The portions were no bigger than a Parisian scoop, no more than two bites. The spoons were sterling silver and tinier than a teaspoon.

The lighting was soft, and the French Mediterranean blue shutters were drawn against the darkness. Intimacy was served with the sorbet.

The hostess seated them at a linen-covered café table. The chairs were an intricate white wrought iron. A server soon arrived. "I'm Alyssa, your water sommelier," she said. Violet looked at Brad, who was trying hard not to grin. "I'll bring your sparkling water and Marissa will take your order. Do you prefer San Pellegrino or Perrier?" she asked.

"Tap," Brad said from the corner of his mouth.

Violet held back her smile. "Perrier, please."

"A good choice," Alyssa complimented. "Perrier has nice fat bubbles." She went for their drinks.

"A server to taste water," Vi said, amazed. "This place is elegant."

Brad took her hand, twined their fingers. Met her gaze across the table. "I like the way you say server," he said. "Very sexy."

She flicked her tongue to her upper lip. "Maitre'd, wine steward," she said in her most sultry voice.

"You're making me horny."

She couldn't help smiling. "Naming restaurant staff is hardly sex talk," she teased him.

"It's your tone, babe. The words come from deep in your throat, warm, low, and breathy." He shifted on his chair, then gave her a hungry look that curled her toes. "You turn me on."

Violet stopped talking when Alyssa returned with their tall, fluted glasses of sparkling water. No ice.

The crystal made the water sparkle twice as bright. Vi took a sip.

Shortly thereafter, Marissa arrived. She set a sheet of lavender parchment paper before each of them. The menu curled slightly, and was as thin and delicate as tissue paper. Vi and Brad looked at each other with a skeptical eye. They were both afraid to touch it. Ever so gently, Violet ran her finger along the edge and read the selections.

"We have two specialty flavors on our list this evening," Marissa pointed out. "Limoncello-mint and Bittersweet Chocolate-cherry."

Violet decided on the burnt-sugar plum sorbet and Brad selected coconut-caramel. Alyssa was quick to bring their orders. She set the cut-glass bowls on a lacy ecru doily.

"These are too pretty to eat," Violet said, reluctant to spoil such a lovely arrangement. Her scoop of sorbet was artfully topped with a sprinkle of lavender-colored sugar. Thin slices of plum framed the scoop of sorbet.

She watched as Brad picked up his spoon, a utensil so small he was forced to hold it with his fingertips. He scooped up a small portion, mindful to include flakes of coconut and shredded caramel.

She planned to eat slowly and savor every bite. Her body heated as the sorbet melted in her mouth. She had the urge to kiss Brad, to mix the sweet, sensually smooth flavors of their desserts on her tongue.

She shook herself. Lavender's was not the place for deep kisses, yet it was always fun to fantasize. She stretched out the two-bite dessert, turning it into four.

She fell in love with Brad all over again when he switched their sorbets, giving her the last bite from his bowl. Pure decadence, and nearly as good as having sex.

She took a slow sip of her Perrier, then said, "I'm feeling very appreciative toward you at this moment."

"How grateful?"

"Naked grateful."

He motioned to Alyssa, who brought their bill. Their desserts were an extravagance made sweeter by the man at her side. Violet noticed he left a large tip. He was generous.

"Home?" he asked as they left Lavender's.

"Bed," she answered.

"How fast can you walk?"

She noticed the bulge in his pants.

"Faster than you," she teased, stepping out ahead of him.

"Don't bet on it, babe."

She felt his hot breath on the back of her neck for the next three blocks. Followed by the warmth of his hands as he stripped off her clothes the minute they burst through the cottage's front door and settled her on cool fresh sheets. It was a night of extreme heat and endless orgasms.

The following day, Violet worked the morning shift at the diner and Brad was scheduled to cover the dinner hour. She couldn't deny she'd been dreading this day, what with the investor coming, but she didn't share her fears with her aunt. How could she? Molly was in her own world, fluttering here and there and not concentrating on her baking. She burned two cherry pies. A first for her. She didn't seem to care. Her mind was elsewhere. No doubt on Joe. Or possibly on the investor.

Violet made it through the noon rush, growing more and more anxious. She kept looking at her watch, wishing she could stop time. The businessman would arrive shortly. Minutes ticked toward the inevitable.

Two fifteen, and the man had yet to make an appearance. Customers had thinned out. The only ones who remained were those lingering over a second cup of coffee. Putting on a brave smile, Vi kept their cups filled with hot brew.

Her stomach dropped when the front door swung open moments later and an unwelcome customer strolled in.

"Lydia." Violet narrowed her gaze on her sister when she entered the diner. She was alone. "Where are your children?" she asked as Lydia took over a counter stool, sitting next to the mailman. Vi didn't try to hide her concern. She couldn't trust her sister to do the right thing, even when it came to taking care of her own.

"My kids are with Mark," she told Violet. "It's his day off from the garage. He took them fishing at Barefoot Cove."

"You chose not to go?" Violet asked. Lydia's boyfriend was nice enough, Vi knew, maybe *too* nice for her sister. Seemed she took advantage of him, too.

Lydia turned up her nose. "Too much sun, too much quiet, and I refuse to bait a hook. I hate the smell of fish." She swung her stool right, then left, and said, "I'm ready to order."

"No dine and dash today, Lydia." Vi was firm and to the point. Her sister always ordered a big meal, then split before she paid the tab.

Lydia flicked her wrist. "Whatever."

Violet planned to keep a close eye on her sister. By the gleam in her eye, she was certain Mark had given Lydia her weekly allowance. No wonder she was flippant. What irked Violet more was that she often spent the money within a matter of minutes, then found herself scamming for handouts the rest of the week.

Lydia tapped her fingers on the counter. "I want the daily special: fried chicken dinner, white meat; mashed potatoes; corn; and cole slaw. Possibly a piece of pie, if I don't bust a gut."

Violet jotted down her order, then clipped it to a revolving wheel in the cook's window. Joe grabbed it, then got busy preparing Lydia's meal.

"Coffee, too, Vi," Lydia requested.

Violet poured her a cup. Her sister sweetened the Colombian blend with three packets of Sweet'n Low. Vi caught her pocketing several more sugar packets. No surprise there. Lydia's kids liked sugar on their morning cereal.

By four o'clock, Molly announced she'd received a phone call from the investor. He was running late. Vi exhaled her relief. Perhaps *late* meant a year from now or maybe never. She could only hope so.

She wished she didn't have to be around when he arrived. Unfortunately, her shift didn't end until five. She'd get a good look at the guy with a long résumé in the food industry.

The diner soon began to fill with the late-afternoon coffee crowd. Regular customers claimed their favorite tables; a few older men preferred to sit at the counter. This was their home away from home.

Lydia had finished her meal, but she had yet to move on. Unless she physically tossed her butt out the door, Violet knew her sister wouldn't leave until she was good and ready. Lydia had drunk an entire pot of coffee and polished off two pieces of lemon meringue pie. She was too full to walk to the door.

Keeping an eye on her sister, Violet circled the diner and took everyone's standard order. Her regulars ate the same flavor of pie every single day. She sensed an undercurrent as the table talk centered on the new investor. Word had spread fast. Most of the customers were curious; a few were apprehensive.

Vi served them in record time. She then moved to the edge of the waitress station and leaned against one of the shelves. Closing her eyes, she breathed deeply, and collected herself. She thought about all the good times she'd had here at Molly Malone's. Laughing and joking with Molly and Joe, chatting about life's highs and lows with the customers, and, most of all, working with Brad. And how that might soon change. Fear of the unknown left her feeling low.

"Wow, check out the Mercedes," Lydia said, her voice pitched high to get everyone's attention. "Someone's owning Center Street."

Violet blinked, straightened, then looked out the

window. She watched as the driver parked the black luxury vehicle near the curb.

"Money, money, money," Lydia chanted.

Violet's heart dropped so fast she felt dizzy. So the investor had shown up after all. Somehow, she had convinced herself he wouldn't. Now she couldn't hide, run from the truth. Whether she liked it or not, life at Molly Malone's was about to change. Forever.

She grasped the side of the soda machine, steadied herself. Sadness swelled in her throat. She had the urge to escape into the kitchen, to hide in the storeroom, while the investor took inventory of the diner.

She didn't want to face the man who could turn her world upside down. She desperately wished Brad were there. He'd give her the courage she needed to get through this. Unfortunately, his shift didn't start for another hour.

Molly swung through the kitchen door. Joe took off his apron and followed close behind her. "I just received a text," she said, smoothing her palms over her apron. "I believe my appointment is here."

Violet turned away so her aunt couldn't see the disappointment written all over her face. She felt guilty even thinking about the man not showing up. Molly deserved this chance at happiness, and she was acting selfish thinking about her own future. And Brad's, too, she reminded herself.

"The guy's getting out of his car," Lydia said, craning her neck. "He's got dark hair and nice shoulders."

That he had, Violet agreed, straining her eyes to

catch a glimpse of him. Street shadows made it difficult to see his face. She watched as he closed his car door and stepped onto the curb.

Time slowed, and Vi felt as if she stood in the still-frame of a movie. Familiarity and confusion crowded her. Her jaw dropped along with everyone else's in the diner when he moved into the sunlight. She couldn't believe her eyes.

"Brad fuckin' Davis," said Lydia, unfiltered.

Violet couldn't say a word, only stared.

He entered Molly Malone's, looking like himself, only different. He'd gotten a haircut, shaved, and now wore a tailored navy sport coat over a pair of jeans. A burgundy tie hung loosely about the collar of his light blue shirt. He gave her goose bumps.

The silence held as he nodded to Molly and Joe and walked straight to Violet. Gone was the short-order cook and skimboarder. Before her now stood a man with a sharp gaze and professional shrewdness. He was all business.

She was so stunned that she barely registered the fact that he'd pulled her close, that his presence surrounded her with unsettling warmth.

Her cheek pressed his chest, and his heart beat steadily beneath her ear. He gently stroked her hair. The scent of his Fierce cologne mixed with the starch of his dress shirt. His new jeans pressed her khaki skirt. The toes on her tennis shoes kissed the tips on his leather loafers.

"What's going on, Brad?" she finally managed. "I don't understand." She'd never felt so lost.

She felt his smile against her cheek. "I love you, Violet Cates," he whispered against the background hush of the diner. "You've had my heart since your eighteenth birthday. I will always do my best for you. For us. That best starts today."

She eased back slightly, her breathing uneven. "I'm listening," she said, keeping her voice equally low.

He dropped a light kiss on her brow. "You've always wanted a diner like Molly Malone's," he said without missing a beat. "I'm here to offer you the opportunity to take over ownership of the restaurant."

Her eyes rounded. "So that's your car out there? You didn't arrive by bus?"

"I drove into town," he confessed. "I parked my Mercedes in a private parking garage at Saunders Shores."

"You're rich?" It was difficult to believe.

He nodded. "Comfortably well off," he assured her.

Her knees grew so weak, she could barely stand. She clasped his forearms, needing his support. She had so many questions, but her throat had closed and her mouth was dry.

"Speak up, Brad," Lydia called from the counter. "We've got a right to know what's going on. We're all family here at the diner."

A murmur of agreement came from the customers.

With his arm still curved about her shoulders, Brad turned slightly, so he faced the locals. Violet leaned against his side and listened along with everyone else as he spoke about his travels. "I left Barefoot William five years ago, a man out to prove himself," he began, making no excuses. "Violet and

I had big dreams. I had to find a way to make our goals a reality."

Molly and Joe nodded encouragingly for Brad to continue. The mailman took that moment to lift his coffee cup. "I could use a refill, Vi, while I hear Brad's story."

"I can listen and eat at the same time," said a second man at the counter. "A slice of blueberry pie would be nice."

Violet made a move to serve them, only to stop when Lydia surprised her by hopping off her counter stool and taking charge. She warmed coffee cups along the counter before slipping a piece of blueberry pie from the revolving pie case onto a plate. She added the cost to the man's bill. Then she returned to her stool.

Vi was as shocked by her sister's assistance as she was by Brad's accounting of his time away from Barefoot William. He ran one hand down his chin, and continued. "I stayed in Florida, closer to Violet than she ever realized. My first stop was Tampa— that's where I sold my car. Success didn't come overnight, but my earning potential finally took shape. I bought a hot dog cart, then staked a claim on a street corner near Tropicana Stadium. Football, baseball, sports fans love their dogs."

"I like chili dogs," said the mailman.

"I made enough money from selling hot dogs to invest in a run-down hamburger joint on the beach in St. Petersburg. I renovated the place and sold it for a nice profit. I continued to flip small businesses, and I made a lot of money. I called Molly after a major shopping mall offered to buy my ramshackle clam shack. The restaurant was old and I had yet to fix it up. The corporation paid big bucks, then went on to level the building so they could expand their parking garage."

Brad slowly massaged the back of Vi's neck. She welcomed his touch. "Once the sale closed, I got in touch with Molly," he added. "I told her that I was coming home. I made a solid offer on the diner, which she accepted."

Molly had known all along, and kept his secret. "Conspirators," Vi said on a sigh, feeling loved.

"His offer was all for you, Violet," Molly put in then. Her smile was soft, her eyes misting. "Brad knew I wouldn't sell the diner to just anyone. I wanted it to go to you, sweetie. You've worked so hard for me. The time has come for you and Brad to take over."

"You'd be doing me a favor, too," said Joe, drawing Molly to his side. "I have a decent pension and I want to show Molly the world, but she refused to leave Barefoot William. Brad's proposition came at the perfect time. It changed our lives. Molly can leave town with a happy heart, knowing the diner is in capable hands."

Capable hands. Vi looked up at Brad, marveling over her good fortune. "We're going to spend the rest of our lives together."

"Together as husband and wife." He surprised her further by reaching into his sport coat pocket and producing a small, black velvet box. "I came back to town, hoping you still loved me. You didn't blink an eye, even when I appeared as poor as when I left."

He gazed deeply into her eyes. "We've been married in my heart for a very long time, Violet. Today, I want to make us official."

Her fingers shook, and she nearly dropped the gift box. Brad cupped his hand beneath hers. It took her several attempts to tip back the top.

During those moments, three surfers stood their boards against the outside window, then bumped shoulders as they came through the door. Lydia was off her stool in less than a second. She crossed to the boys, shaking her head. "Sorry, guys, no shirt, no shoes, no service," she said firmly, turning them away.

The bare-chested, shoeless surfers shrugged, then left. They headed down the boardwalk toward the vendors selling cheese nachos and corn dogs.

"Let's see your rock," Lydia said, crossing back to Violet. "Bet it's big enough to blind me."

The spring on the box released, and a pink diamond flashed. The ring sparkled brightly beneath the overhead lights. Emotion swept through Violet, so powerfully, her entire body shook. "The ring from Saunders Shores," she said, fighting back tears. She gave Brad a watery smile. "You saw me staring a hole through the jewelry store window."

He kissed her lightly. "The pink is soft but vibrant. It suits you." He slipped the ring on her finger. It fit her perfectly.

The customers in the diner rose as one. They crowded Brad and Violet with words of congratulations. The men thumped Brad on the back; the women wanted a glimpse of Vi's engagement ring.

The locals took their leave shortly thereafter. Molly and Joe went back to the kitchen to prepare for the dinner rush. Violet stood in Brad's embrace.

His arm was tight around her waist, his heart entwined with hers. She'd never been so happy in her life.

The clank of dishes drew her gaze to a nearby table. The sight of Lydia busing tables seemed surreal. Her sister looked up, glared back. "What are you looking at?" she asked. "New customers can't sit at dirty tables."

"You're doing a great job," came from Brad.

"I've watched Vi work over the years," Lydia tossed back. "There's nothing here I couldn't handle."

Violet glanced at Brad and he nodded, reading her mind. "Molly and Joe will be packing up in a month or so," he told Lydia. "Violet and I will be hiring additional staff before then."

Lydia wiped down a tabletop. "And that affects me how?"

"We're offering you a job," Violet said. "Waitressing brings in good tips."

Her sister straightened the condiment stand, taking her time before she said, "There's more money in management."

"Prove yourself first," said Brad, challenging her. "Don't give us a hard time, keep your nose clean, and don't eat our profits."

Lydia scrunched her nose. "You have a lot of rules."

"Take them or leave them," said Brad.

"When would I start?" asked Lydia.

"As early as tomorrow," said Vi. "I'll schedule you on the dinner shift. That way you can be with your kids during the day and Mark can watch them at night."

Lydia grew quiet. "Why are you doing this for me?" She needed a reason for their offer.

"Because it's time you stood on your own two feet," said Violet. "Here, you'll get support from family."

"Yeah, fine, maybe . . . okay." Lydia was slow to make up her mind. She slid her hand in the front pocket on her skinny jeans, tossed a twenty-dollar bill on the table. "Cost of my meal including your tip," she said. Then moving toward the door, she paused with one hand on the knob. She dipped her head, said, "Thanks, sis." Then she was gone.

"You're welcome," Vi called after her, the door closing on her words.

Brad kept his arm around her. She never wanted him to let her go. "I think we need to take a look around our investment," he said in a casual but loving manner. "Nice dining room," he noted, then led her into the kitchen.

Molly was at the stove, stirring a pot of gravy. Joe was slicing roast beef. Violet had never seen them look so happy. "The back half of the diner is modernized with plenty of work space."

"Then there's the storeroom." Violet kept her voice low.

"Lots of good memories among the buckets and brooms," he agreed, then squeezed her waist.

She felt daring with her man. "Care to make one more memory, tonight after the diner closes? Initiate our place."

His dimple flashed. "I like the way you think, babe."

FISH OUT
OF WATER

Cat Johnson

Chapter One

"*Stillwater, Oklahoma's Lake McMurtry offers both primitive and improved campsites.*" Mark Ross read the description from the computer screen, and then glanced up. "Primitive or improved? I hate to even ask, because I doubt I'll like the answer, but what's the difference? And more importantly, which one are we going to?"

Logan Hunt grinned back at him from the other side of the desk. "Why? You worried?"

"Yes. Do you blame me? Primitive. What kind of descriptor is that to try to sell this place to the public? They need some help with their marketing materials, I can tell you that." With one finger, Mark pushed his glasses up onto the bridge of his nose, from where they'd slid down. "And you still didn't answer my question."

"The difference is that the primitive campsites only supply water, while the improved sites have both water and electric." Logan leaned back and rested one heavy-looking combat boot on the camouflage-covered knee of the opposite leg. Logan tended to make himself comfortable anywhere, whether he was lounging on Mark's office furniture, or in an easy chair in his living room.

Mark, on the other hand, was not at all comfortable with the idea of this camping trip. "And we're going to which site?"

By the smug expression on Logan's face, Mark had a feeling he knew which the man had chosen for the staff retreat even before he answered. "The primitive."

"Of course." That's what the university got for turning over the planning of the year-end faculty event to the military science department. Soldiers had a different idea of fun and relaxation—and comfort—from English professors.

"Stop scowling, Mark. We take the ROTC cadets there for overnight trips a few times a semester. Never lost one of them yet." Logan's persistent grin was enough to make Mark want to wipe it right off his face.

As if he could. Mark had a feeling the six-foot-two lieutenant colonel seated across from him had been trained well during his years in the army. At least well enough to defend himself against a disgruntled English professor armed with nothing more than a pen. Though they did say the pen was mightier than the sword, Mark figured Logan's combat training would win out in this case.

"Jeez, Mark. Back out if you're that miserable about going."

"I can't. I'm a department head. I have to lead by example." Besides, it had been *strongly suggested* by the powers-that-be at Oklahoma State University that all heads of the departments go, whereas the assistant and associate professors working beneath him could choose not to, and quite a few had. "It is still one night, correct? Or did you tack on a few more fun-filled days?"

"Yes, we're only staying for one night. And stop acting like the whole time is going to be torturous for you. Come on. It'll be fun." Logan's enthusiasm, whether fake or not, still wasn't very convincing.

"Oh, I'm sure." Tons of fun.

Sleeping in a tent, in the pitch dark no less, since there was no electricity. Yeah, sure. That sounded like a blast. He'd be lucky if some animal didn't crawl in with him in the middle of the night.

"Seriously, Mark. The site's laid out real nice. The lake has separate areas for swimming and for fishing."

"Mmm-hmm." Meaning he'd be in the water right along with the fish that probably all congregated in the designated swimming area, knowing fishermen couldn't get them there. "What other fun things do you have to entice me?"

"Come on. There's nothing like it. Think what a sense of accomplishment you'll have when you catch your own dinner and cook it over an open fire." Logan leaned forward, looking truly excited at the concept.

Landing his position as the youngest head of the English department at OSU—*that* had given Mark a sense of accomplishment. Landing a fish? He wasn't certain that would qualify as being in the same league.

Oh, well. Nothing Mark could do about it now. The plans had been made, and if nothing else, he'd learned his lesson. Next year, he'd plan the faculty retreat, and it wouldn't entail fishing. He'd have to look into the local winery. They did tours and tastings. They could probably host a faculty retreat. Now there's a place he wouldn't mind camping out. Rather than catching a trout, or whatever species of fish he'd be swimming with shortly, he could catch a nice wine buzz.

Speaking of camping and biting insects that went buzz in the night . . . "You're still bringing an extra tent for me, right?"

Sleeping in a tent might be pretty low on the list of things Mark wanted to do in his lifetime, but sleeping outdoors without one was even lower. The thought sent a chill straight up his spine.

"Yes, sir." Logan nodded. "Tuck has an extra tent he's bringing. And I've got a spare sleeping bag for you to use."

He hoped Logan's friend, Tucker, was aware he'd not only be loaning the tent, but also instructing Mark on how to erect the damn thing. These guys were used to camping if they owned extras of both tents and sleeping bags, while Mark didn't own a single one of either.

Tucker Jenkins was one of Logan's military science and ROTC instructors. Mark knew the man, though not well. He should try to get to know him better since Tuck was engaged to Becca Hart, one of the associate professors in Mark's department. She had conveniently planned to be visiting her home in New York this week.

No dummy, that girl. Her fiancé, the owner of not one but at least two tents, had probably already taken her camping, or at least tried to. City girl that she was, Becca knew to get out of town or she'd have to go on this overnight trek into the great outdoors.

Mark had no doubt he'd have plenty of time to bond with Tucker this weekend. With no electricity, there wouldn't be much else to do except get to know each other. He should pack a deck of cards and some poker chips, just in case they all got bored.

"Oh, and good news. I grabbed my extra fishing rod last time I was home visiting my parents. It's light action, but it'll be good for what's in the lake, so I'll bring that along, too."

Mark had never held a fishing rod in his life and chances were Logan damn well knew that.

It looked like Mark would be learning how to fish on this trip as well as erect tents. "Okay. Thanks. I'll, uh, bring along my extra eReader, if you'd like."

Logan's dark brows rose at the offer. "Uh, yeah, thanks, but that's okay."

Mark shook his head and let out a short laugh. "Why are you friends with me again?"

Logan raised one shoulder in a half shrug. "Because you invited me to be the fourth for your weekly poker game when what's-his-name left."

"Ah, yes. I remember it all now. Old Percival from the math department. Damn man hardly ever lost a hand or a dollar. I swear, he had some sort of mathematical system he used against us to win. I'm glad you agreed to fill his spot."

His friend let out a snort. "Why? Because I hardly ever win?"

"That's one reason." Mark grinned. "But mainly because a man just can't have enough fishing and camping buddies in his life."

"Mmm-hmm. Yeah, I'm sure." Logan didn't seem at all convinced by Mark's faux enthusiasm. "So, you all packed?"

"Yes . . . mostly." The only things Mark had put in his overnight bag so far were sunscreen, bug repellent, a beach towel, two pair of swim trunks because he hated sitting around in a wet bathing suit, and a folding chair. Just because they were camping, and primitive camping at that, was no reason to sit around on the ground like cavemen.

He'd get the rest packed after work today, not that he was all that sure what he'd need to take.

"Good. Tuck's picking me up at zero-six-hundred and then we'll swing over and get you."

Zero-six-hundred. In military time that hour sounded even more insanely early than usual. Mark cringed. "Why are we leaving so early again?"

"You know what they say. Early bird gets the worm." Logan grinned.

"Yes, I've heard the saying. But we're fishing. I assume for fish, not worms."

"We are, but we need worms to catch fish, now don't we?" Logan raised a brow as Mark felt both his jaw and his spirits drop.

"We have to catch our own worms?"

How the hell did a person go about catching worms? Mark could imagine it must involve digging in the dirt. Hopefully, he wasn't expected to bring a shovel since he didn't own anything even resembling one. He happily paid a hefty maintenance fee at his condo complex to have groundskeepers do things such as dig, and deal with worms.

Logan broke out laughing at what must have been a pretty stricken look on Mark's face. "I'm kidding. I'm picking up the night crawlers at the bait shop. We don't have to catch 'em ourselves. But we still want to get there early because the fish are more likely to bite earlier in the day."

"Ah, yes, of course." Mark figured there was no fighting Mother Nature. Logan and his friend Tuck were early risers, and the fish they'd be after were early birds as well. He was clearly outnumbered.

"I need to get going and finish some stuff before morning." Logan planted a hand on each arm of the chair and hoisted his six-foot-plus frame up.

"All right." Mark had quite a bit to do before morning, too, apparently. This trip was sounding more and more rustic than he'd ever imagined. He'd better pack a first aid kit. Who knew what could happen out there.

Logan turned to go, but paused in the doorway and glanced back. "It'll be great, Mark. The best, most relaxing time you've had in years. I promise you."

Mark sighed at his own doubts, in spite of Logan's obvious sincerity. "Okay. See you in the morning."

"Zero-six-hundred," Logan reminded.

"I'll be ready," Mark assured him. He might not be a camper by nature, but neither was he tardy.

"All right. See you in the morning." With one final nod, Logan was off to go buy bait.

Night crawlers. Even the name was disturbing. As the sound of Logan's boots echoed farther down the hall, Mark sighed, "God help me."

* * *

"Are you sure you can get away? It's not mandatory that you come, you know."

Carla Henricks balanced the cell phone on one shoulder as she dumped another scoop of horse feed into the bucket. She laughed at Tuck's suggestion she stay home. "Are you kidding? I wouldn't miss this weekend for anything. It's been far too long since I've taken a day to get away to just fish and relax."

"Your mama is okay at your place without the help? I know your pa's out on the road at that stock auction right now."

"Tucker Jenkins, I know you're a natural-born worrier, but stop. Mom will be fine." Carla finished filling the pink bucket in front of her and moved on to the empty blue one. "I rearranged the lesson schedule so tomorrow will be light. Craig is on the road with Dad, but my other brother is around. And there's always a bunch of kids here willing to help out in exchange for riding time."

"Yeah, you're right about that." Tuck chuckled. "I remember back when I was young, I'd shovel manure or move stock for whoever'd let me, just for the chance to get up on a cutting horse or a good bucker."

"Well, hell. Feel free to stop by anytime. We can always find some shit for you to shovel in exchange for some time in the practice pen."

"Thanks." He laughed. "I'll keep that in mind."

She smirked, knowing Tuck had moved past that stage in his life years ago. The former rodeo champion was a full-time ROTC instructor now. He was also Carla's boss in her role as assistant coach of the rodeo team. She'd made an extra effort to rearrange her schedule so she could attend this faculty retreat he'd invited her to because what she'd told him was true—she needed some time away.

Away from the never-ending work at the family farm. Away from competing on the rodeo circuit. Away from all the rodeo cowboys, and the trouble that came with them.

Carla sighed. Her most recent troubles with cowboys were over. After the last one she'd dated, a steer wrestler who liked to wrestle buckle bunnies as well, she'd sworn off cowboys. Every last boot-wearing one. That was yet another reason she needed diversions such as this camping trip, to keep her mind off men. A nice calm day of fishing on a peaceful lake would be exactly the right thing to take her mind off her sexual frustration.

She dug into the bin for another scoop of feed. "So who else is going?"

"I think it'll be about two dozen staff members total, but they're from the other departments so I don't know most of them."

"Is Becca coming?" It would be nice for Carla to be able to spend some time with Tuck's fiancée. Carla didn't have all that many close female friends.

"Becca? Camping?" Tuck let out a snort. "Nah. There was conveniently a baby shower for her cousin back in New York she said she had to attend. Plus she scheduled some fittings or something for her and her sister's dresses for the wedding. I love her more than my own life, but the truth is my little city girl is allergic to too much outdoors. I think camping and fishing would be way more than she could handle."

Carla smiled at the image Tuck painted of Becca, the New York city girl, and him, the rodeo cowboy. "They do say opposites attract."

"Ain't it the truth. Guess she and I are living testament to that. Anyway, I'm getting Logan at six tomorrow morning."

"Six? So late?" Carla had figured to leave her house closer to four thirty. Her truck was already packed and ready to go except for the cooler of water and beer, which she'd ice up right before she left.

"Yeah, I know. I'm traveling with Logan and his poker buddy, Mark Ross, who also happens to be the head of the English department."

"Which makes him Becca's boss." Understanding dawned.

"Yeeeup." Tuck dragged the word out and Carla got the idea that spending the weekend with his fiancée's department head wasn't exactly what Tuck had in mind by way of fun. "I think Logan's trying not to scare the guy off by making him get up too early. Ross is more the type to read a book than wet a line. And it's not as if I could tell my superior officer to tell Becca's boss to get his ass out of bed before the fish stop biting."

"Nope, guess not. But I'm not afraid to tell you, *boss*, that I'll be waiting on you at the lake with a nice pile of fish by the time you arrive."

"Yeah, thanks." Tucker snorted. "Good to know we'll have something for dinner so we won't starve."

"You can leave it up to the cowgirl to put food on the table, but I'm telling you one thing—I'll catch it, but I'm not cooking it." Carla could saddle break a horse as well as any man, better in fact, but don't ask her to cook. Her mama had a few burnt pans still in the cabinet as testament to that.

"That's fair. I can filet and fry a catfish with the best of 'em. A little oil and some salt and pepper and cornmeal. Mmm, mmm. Can't beat it. Or hell, we'll tie an apron on Ross and make him cook it. How's that? Not like he'll be catching anything, so he might as well be useful."

"Sounds like a plan." She filled the last bucket, and dropped the metal scoop into the feed bin. After she slammed the lid shut, she latched it to keep the animals out and turned toward the cart filled with the horses' afternoon meal. "All right, let me go and get these animals fed. See you in the morning. *Late* morning . . ."

She'd added the last as one final dig. It hit home. Tuck groaned. "Don't remind me. See ya tomorrow."

"Tomorrow." With a smile, she disconnected the call and shoved the cell into her jeans pocket.

Quite the cast of characters she'd be hanging out with this weekend. Tuck, his commander, an English professor, and her. It should be interesting.

Chapter Two

The early morning sky, streaked with vibrant colors, made for a breathtaking start to the day. No doubt about it. For millennia, man had waxed poetic about sunrises this magnificent. Mark knew he should be more appreciative. Take note of the experience. After all, it's not as if he was up and outside early enough to see the beauty of this natural phenomenon all that often. But instead, he couldn't take his eyes off her.

To be fair, she was a natural beauty as well, silhouetted in profile against the hues painting the sky. She stood on the shoreline of the lake, holding a fishing pole. His first glimpse of her had him tripping over his own feet.

A few steps ahead of him, Tucker strode toward the lakeshore. "Hey, Carla. You catching anything?"

"More than you got while you were sleeping in, that's for sure." She turned and Mark got a better look as she faced them and teased Tuck with easy familiarity. Of course she did. Tucker wore a hat that looked almost a mate to the cowboy hat she wore. Or perhaps hers was a cowgirl hat. Mark didn't know these things. That was probably obvious to the stranger from the canvas bucket-hat Mark had chosen for this excursion. It had looked pretty sporty on the mannequin in the store, but here and now, up against Tuck's headwear, or even Logan's baseball cap, not so much.

Mark watched the interaction between Tucker and the cowgirl fisherwoman. He didn't recognize her as one of the faculty. Not that he knew everyone, but still, he thought he'd remember seeing her.

"Is she with our group?" he asked Logan.

Logan dumped a load of camping gear on the ground and glanced up. "Carla? Yeah. She coaches the rodeo team with Tuck."

"Ah." The university's rodeo team had never been on Mark's radar before. After seeing Carla, it would be from now on.

How could a woman manage to look so tempting this early in the morning? And while fishing?

Maybe it was the long, brown braid draped over one shoulder. If he loosened that braid, set those waves of hair free, it would reach all the way down her back. Her cowboy hat was pulled low over her eyes so that it accentuated the heart shape of her face. He wanted to peer beneath the brim of that hat and discover what color those eyes were.

All in good time. For now, this view would have to do. And oh what a view.

The contour of her Cupid's bow lips drew him. He couldn't help but stare and want to see it all closer. Even this distance, just a couple of yards away from her, seemed frustrating. Was her complexion genuinely that rosy, or was it a trick of the light? He needed to find out.

She stood in the ankle-deep water with her jeans rolled to her knees. Most of the women Mark had dated wouldn't even venture outside in the rain. Everything about her seemed to be the opposite of the females he was used to, and he liked the differences.

The weight of the overnight bag in his hand finally drew Mark's attention away from his ponderings. He lowered it to the ground and glanced up to find Logan staring.

"I'll introduce you if you want." Logan wore an amused expression.

Mark managed to maintain a poker face while playing poker, but judging by Logan's smirk, he wasn't doing too well at hiding his interest in Carla now. He swallowed hard. "Oh, sure. That would be good, since we'll be fishing together."

Sure, fishing. That's what he wanted to do with this vision in denim before him. Fish.

"Yeah, that's what I thought, too." Logan grinned. "Come on."

Leaving the pile of gear on the ground, Logan led the way toward the shoreline. Every step they took ramped up Mark's nerves until his heart pounded. It was insane. He lectured to an audience of hundreds on a regular basis, he'd shaken hands with a former president of the United States, as well as the current poet laureate, but meeting this one woman made him anxious.

Logan stopped just short of the water. "Hey,

Tuck. Do you wanna make the introductions for me while I go grab the bait outta the truck?"

"Sure, no problem." Tuck turned toward the goddess wielding the fishing pole. "Carla Henricks, this is Mark Ross."

"Becca's boss." Carla nodded to Tuck and turned to look at Mark.

She knew who he was? Mark didn't know how to feel about that. Had Tucker talked to her about him? And what in the world could he have said? Paranoia kicked in as he wondered if it had been good or bad. Either way, here was his opportunity to make a good impression. Mark couldn't help what others said about him, but he could control how she saw him now. He'd show her who he was, and that was a gentleman.

"Very nice to meet you, Carla." Mark stifled a groan at his own mundane words.

The head of the English department, with a PhD in linguistics, and yet he couldn't come up with a better greeting than that? He stank at this male/female stuff. He stepped forward and extended his hand, hoping it didn't feel as clammy to her as it did to him.

"Pleasure meeting you, too, Mark." She wiped her hand on her jeans before reaching out to grasp his. "Sorry. Fish guts."

"Oh, no problem at all. To be expected, really. Considering."

"True that. All part of the sport." Her smile lit her face and possibly outshined the morning sun rising in the sky.

Her grip was strong and firm in Mark's hand,

and it wasn't until he noticed he'd held it longer than was proper that he let go.

All right. The introductions had gone well enough. So far, so good. Now all he had to do was not look like a fool trying to fish, since this girl seemed to be an expert. He could tell that just from the confident way she held her pole, not to mention all the fishing paraphernalia littering the ground around her.

Tuck peered into the big white bucket resting on the ground. "Nice-looking bass."

"Yeah, I only got the one but it's not a bad size. Still, I'm catching crap here with the rod. I was fixin' to do some noodling. If you're up to it, that is." Carla glanced at Tuck.

"Damn right, I'm up for it. I didn't know you'd be, though." Just as Logan returned from the truck, Tucker began to strip. In seconds he was out of his boots and working on unbuttoning his jeans.

"Hell, boy. I've been noodling since I was four years old. What's the biggest one you ever caught?" she asked.

Tuck paused in his stripping and eyed her. "Fifty-five pounds."

"Ha! Seventy-five-pounder for me." Carla's smile was triumphant.

As the conversation and Tucker's stripping continued, Mark turned to Logan, more confused than ever. "Noodling?"

What the heck was that? Mark had to wonder, since it required that Tuck strip naked for him to do it with Carla.

"It's hand fishing for catfish," Logan answered, resting the bait on the ground.

With a relief, Mark saw Tucker had been wearing swim trunks under his jeans. The man wasn't naked after all, only sans pants. And now shirt, as he exposed suntanned muscles worthy of a men's health magazine cover model.

So much for Mark impressing Carla with his own physique. That wasn't going to happen with Tucker there, looking like a Greek god. Maybe Mark should start working out with Logan and the ROTC cadets if those muscles were the result. Until then, it was best Mark leave his shirt on. The Total Gym he stored in the spare bedroom kept him toned, but jeez, nothing like this guy.

When Mark could wrestle his eyes off what was happening between Tuck and Carla, what Logan had said about the noodling sank in. "Wait. What? They're going to catch fish by hand? That's what noodling is?"

He watched as Carla reeled in her line and then proceeded to peel off her own clothes to reveal a sexy as sin bathing suit that captured Mark's attention far more than Tuck's stripping had. Wow. A woman who could catch a fish with her bare hands while looking that good in a bikini. He'd never met anyone like her before, and he doubted he ever would.

"Mark. You're staring." Logan's touch on his shoulder brought Mark's head around.

He swallowed hard. Logan was right. He had been staring. He hated to admit it but his jaw had dropped open at the sight of her and all that exposed flesh. Mark slammed his mouth closed now. "Sorry. I've just never heard of anything like this noodling before."

"Yeah, I'm sure." Logan didn't look convinced that was the reason for Mark's openmouthed shock, but he continued anyway. "This time of year the catfish are spawning. The females lay their eggs in underwater holes in the banks of rivers or lakes, but the males protect the eggs. Carla and Tuck are going to feel around and try to find one of those holes."

"And then grab the fish?" It sounded pretty difficult. Mark could only imagine the fish would be slippery and hard to hold.

"Not exactly." Logan laughed. "More like they wait for the catfish to bite them. Once his mouth is clamped onto their arm, they pull him up."

"No." Mark's eyes opened wider.

"Yup. You have to have two people because some of these catfish can grow to be over a hundred pounds. And then, you know, it also helps to have a second pair of eyes to watch out for water snakes. Or beavers, depending on where you are. Those bastards can get nasty." Logan spoke while prying the lid off a small plastic tub. Mark assumed it contained what would be their bait for the day.

"You're messing with me." Mark screwed up his face. Real funny. Make fun of the nerdy English professor who grew up in Chicago and never fished in his life. Ha, ha.

"Not at all. Mark, I swear, my hand to God, it's true." Logan went so far as to hold his hand up along with the pledge.

After Logan's impassioned declaration, Mark could see the man wasn't joking. "You're serious? They're going to catch catfish with their bare hands?"

"Yes. Watch. You'll see." Logan turned away and

started to root through the things they'd brought, as if what their two companions were about to do was nothing out of the ordinary. "I'm going to assume you're not up for any grabbling."

Mark sighed. "What's grabbling?"

Logan paused in his search and glanced up. "Same as noodling, but grabbling is what my granddad and my dad always called it."

"Ah, yes. Of course." Mark began to see an untapped market here. An opportunity he might have to take advantage of. He could write a dictionary of fishing terms for the novice sportsman. He could see it now on the shelf in his library right next to the linguistics textbook he'd contributed to.

Unperturbed, Logan continued, "I'll set you up with a light rig. The night crawlers I bought will attract pretty much anything in this lake."

"Okay." Mark wasn't sure he had an opinion, or wanted to have one, on the creepy-sounding and unfortunately named night crawlers.

"You're going to want to cast close to the shore near the reeds, but as far away from Carla and Tuck as you can. They'll likely spook anything nearby just by being in the water." Logan spoke while he worked. Mark cringed as he watched Logan impale a worm on the hook.

"All right." He'd have to take Logan's word on all of this. Besides, Mark was too fascinated by this whole hand-fishing scenario to think too much about his own pole. He glanced back at Carla, wading out into the water with Tuck at her back. "Logan, I don't know much about fishing, but do women usually do that? This noodling grabbling thing, I mean?"

"Yeah. Some." Logan handed the rod to Mark and then reached for the second one on the ground.

"Oh." Apparently, Mark hung out with different kinds of women than Tucker and Logan. Maybe he needed to start spending more time with these two men.

"Let me get my rig set up and I'll show you how to cast."

"Sure." Mark could stand there looking at her all day and be very happy. No fishing required.

He noted how the rising sun caught the golden highlights in Carla's brown hair. She'd taken off her cowboy hat when she'd stripped down to her bathing suit. Now, Mark could see how light in color the strands were, except near the bottom where the braid had turned dark from trailing in the water.

As he watched, she sank shoulder deep. She laughed and said something to Tuck—all while she tried to feel around underwater for a hole with a hundred-pound catfish inside to bite her so she could catch it.

Fascinating. Absolutely fascinating.

"So what's up with the professor over there?" Carla glanced at the shoreline where Tuck's boss, Logan, was showing Professor Mark how to cast. Something about this shy, unassuming English teacher intrigued her. With his pink, collared polo shirt and khaki shorts that looked as if they needed to be ironed, it wasn't like he was her usual type. But there was something in his blue eyes, a kindness that showed through from behind those glasses that kept slipping down his nose. It made her want to learn more about him.

Tuck glanced at the two men standing a pretty good distance away, and then back to her. "What do you mean?"

"You know. What's the four-one-one?" As Carla felt along the underwater bank with one hand, she kept her gaze focused on the object of the conversation up on shore.

"*The four-one-one?*" Tucker laughed. "Jeez, girl. You've been hanging around with the students too much. You're starting to talk like them. I don't know what else I can tell you. He plays poker with Logan once a week. He seems like an all right guy. I've only hung out with him a few times. Why?"

"No reason."

Tuck splashed his way closer to her. "Wait a minute. You're not interested, are you?"

Carla turned to see a frown that creased Tuck's forehead so deep, it made her laugh. "Well, jeez, don't look at me like that. First off, I didn't say I was interested, but even if I were, you said he was an all right guy. Right?"

"Yeah, I guess. I mean I wouldn't worry about you if you and the nerdy professor went out together or anything. But I didn't think he was the type of guy you'd date." Tuck whispered the last word, as if the professor on the shore might hear.

Carla gave up on finding any catfish in the section she'd been working and stood. She moved a few feet over and felt for holes, resuming the conversation when Tuck followed her. "Exactly. I've had it with my usual type. I thought it might be nice to get to know a guy who doesn't ride horses."

"Or ride buckle bunnies?" He grinned, even as she scowled at the truth of that comment.

"Yeah, that too. And remind me not to tell you my personal business from now on."

"Sorry. I'm not making fun. I'm just surprised. But hell, you're right. You could do way worse than him." Tuck tilted his head in the direction of the professor, who'd just made a surprisingly good cast for a novice. "He's got a good job with a steady paycheck and benefits. And I bet he's got shelves and shelves full of books at his house. You know, in case you two had nothing else to do at night, you could read or something."

His smirk had her frowning. "Tucker Jenkins, you can be a real bastard, you know that?"

"Now, why would you say a thing like that?"

Tuck's innocent act wouldn't work on Carla. She knew him too well and she wasn't about to put up with his teasing her about her possible interest in Mark just because, at first glance, he was the typical nerdy professor type.

"You're marrying an English professor yourself, so don't pick on me for asking a casual question about this one. And don't think I didn't notice that bite mark on your chest, Tucker Jenkins. Don't you tell me all you do with your professor at night is read books." She let out a snort and attacked the mud beneath the water with new enthusiasm.

Glancing over her shoulder, she took great satisfaction in the way Tuck's face turned beet red at her bite mark comment. Good. He deserved to be embarrassed for teasing her.

When he started to wade toward the shore, Carla frowned and stood. "Hey. Where are you going?"

"To put my shirt on."

His mumbled answer made her laugh. "Why? Too late now. I already saw your hickey."

"It's not a hickey. It's . . ." It seemed Tuck didn't have the words to finish his hissed reply.

"A love bite?" She happily supplied that suggestion and watched his face color deepen.

"Whatever. And you may have noticed it, but hopefully my fiancée's boss hasn't. I'd like to keep it that way, if you don't mind, so keep your voice down." With a scowl he proceeded toward his clothes, which were piled on top of the cooler.

"Yes, sir." She grinned, thankful she and Tuck didn't have the typical work relationship that Becca and this Mark Ross probably did.

Thankful, too, that for the next day and night there'd be no rodeo cowboys around to tempt her. Just one alluring, nerdy professor whose eyeglasses she wouldn't mind steaming up a bit.

She'd been so busy teasing Tuck, she'd almost failed to notice the professor was not only alone now, but wrestling with something on the end of his line. Glancing at the shoreline, she saw Logan was nowhere in sight, and Tuck was still fighting what looked like a losing battle to get his T-shirt on over his wet skin.

Carla didn't think twice. She bounded out of the water and ran to Mark, who obviously needed help reeling in whatever was on his hook. It had the tip of his rod bent low over the water.

"Where'd Logan go?" she asked when, dripping wet and out of breath, she reached him.

"To the truck." Mark widened his stance and tried to control the rod as the unseen fish nearly tugged it out of his hands. "There's something . . . on here."

The man could barely get the words out while he gripped the pole with white knuckles. As if his life depended on it.

"Yup, there's definitely something on there." She nodded.

"Maybe you should handle this." He glanced at her through glasses that now were askew and half-way down his nose. She fought the urge to slide them back into place for him.

The teacher in Carla kicked in. "No, you can do it. I'll tell you how."

"I think you should do it." He thrust the rod at her, just as the fish gave another hard tug.

No time to fight with him now or they could lose whatever he'd hooked. She took over manning the rod. "All right, I'll do it for you, but watch me so you can do it next time. Okay?"

He let out a short laugh. "I'll watch but that's no guarantee it will help me next time. If there is a next time."

Carla shook her head at his pessimism. The best fishermen were natural-born optimists. They had to be, to sit for hours, sometimes without even a nibble. But apparently professors, or at least this particular professor, was not.

Turning the handle, Carla reeled in the line, slow and steady as the fish kept the tension tight enough to bend the end of the rod. Mark's catch fought and tugged until it broke the surface of the water, but then it couldn't fight anymore and just dangled. She reached out one hand and grabbed the line to keep it from swinging.

"It's a bluegill. They tend to swim sideways when you reel them in. That's why it felt bigger than it is. They're real good eating, though." Carla gripped the fish behind the gills and unhooked it. "Here you go. It's all yours. Your first catch of the day."

He let out a short laugh and stared at the wiggling fish she tried to hand him. "Not just the first of the day. This fish is my first catch ever."

Finally, he took it, looking at a loss what to do next.

"Well, then, you should be very proud. That's a nice one, too. Probably about a pound. Maybe more."

"It does look like a nice one, doesn't it?" Mark smiled and held the fish, considering it. "Can I keep it? I mean it's not too small, is it? Do I have to throw it back?"

Mark's rambling enthusiasm made Carla smile. "No, you can keep it."

Tuck, finally in his shirt, the telltale bite mark safely hidden from view, made his way over. He eyed Mark's fish. "Yeah, you can keep that one. It's just a sunnie. There're no regulations on size for those. That's why little kids usually start out catching them."

Seeing the pride over his first fish beaming from the professor even in the face of Tuck's smart-ass crack about it being a kid's fish, Carla shot Tuck a warning glance and then turned back to Mark.

"*Or*, this type of fish is sometimes called a perch, and as I said before, a bluegill. Just a lot of different names for the same thing." She finished her speech and looked up in time to see Tuck trying not to laugh at her.

"What do I do with it?" Mark turned to her as the fish remained in his hand.

She forced herself to ignore Tuck as she dealt with Mark and his catch. "You put it in a bucket with some water until we're ready to cook it."

"I didn't bring one. I didn't know I should." His gaze met hers as he looked a bit distraught about his lack of a bucket.

"Not a problem. Plenty of room in mine." She tilted her head in the direction of the big bucket of water currently holding her bass. "Go on and put it in there."

A frown knit Mark's brow. "With yours? Is that okay? They won't, I don't know, fight or anything?"

Carla smiled. "Nah, it'll be fine."

"Okay." Holding the fish out at arm's length and looking like an excited ten-year-old rather than his thirty-some-odd years, Mark made his slow but steady way toward the bucket.

The moment he was out of earshot, Carla spun to deliver a warning to Tuck. "You be nice."

"Me?" Tuck drew back. "What'd I do?"

"You made fun of his fish." Carla had learned how to put a man in his place from watching the best. She had a mama who had never allowed any crap from Carla's two brothers. Right now, Tuck needed reprimanding.

"I did not." When she continued to glare, Tuck backed down. "All right. Maybe that kid crack was out of line, but you didn't do any better."

"Me?" Her voice cracked with a squeak. "I didn't do anything except help him. Somebody had to. Both you and Logan were ignoring the poor guy."

Tuck laughed. "Yeah, sure. You think a man really wants help reeling in his catch? Especially from the girl he's hot for?"

"You really think he's hot for me?" She didn't bother defending herself to Tuck by telling him Mark had *asked* her to help reel it in. He'd practically thrown his pole at her, but that didn't matter now. Not in light of this new revelation. Tuck thought Mark was hot for her. Hmm.

She glanced over her shoulder at Mark. He stood staring down into the bucket, probably to make sure the two fish didn't fight. She turned back to Tuck. "How do you know?"

"Holy crap. Look how excited you are. You do have your eye on Ross. Jeez, girl. You need to get yourself another boyfriend if even the professor over there is getting you squirrelly in the drawers." Tuck's focus on Carla and her love life was a little too intense and personal for her liking.

"Oh, hush up." Carla shot Tuck what she hoped was a withering glance but most likely fell short, since he chuckled at her.

She allowed herself one more quick look in Mark's direction. Tuck was right, she needed something but it wasn't necessarily another boyfriend. At least not one like the last one . . . or three.

Maybe just a nice fling. That would be lovely at this point in the man drought in her life.

So Mark wasn't her usual type. So what? She wasn't going to count him out of the good-in-bed category because of that. Cowboys didn't hold the monopoly on sexual prowess. Hell, it was the quiet guys, the ones you'd least expect it from, you had to watch out for. They could be the wildest once the lights went out.

Oh, yeah, she'd like to get him to let his hair down—figuratively speaking. It was true what they said: still waters ran deep.

Checking out Mark as best she could without having anyone notice, Carla decided he was a damn attractive man once she looked past the surface. There appeared to be a nice and firm, although lean, body beneath those clothes that belonged more on a catalog cover than a fishing trip. Not to mention those high cheekbones and chiseled jaw. The man definitely had good bones. He was like the male equivalent of the sexy librarian hiding behind staid clothing and studious eyeglasses.

Carla wouldn't mind being the one to get him to whip off those glasses. Then he could sweep aside piles of books and lay her down on top of his big, sturdy oak desk—

"What did I miss?" Logan's question broke into the porn movie playing in Carla's head.

"The professor caught a sunnie, and Carla yanked the rod right out of his hand and reeled it in for him."

"No! You reeled it in for him? Ah, Jesus, Carla." Logan slapped his palm to his forehead and let out an exasperated breath. "At least let Tuck or me filet it. Don't you do that for him, too."

Apparently, Carla had committed the ultimate in sins, at least according to these two guys.

"Jeez. I'm sorry. I'll never touch another man's fishing pole again. Promise." With that, she stalked over to Mark to see if she could repair this horrible damage she'd supposedly caused to his delicate male psyche.

He turned to her with the biggest grin she'd seen

since her brother had won the high school rodeo championship buckle. "He's not as big as the one you caught but he's still pretty nice."

She looked down into the bucket. "Well, mine's a bass. They tend to run a little bigger than bluegill. But you're right. You've got a real nice one here. Though it's probably a *she* rather than a *he*, judging by the size and the way it fought. The females get more aggressive this time of year because they're laying eggs. But bluegill are tasty. It'll cook up real good tonight."

"How do you think you'll prepare him?" He looked a little crestfallen at the idea of turning his prize over to her for dinner. Little did he know, the camp cook she was not.

Time to invent some rules of fishing. Mark would never know the difference, she was sure. "Well, now, that's up to you. It's your catch. That means you get to fix it any way you want. Hell, you know what? I'll even let you cook up my fish with yours, if you want."

"Really?" Mark perked up at the offer. "You wouldn't mind?"

"I don't mind at all." She dismissed his concern with a wave of her hand.

"Hmm, I'll have to look at what we brought with us, but I have a few ideas." He crossed his arms and considered the two fish in the bucket before looking back to her. "I fancy myself a bit of an amateur chef. And I cook a lot of fish at home."

"Sounds like we're in good hands. I look forward to dinner." Pleased with herself, Carla slapped his shoulder.

Problem solved. He'd never know she could barely

boil water. Actually, she'd even failed at that once when she'd run out to check on something in the barn and forgotten she'd left the pot of water on the stove until all the water had boiled away and ruined the pot.

Mark the professor was turning out to be a surprise, as well as quite a catch. Cute, smart, modest, and he could cook. What more could a girl ask for?

Okay, maybe one other thing . . . and she hoped to explore that area with him real soon.

Chapter Three

Mark watched as Carla raised the fork, laden with the first bite of the flaky white fish he'd cooked, to her lips.

When she closed her eyes and released a sultry, low "mmm" from deep in her throat, he feared he might embarrass himself right there. Her groan seemed to cut straight through him, awakening carnal desires he shouldn't be having in public, and especially not for a woman he'd just met today.

"What did you put on it?" When her golden-brown eyes opened and focused on him, he had to force his attention off her mouth and what he'd like to do with it, and on her question.

"I didn't do too much to it, really. Logan brought salt and pepper and a few lemons. And Tuck had aluminum foil. I wrapped it all up with the fish, and put it over the coals. But of course, there was one more secret ingredient I added."

Carla lifted one eyebrow. "Is it so secret you won't even share with me?"

Her flirtatious question set Mark's heart speeding. "I think I might be able to, *if* you promise not to tell."

"Cross my heart." Her motion as she trailed a finger across the skin of her chest exposed by the bikini top drew all of his attention. He imagined following that path with his mouth.

It was an effort to wrestle his gaze away as his misbehaving cock woke up and took notice.

He drew in a deep breath to settle himself and then said, "Beer."

"Beer?" Her eyes opened wide.

"Yes. At home I would have used white wine, but since we didn't have any with us, I figured I'd give the beer a try." He shrugged.

She laughed. "Well, I'm glad you did, because it worked. This tastes amazing."

"What's amazing?" Tuck returned from where he and Logan had the propane burner hooked up beneath a fry pot filled with oil.

"The fish Mark cooked." She took another bite. "Oh, my, God. Absolutely amazing."

Carla's eyes nearly rolled back in her head with her obvious satisfaction. Mark's mind went to bad, bad places as he pictured her beneath him, her face contorted with pleasure from his loving her, rather than from the food he'd cooked.

Where had that thought come from? Mark pulled his brain off naughty thoughts of making love to the sexy woman in front of him and back to more appropriate topics—such as campfire cooking.

He cleared his throat. "It was nothing. Really. I just threw on what we had."

Logan followed close behind Tuck with a plate loaded with fried catfish. "First batch is done. Second batch is in the fryer."

"I don't know if the catfish I caught and you cooked can live up to Ross's sunnie, here. According to Carla, it's unbeatable. Too bad it was too small for all of us to have a taste." Tuck grinned at Carla.

"Don't worry, smarty-pants. There's more. Mark cooked my bass, too, and it's excellent."

The sound of his first name on Carla's lips had Mark warming further. Her calling him by his given name sounded even more intimate in contrast, since Tuck always referred to him by his surname.

But all this discussion about his cooking made Mark self-conscious. He tilted a chin toward the overflowing plate Logan held. "I'd love to try a bite of the catfish you and Tucker fried, Logan. And here, let me get you both a plate so you can try some of Carla's bass."

"Thanks." Logan put the dish of fried fish on top of the cooler, which seemed to now be functioning as a serving table. "I was talking to a few of the guys from the phys ed department. They set up camp right next to where I had my fryer going. Anyway, they're going over to see what they can catch on the other side of the lake tonight. Tuck and I are going to join them right after we eat. You two in?"

More fishing? It had been fun once. No doubt Carla's presence had added greatly to his enjoyment, but even with her there, Mark wasn't sure he was up for a repeat. Not at night, following a day that had started very early that morning. After eating the meal and drinking a few beers by the campfire, he was happy to not do much of anything.

They'd already fished for hours, for the better part of that day, but except for some faculty stopping by to say hello to him on their way to the swimming area, it had been just the four of them. He hadn't totally embarrassed himself fishing today with Tuck and Logan, and he'd impressed Carla with his cooking skills tonight. His instincts told him it was time to end this day on a high note.

Who was to say what would happen tonight with these other people? It was best that Mark quit while he was ahead. He could imagine how inadequate he'd feel next to the iron-pumped linebackers from the phys ed department. Jeez.

With a plate held in one hand, Mark pushed his glasses up his nose with the other.

"Uh, thanks, but I think I'll pass." He reached out and gave the dish to Logan and then bent to pick up the second plate, which would be for Tucker.

"You know, I'm not gonna want to go out again tonight, either. I'm thinking after such a good meal, all I'm going to want to do is relax." Carla's answer almost made Mark trip and drop the plate in his hand.

She wasn't going fishing? When the others left, she was going to stay there. With him. Alone.

He forced himself to pay attention to where he was walking only to find when he did glance up from the tricky terrain, Tuck was grinning at him.

Mark thrust the fish-laden paper plate forward. "Here you go."

"Thanks, Ross." Tucker had a way of smirking that made Mark feel like a bug under a magnifying glass. As if Tuck could somehow know what Mark was thinking, and it amused him greatly.

If Tuck could read minds, Mark's romantic thoughts about Carla would amuse the cowboy to no end, because women like Carla didn't go for men like Mark. Historically, inevitably, they went for guys who could wrestle giant fish with their bare hands, the way Tucker had today.

Meanwhile, Mark had done nothing to help Tuck with his struggle in the water except stand by, openmouthed and amazed. Then he'd whipped out his cell phone to take a picture of the action, because really, without proof, who would believe it if he told them?

Women like Carla went for guys like the bruisers from the phys ed department who coached the OSU Cowboys football team to victory. But men like Mark? Pale—make that slightly sunburned, since he'd forgotten to reapply his sunscreen today—professors who spent their days behind a desk or in front of a classroom?

No. He couldn't see a woman like Carla with someone like him.

As unfortunate as that was, Mark feared it to be the truth. As an Oklahoma cowgirl, Carla was used to the rough and tough outdoorsmen she encountered in her everyday life. Her perfect man would be a fish wrestler, or a cattle rancher, not a pencil pusher. Not even one who could cook.

Tucker took a plastic fork full of the bass Mark had so painstakingly prepared because it was Carla's catch and tasted it. "Mmm, Carla's right. That is damn good."

Logan laughed between forkfuls from his own plate. "Uh-oh, Mark. You may have just nominated yourself camp cook for the next fishing trip."

"Next fishing trip?" Mark paused in his path back to his chair.

"Yeah, sure." Logan nodded. "Tuck and I go as often as we can. At least a couple of times over summer break."

"Really? Oh, okay," Mark agreed, figuring when the time came, if they did invite him, which he doubted, he'd come up with some kind of an excuse to back out. Unless of course, Carla would be there again.

Would she? Did this group he'd fallen into today all hang out together on a regular basis? Or was she on this trip strictly because she was part of the OSU rodeo team and this was a university retreat?

Mark didn't know, but he'd like to find out because although Tuck was engaged and a taken man, Logan wasn't. Logan was single and available and could definitely make a play for Carla should he wish to. The university's nonfraternization rule wouldn't even apply in this case since the rodeo team was classified as a club and not an official part of the sports program.

All of his pondering raised another, more important question—was Carla even single? She didn't wear a wedding or an engagement ring, but that didn't mean she wasn't in a serious relationship with some cowboy off tending his herd somewhere.

When Tucker and Logan went off fishing tonight, and Carla was all his—and God how he wished she were his—then Mark would have to see what he could glean. Words were his life, and although it seemed she made him as tongue-tied as a teenage boy, Mark would find out more about this woman. Once he set his mind on a goal, there was no stopping him.

*   *   *

"You sure you don't want to come?" Tuck asked.

Carla shook her head. "Nah. Thanks. I'm ready to turn in for an early night."

Hands filled with what he'd need, Logan paused just on the edge of the firelight. "You two will be okay here until we get back?"

"I'm sure we'll be just fine." Mark covered a yawn with his hand. "Excuse me. I'll probably be turning in pretty soon myself."

"All right." Tuck nodded. "If you're both asleep by the time we get back, we'll see you in the morning."

"All right." Mark raised a brow. "Uh, are we fishing again at sunrise?"

The tone of Mark's question had Carla smiling. He might be trying to hide it and sound enthusiastic, but she saw right through that act. The last thing he wanted to do tomorrow morning was get up before dawn to fish.

"Nah, we'll break down camp after breakfast, maybe take a dip in the lake, and then head out," Logan answered.

"Oh, okay. Great." Mark visibly perked up. "See you in the morning. Happy fishing."

When Tuck and Logan were out of sight, Carla stood. She had a plan and now was as good a time as any. She dumped the paper dinner plates into the garbage bag they'd brought along and glanced up at the professor.

"So, how's about a little dip right now?"

"Dip?" He pushed his glasses up his nose one more time, where she knew from watching him all day they wouldn't stay for long before they'd slip down again.

"Yeah. I love swimming at night. The air's just starting to cool off but the water's still holding the heat of the sun. It's the perfect way to end a perfect day. And I can go to sleep feeling clean and fresh, instead of smelling like campfire smoke."

"Is that allowed? Swimming at night, I mean?"

She grinned at his hesitation. It was adorable how he worried about every little thing. If her last boyfriend had been even half as concerned with the consequences of his actions, Carla might not have found him buried inside a buckle bunny on the night he'd canceled their date because he supposedly had to help a buddy move.

Just thinking about it pissed her off, even months later. She buried that anger and concentrated on the man in front of her. Mark couldn't be more different from her ex-boyfriend, and he didn't deserve to be subjected to her anger over something he had nothing to do with.

"Is it allowed?" Carla shrugged. "Hell if I know. I didn't stop to read the rules posted on the sign when I drove in."

He smiled and started to gather the cooking utensils. "No, you wouldn't. You're not the kind of woman who'd let rules tie her down."

In reality it was because she'd been tired this morning and it had still been dark out, but yeah, his excuse sounded good, too. It made her seem like an independent, strong individual, which was way better than what she was—kind of smoky-smelling and a little bit sex deprived. She wouldn't mind getting closer to this man, much closer, while washing away the remaining scent of dinner.

"You're right. Nothing ties me down, so put back that frying pan and let's go." She reached out and grabbed his free hand.

"I should clean that pan—" As Mark started to protest, Carla paused in her quest to pull him toward the water. She turned to stare into his eyes. She watched as he bit his lower lip, and a small frown furrowed his brow. Finally, he put the pan down. "You know what? Forget about cleaning up. I can do that later."

"Good." She smiled. "Now let's go."

"Do you know where the swimming area is? Logan said there are separate designated swimming and fishing areas." He continued to question the rules as she dragged him forward.

"Yup. I know right where it is." As far as Carla was concerned, for her purposes, the swimming area was wherever there were no people nearby. She wasn't in the mood for idle chatter with some OSU faculty member she'd never met. She was in the mood for some alone time with Professor Mark, though.

Mark took her hand in his with a firm, warm grip. No wishy-washy hand-holding with this man. When he held on to her, she felt held. It was nice. She liked the feeling. She'd like it better if it were his arms wrapped around her body rather than his fingers wrapped around hers, because she hadn't had that satisfaction with a man in far too long.

Just one more motivation for her to find a secluded spot.

She stopped at the shore and glanced around

her. The campsites were farther in. Not that it mattered to her, but this might well be the official swimming area since she didn't see anyone fishing here.

It was early, just getting dark, and most people would still be occupied, enjoying their s'mores by the campfire. That might explain the current peace and quiet here by the lake.

"This looks like a good spot." Carla dropped her hold on his hand and turned toward Mark, just in time to catch him eyeballing her. She'd chosen the bikini for today because she hated having the white belly and brown arms she got when she wore her one-piece swimsuit for a day out in the sun. But now, seeing his admiration of her when he thought she wasn't looking, she was doubly pleased with her choice of attire.

"Um, uh, sure." He'd yanked his gaze back up to her face so fast, she nearly laughed.

It was dim enough she couldn't see him blush but she'd bet money he was beet red at having been caught checking her out. Little did he know she took it as a compliment. She was used to cowboys ogling her at rodeos. But to have a smart, educated, and important man like Mark be interested—that was a nice change.

"Good. Then come on." She led the way into the water, turning to see him still by the shore.

After first toeing off one slip-on canvas shoe, and then the other, Mark bent to line them up on the ground a safe distance from the lapping water. He peeled off his shirt next, meticulously folding it before laying it on top of his shoes.

Since it looked as if this might take awhile, Carla dipped to her shoulders and floated weightlessly in the water as he took his time getting ready. She watched his preparations, fascinated. Men weren't like this. At least, not the ones she knew.

Sure, Tuck tended to be neat at rodeo practice, always making sure the students' gear was cleaned and stowed before they were allowed to leave, but she'd figured that was his military training. And that he was trying to teach them to do things right. Her brothers were both slobs. Her exes had been, too. But this man took the time to fold his clothes before he went swimming in a lake.

Finally, when he was down to just his swim trunks, Mark waded ankle deep and paused. After a few seconds, he came in to his knees, and paused again. By the time he reached her, she was full out grinning.

"Something funny?" he asked.

"You're very careful, aren't you?"

"What do you mean?" The frown she'd gotten used to seeing on Mark appeared again.

Putting her feet down on the sandy lake bottom, she moved closer to him. "You don't jump into anything without proper preparation and consideration, do you?"

"I could, should the right opportunity present itself." He could have sounded defensive, but he didn't. Instead, he sounded almost flirty, challenging her to make him abandon his careful ways. Throw caution to the wind. With her.

"Nope. I don't think you could. You'd have to consider it first. Weigh all the options. Then take your time deciding how best to go about it." At his frown, Carla stopped. Crap. She hadn't meant to insult him, but she'd gone too far in her teasing. "Don't get me wrong. That's a good thing. I wish more men thought about things before they just went out and did them."

"Really?" He looked doubtful, which made her want to reassure him and get back to the place they'd been before.

"Yes. The world would be a better place if all men were as careful as you are. At least my world would be." And this conversation had gotten serious damn fast. Carla noticed him watching her, so intense she almost looked away.

They'd drifted into slightly deeper water. She found they were closer than before, her toes just touching the sandy bottom of the lake as she bobbed. They were only inches apart now and she found she wanted to be even closer, in more ways than one.

"So, I don't know very much about you," she said.

"What do you want to know?" His voice was low, just loud enough for her to hear. It made the situation feel even more intimate.

In the darkness, the sky lit only by a partial moon and a few stars, she let herself drift closer to him. "Are you married? Have any kids?"

"No, and no."

Good answer. Carla was concentrating on coming up with another question when her big toe touched bottom again on top of a rock, pitching her forward. Mark caught her. His hold on her arms was the only thing that kept her upright.

"So what about you? Married? Children?" He continued the conversation as if she hadn't just tripped like a klutz, like nothing had happened, but there was one big difference now—both of his hands were on her arms and he hadn't made any move to change that.

"No," she answered, feeling the heat of his touch in stark contrast with the chill in the water.

"Boyfriend?" His tone dropped even lower. He ran his hands up to her shoulders and back down, lightly. Goose bumps rose on her flesh even as inside her core heated for this man.

"Nope. Girlfriend?" Her heart began to pound as she awaited his answer.

"No." Mark was so close now, her chest bumped against his when the water moved them. "Carla?"

"Hmm?" She didn't wait to hear what he wanted to ask. They were so temptingly close. On her tiptoes, she was almost as tall as he was standing flat-footed. She only had to reach up, just a bit . . .

He dragged in a deep breath through his nose as her mouth touched his in a gentle kiss. His hold on her arms tightened and she found herself pressed against him. All of him, from chest to thigh.

Mark Ross might be a cautious man about many things, but he wasn't acting that way now as he kissed her back with enthusiasm. His body wasn't taking it slow. Carla felt his arousal outlined through the thin fabric of his swimsuit. There was no hiding it, considering how close they were holding each other and how little they both wore.

Rather than back away, Carla did the boldest thing she'd ever done—she wrapped her arms around his waist, ensuring her pelvis pressed harder against his.

Mark responded with a groan as he tilted his head and changed the angle of the kiss. He moved his hands down and gripped her hips. He held her right where she was, tantalizingly pressed against the hard length between them. His possession of her mouth increased as he teased her lips with his tongue.

How long had it been since she'd made out with a guy? Not just a quick kiss and fumble before the sex, but actually did some long, hard kissing? Too long, if how good this felt was any indication. The pleasure filled her, heating her from the inside. She met the intensity of his kisses with some pretty crazy enthusiasm on her own part. Opening her lips, she invited more and he took it, thrusting his tongue into her mouth until they were both breathing heavier.

Carla found herself gyrating against the bulge between them, dry humping this man in the water, which probably made it wet humping, technically. The movement hadn't been conscious on her part. She didn't realize she was doing it until her body tightened and the fingers of pleasure gripped her and spread.

Breaking the kiss, she pulled back just enough to see his face. His eyes were heavy-lidded when he opened them and stared back at her through the lenses of his glasses.

Mark sank lower in the water, moved his grip down to her thighs and lifted. "Wrap your legs around my waist."

She did and he began to move her against him. Her mouth opened on a gasp. They were lined up perfectly to rub just the right spot. A few minutes more of this, given her current needy condition, and she'd come, and she had a feeling he knew it, too.

Mark was taking control of the situation, and of her pleasure, showing an assertive side she found incredibly attractive. She didn't have time to consider how much she liked the new decisive side of him, because she was gasping for breath and trying not to moan.

As she teetered on the edge of a climax, Carla hoped Mark was prepared, because it was going to be a big one.

Chapter Four

Carla gasped his name against his wet skin and Mark felt her come apart in his arms. Her entire body trembled as he held her pressed to his erection. The only thing between them was the fabric of their suits.

With her face buried against his neck, he felt her moans vibrate through him. A small part of his brain registered that they should be quieter. If anyone was close enough to hear, there would be no mistaking what was happening here in the water, under cover of the darkness.

These were the sounds of two people taking pleasure in each other. No doubt about it.

The weight and feel of Carla in his hands, causing friction against his cock as he continued to rock her against him, was more than enough to have him breathing pretty hard himself. He held back a groan as he relished each move and every sound she made. He'd made this woman come while he held her in his arms, and it was even better than he could have imagined. One thing would make this night perfect, and that would be him buried inside her feeling her muscles pulse around him.

That thought alone did elicit a shaky groan he couldn't control.

He felt the warmth of her breath against him before she pulled back. Her eyes met his as she reached between them and pushed at the waistband of his swim trunks. When he realized she was struggling to free his erection, his heart raced until the pulse pounding in his ears was enough to block out the sounds of the water sloshing around them.

Breathing was harder than it should be. Maybe it was oxygen deprivation that led him to it, but he reached down. His hand encountered hers between them. He helped her struggle with the wet fabric until it was no longer between them.

The first stroke of her hand on the bare skin of his erection had him closing his eyes and relishing the sensation of it. He could come just from her fingers wrapped around him. How amazing that would be, to—

His eyes popped open as the feel of her fingers was replaced with the heat of her body. She moved to position the tip of him at her entrance.

"Carla. What are you doing?" He hadn't even noticed that she'd pushed the crotch of her bikini bottoms to the side to allow him access.

She bit her lip, her eyes mere slits, narrowed with need. "I think you can figure that out."

Yes, he could, which was why the rational part of his brain, the portion that was rapidly shrinking with every passing moment, protested. As the need to plunge into her increased with each breath he took, Mark somehow remembered his objection.

"I don't have a condom." And he definitely didn't trust himself to have the control to be able to pull out in time. She felt too incredible and he was too damn close already from what they'd done so far.

"It's okay. I'm on the pill." As she said it, she pressed lower.

He felt the tip of him slip into her wet heat, as his resolve slid away. He'd had a small sample, and he wanted more. She obviously did too. With her legs still wrapped around his waist, she let the weight of her body force him all the way home.

There was no turning back now.

This was the most incredible thing he'd ever felt. Why didn't people have sex in the water all the time? Hell, when he finally sold the condo and bought himself a house, you could bet he was putting in a pool just for this reason.

They were so buoyant in the water that the slightest move on either of their parts had her sliding up and down his length. It was almost effortless, leaving him free to concentrate on every sensation assaulting him.

Her breath, quick, short pants that were coming closer together now, told him that she was as affected by this as he was. That they both were getting closer to the culmination he feared as much as anticipated.

Mark prayed no one would hear them because it wasn't going to be easy to be quiet. Not with her hot body surrounding him, squeezing him tighter inside her. More, he hoped no one interrupted them before the end, because he might just die if they did.

A frenzy he'd never felt before overtook him. He clasped one hand to the nape of her neck beneath her braid and pulled her to him for a hard kiss. With his other hand cupping her ass, he guided her up and down his length. Her arms wrapped around his neck as she clung to him. Rode him.

It was surreal. Dreamlike. Yet at the same time, his senses had never been so sharp. He heard each breath she took, as if it were his own. He smelled the combined scents of the lake, the campfire smoke, and her. He felt every quiver her body made, both inside and out. He definitely felt it as the second orgasm hit her, making her muscles grip his cock with a rhythm that did in his already tenuous hold on his control.

The feel of her coming around him sent Mark careening over the edge himself. He thrust one more time and shot off deep inside her in what had to be the most amazing experience of his life.

Still pulsing with aftershocks while partially hard but fading inside her, he held her close and hard, unwilling to let her go. She panted against him, but otherwise she didn't move. That was fine with him. They could stay here, just like this, until the sun came up.

Once he let her go, this opportunity might never come again. He wasn't sure how it all had happened to begin with. One moment they were cleaning up dinner, the next they were swimming, and then . . . The heat of her still surrounding him reminded him of what had happened next.

He was afraid to speak, or even move, or he might break whatever magic spell had brought them to this point. Women like her didn't go for guys like him, he reminded himself. Yet her body against his told him differently. She had gone for him, at least once, anyway.

The one question that remained was this—could a woman like her stay with a man like him?

Carla had begun to wonder if they were ever going to speak, or move. Or if they would just drift in the water, clinging to each other, until morning. Eventually, nature took its course and Mark's spent hard-on faded and slipped out of her body.

He continued to hold her close as he asked, "Are you all right?"

"I'm fine. Are you?" she asked.

He let out a short laugh. "Yes. More than fine."

"You sure about that?"

Gone was the man who threw caution to the wind and let himself get lost in the moment. The man who considered everything so deliberately and carefully was back. She could feel the switch. His arms were still wrapped around her, yes, but a polite distance, which the heat of passion had erased while they'd been tangled together, had now returned.

"Carla, believe me, I wanted nothing more than to make love to you. And here, like this?" He shook his head. "It was as amazing as it was unexpected. And perfect. The dark night, a canvas for the moon and the stars above us. The sound of the lake lapping against the shore. The chill of the water, in contrast to the heat of your body surrounding me. The feel of you when you . . . God, I've never felt anything like it before in my life."

Damn, the man had a way with words. He was turning her on all over again just with his silken sentences, and the best part was, he didn't even realize he was doing it. It was like poetry dripped from his tongue. Meanwhile, most days she was lucky if she could string two sentences together without a cussword in the middle somewhere.

"Good. There's no problem then." Even though Carla couldn't put it as eloquently, she felt the same.

"Yes, good, but I thought I should get to know you better first. All about you. I guess I wanted to at least take you out on a date. Buy you a nice dinner before we . . . did this." He glanced down between them to where she was still straddling his hips.

"You cooked me a nice dinner. That's even better than taking me out and buying one for me."

He smiled. "Yes, I guess so."

"No guessing about it." Releasing the hold her thighs had on him, she let her feet touch the ground.

She turned and leaned back against him. A low groan of contentment rumbled through her. He answered with a sigh of his own as he wrapped his arms around her from behind.

They bobbed in the water for a while, him holding her close, her back against his chest as they stared into the night sky together. She felt weightless. Every once in a while he'd kiss the top of her head and squeeze her closer. His fingers traced light patterns on her skin, making her crave more. She wanted his body naked against hers. All of it. Dry and warm.

Later. For now, this was perfect . . . until she heard the sound of a distant voice and was reminded they weren't alone. "I hate to say this, but we should probably get out."

"I know. You're right. Just one more minute."

If Mr. Cautious wasn't worried, Carla sure wouldn't argue the point. She felt too boneless and content.

"Okay." Leaning her head back again until it was cradled against his chest, she let her eyes drift closed. The movement of the water. The warmth of his embrace. It lulled her into a relaxation that consumed her until she heard him say her name through the darkness.

"Carla," he repeated it again. "You're falling asleep, sweetie."

"Mmm. Sorry."

"Don't apologize. I liked it, but you were right. We should get going."

Reluctantly, she stood on her own two feet and they waded to the shore. He gathered his things in one hand and held her hand with the other. Holding hands was foolish, she knew that. If Tuck and Logan were back, they'd see her and Mark looking like they'd just had sex, but she didn't care. They walked hand in hand all the way back to the camp. Only then did she realize that in her enthusiasm to drag Mark swimming, she hadn't considered how they'd dry off. "I don't know where my towel is."

"Oh, sorry. I hung up all the wet towels to dry before I cooked dinner. Let me go get yours." He trotted to somewhere behind his tent and emerged with a towel, which he wrapped around her shoulders until she was cocooned in dry terry cloth.

"Thank you." So sweet and kind and generous. She felt warm in spite of the cool air. "So, your tent or mine?"

"Are you serious?" His eyes opened wide at her question, but his tentative smile told her he was interested in her offer.

"Of course, I'm serious." Little did Mark know, she never joked about things that were important to her, such as more sex with him.

"My tent's borrowed, so I guess yours. If that's all right with you."

Mark didn't want to have sex in his tent because it didn't belong to him. How considerate could the man get? She liked him even more for it. "Yes. That's very all right with me."

He shoved his glasses up his nose for the thousandth time that day. Carla vowed she would change that at the earliest opportunity. She wanted to clearly see the heat of his desire in his eyes without anything obscuring it. She'd get those glasses off Mark, even if she had to wrestle him to do it.

"Good, then let's go." As she reached out to take hold of his hand, she half expected him to say they had to do the dinner dishes first.

When he didn't protest, or even take a second look at the mess they were leaving behind as they made their way to her tent, she smiled at the small victory. Moments later, inside her tent, they both stripped out of their wet suits. He lowered his head between her spread thighs, pausing just long enough to take off those glasses and set them aside.

Carla took great pride in noting Mark didn't look for his glasses again for the rest of the night.

Chapter Five

Tucker stumbled past the flap of his tent and sniffed the air. "Is that coffee I smell?"

Mark felt a bit too self-satisfied that this morning he was up and about a good hour before the two ROTC early birds. Even after he'd been in Carla's tent half the night doing things he didn't dare think about now or risk the embarrassment of a hard-on.

The memory of last night gave him even more satisfaction, while making him want—need—more with her. He forced his focus back to Tuck. "It is. Fresh brewed. Can I pour you a cup?"

"God, yes."

Finally, something he could do that would impress the manly sportsmen at camp. Mark stood from his comfortable seat in the folding chair, grabbed an empty cup, and poured the steaming dark liquid. "Here you go. There's cream and sugar and a spoon set out on top of the cooler."

"Thanks." Tuck took his first gulp black and

groaned. "Damn, Ross. We're going to have to invite you camping with us from now on if this is the way I get to wake up."

"Or I could just loan you my French press and show you how to use it." Making coffee, Mark was skilled at. Camping? Not so much. "So how was fishing last night?"

"Good. I didn't catch shit, but there was lots of beer, so how could it be bad?"

Mark laughed. "Very true."

"What did you and Carla do here for entertainment last night?" Tuck's question might well have been perfectly innocent, but Mark hadn't been prepared for it.

Mark realized it was his own mistake. He'd brought up the topic of last night by asking Tuck about the fishing. He and Carla should have talked about a cover story when they were alone, but they'd been far too busy doing other things. Many other things. A couple of times. For hours.

And now Mark was starting to get an erection as Tuck waited for his answer to a casual question that should have been easy to answer. "Uh, we—"

"Morning." Logan emerged from his tent.

"Logan, good morning. Coffee?" Mark could have kissed Logan for saving the day, or at least for saving him from answering when he had no good answer.

"Yes, sir. I'd love some." Logan nodded.

Mark had never been so happy to see someone in his life, until the flap of Carla's tent flipped open and she ducked out. Then he knew true happiness. Seeing her, all sleepy with her hair loose down her back in the early morning light, took his breath away.

"Mark?" Logan's voice dragged Mark away from his blissful occupation of staring at Carla.

As his heart battered the inside of his rib cage, Mark realized Logan was standing next to him, holding out an empty cup, waiting for Mark to pour the aforementioned coffee he'd forgotten he held in his hand.

"Of course. Sorry." Mark took the cup from Logan to fill it when he realized his hand was shaking. He didn't trust himself to pour the hot liquid.

Cup filled, though it had been more difficult a task than it should have been, Mark handed it back.

Logan took it. "Thanks."

"You're welcome." Glancing up, Mark realized he was the sole object of Logan's scrutiny. Self-conscious, he tilted his head in the direction of the cooler. "Um, cream and sugar's over there."

Logan glanced from Mark to Carla, and then back again. A small smile crooked up one corner of his mouth. "Yeah, I see it."

Mark was sure it wasn't just the cream and sugar Logan saw. He always had been an open book when it came to his emotions, and Logan was more observant than the average man. The combination meant his friend, at the very least, suspected Mark was attracted to Carla.

Attracted to her. That was the understatement of the year.

One night with her had Mark, after he finally did sneak back to his tent, lying awake for long hours. His mind flew to crazy places as he considered their

possible future together. Insane things such as property values and school districts and which cut of diamond Carla might prefer if things progressed that
far.

Not to mention the far bigger *if*—that he'd be
able to get up the nerve to ask her out on a real
date. That was a hurdle to get over before he could
even consider being the steady man in her life.

The prospect was unreal, but at the same time
felt more real than anything had in a long time.
He'd only known her for twenty-four hours, yet he
wanted to know so much more. Mark was certain
that learning everything about her would only rein-
force what he was already sure of, that she was the
most amazing woman he'd ever met . . . and ready
or not, she was headed in his direction at that very
moment.

"Morning." Carla looked at the carafe in his
hand. "Mmm. Coffee."

Her soft groan cut right through him. "Ah, yeah.
Hold on and I'll pour you a cup. Oh, and, uh, good
morning to you, too."

Jeez, he sounded like an idiot. Next to him,
Logan chuckled, and in his peripheral vision, Mark
saw Tucker grinning.

The morning after was awkward enough without
the added challenge of Logan and Tucker observ-
ing them as if he and Carla were two fish in a glass
bowl. Mark had no hope of playing it smooth in this
situation. He stifled a sigh and poured her the coffee.

When she pressed the cup to her lips and her
eyelids drifted closed, Mark couldn't worry about

Tucker or Logan anymore, because instead he had to mentally talk down his burgeoning erection.

"Good coffee. Thanks." Her gaze collided with his as he glowed with pride.

"You're very welcome." Coffee. Poached fish. Mark had definitely kept this woman well sated in the food and beverage department.

As he thought back to the number of times she'd trembled in his arms last night, he knew he'd satisfied her in another area as well.

And damn, now he was as hard as a rock. Mark dropped into his chair, put the carafe on the ground next to him, and covered his lap with his hands wrapped around his own cup, hoping to look inconspicuous. No more thinking about last night. His hormones, which were acting like those of a teenage boy, couldn't take it.

He glanced up and caught Carla staring at him over the rim of her coffee cup. She yanked her gaze away, but he thought he saw the hint of a blush creep into the part of her face not hidden behind the cup.

No, he wasn't alone in this. Not the only one having problems juggling these feelings—a melding of doubt, embarrassment, and anticipation. Now, the only question remaining was, what did he do next?

"So we're just going to keep pretending nothing's going on?" Tuck put the cooler he'd carried to the parking lot down next to Carla's truck.

Carla paused a second before she recovered and put the rolled sleeping bag she held into the truck bed. "Don't know what you're talking about. Thanks for carrying that."

"No problem, and don't change the subject. You know damn well what I'm talking about."

"No, I don't." Denial seemed the only option at the moment. Carla had managed to get through the faculty group breakfast that morning by keeping her head down, concentrating on the food on her plate, and not looking at Mark. In the group, it had been easy. Now, alone with Tuck, it was much harder to act like nothing had happened.

"Ross."

"What about him?" She shrugged.

"Something's up." Tuck tried to catch her gaze, even as she worked to avoid his.

"What could be up? We all had a nice time and now it's over. End of story."

"Oh, really?" He cocked one brow up.

"Yes, really."

"So you're not into him?"

She let out a breath of frustration. "When is Becca getting back from New York? Because you really do need her to keep you busy." So he'd stop being a busybody.

"And you need a few lessons in hiding your feelings. And your hickeys." The focus of his gaze moved to her neck.

She moved her fingers to her throat. "What? I don't have any—"

Tuck touched a spot just above her collarbone and a memory flashed through Carla's mind. Mark in her tent, latching on to her throat as he tried to stifle the groan as they came together while he was buried inside her. Crap.

"At least mine was under my shirt. Yours is right out there for all to see. Good color, though. A real nice deep purple." He leaned his ass against the edge of the open tailgate and folded his arms. She supposed he was settling in to wait for her explanation or confession or whatever.

If her face looked as red as it felt, there was no denying anything to Tuck. Carla sighed. "Please don't tease me."

"I'm not planning on it." Tuck shook his head. "Hell, I've been there, darlin'. I know what it's like to do something you regret the next morning."

"I don't, though." She forced herself to look him in the eye. "I don't regret it at all. I like him. A lot. That's the problem."

"Well, I don't see why. The way he looks at you, the feeling is mutual."

Yeah, the feeling was mutual. For now. But what about when Mark realized she was a high school dropout who'd only finally gotten her GED a year ago? Between helping around the family ranch and competing, there had never been time to finish her education.

Thank God the assistant coaching position on the rodeo team wasn't an academic one. She'd landed that with her rodeo experience. Otherwise, if they'd looked into her education, she probably would have been screwed out of that job. But there was no impressing Mark with her skills on horseback. Not when she was sure the man's walls were papered in diplomas.

She shook her head when she noticed Tuck still watching her. "Nah. It was just a one-night thing.

Nothing serious. I'm gonna grab the rest of my stuff and git. Mama will need my help at home today."

As Tuck frowned, she turned and left him where he was. That was one way to end this conversation, because she really wasn't in the mood to continue it.

Chapter Six

"Thank you very much, gentlemen." Logan gathered the pile of poker chips from the center of the table with one sweep of his forearm. "About damn time I won, huh?"

Mark leaned back in his chair, defeated. In that pile had been the last of his own chips. "I guess it was inevitable. No one can lose every single hand. Not even you, Logan."

"Har, har. Joke all you want at my expense. I can afford it, since I seem to have all of your chips, Mark." Logan's winning was so rare, Mark couldn't blame him for his glee, even if it did clean him out and put him out of the game for the night.

"That's okay. I'm done for tonight anyway." Harry, from the philosophy department, rose from his chair, stretching his back with a groan as he did.

"Me, too." Jamey, from the political science department, followed suit. He gathered the small pile of chips in front of him and stood as well.

"Anyone want to hang around for a little while?"

The game was over but Mark wasn't ready to be alone quite yet. "I could put on a pot of coffee. I've got a bottle of Irish whiskey that would be real tasty in it."

"No, thanks." Jamey shook his head. "Time for me to get back home to the wife. She was reading one of those steamy romance novels when I left. She should be nice and warmed up by the time I get home, if you know what I mean."

Harry laughed. "Lucky bastard. Mine will be awake and waiting for me, but only so she can smell my breath to see if I've been drinking, and then bitch that I get one night a week out with the guys away from the kids and she gets none. Thanks anyway, Mark."

That was it then, the party was over. Mark stood, too. "Sure. No problem."

An array of colored poker chips and dollar bills exchanged hands, Jamey and Harry left, and soon Mark was alone with Logan.

"You staying? We can skip the coffee and go right to the whiskey if you want." Mark reached for a short cut-crystal glass from the side table.

"What's up with you?" Logan asked.

"Besides that you took all my money?" Mark joked while reaching for the bottle. "Nothing."

"This is not about the money, and you know it." Logan shook his head. "You spent far more on that bottle in your hand than I took from you tonight."

Very true. Mark poured amber liquid into one glass. He raised a brow and held up the drink he'd poured, glancing toward Logan in silent question. Logan nodded and took the glass before sitting on the leather sofa.

Mark poured himself a nice-sized shot and sat in the chair opposite Logan. This was good. Two single guys kicking back with some fine, aged spirits. Hanging out as long as they wanted. No need to talk, if they didn't want to. No wife to nag if they got home late with booze on their breath.

Really, who needed a woman? Certainly not Mark. As the comfortable silence between him and Logan stretched out, Mark tried to convince himself of that.

"I can sit here all night." Logan eyed him over the rim of the glass as he took a sip.

"All right. You're welcome to do that." Mark shrugged. "I'll get you a pillow and a blanket."

"I meant that I'm waiting for you to tell me what's up with you this week." Logan raised a brow and indeed looked as if he'd wait all night for Mark's answer if need be.

Maybe Mark didn't need a wife to get nagged. Logan seemed to be doing a fine job of it. "I don't know what you're talking about. Nothing is up with me."

"You haven't been yourself. Not since a day or two after the camping trip." Logan's eyes narrowed a bit, as if he'd started to put the pieces of a puzzle together, and the picture had begun to take shape. "Is that what this is about? Exactly what happened on that trip, Mark?"

"Nothing." Except that he'd had an amazing night with Carla and she'd blown him off afterward. That's all.

Mark had waited all the next day for her to call him, then had decided that was foolish. He went ahead and called her. Stupid, stupid, stupid. If she'd wanted him to call her, she would have given him her number. She hadn't, but that didn't stop Mark in his headlong plunge into embarrassment. The OSU staff directory made it all too easy for him to look up her number, confident that she'd had as great a time last weekend as he had.

What a mistake that had been. Oh, she'd been polite. Too polite. And extremely busy, apparently, since every one of his suggestions for them to get together again had been met with excuses.

"Mark, we're friends. I'm here for you to talk to if you need. And I promise, no jokes. No judgment. Just a sounding board."

Mark let out a snort of a laugh. "I can picture you saying that to your cadets."

"Yeah, but it works on them. They spill right away. Apparently, I don't intimidate you the way I do them." A crooked grin lifted one corner of Logan's mouth. "What I said is still all true, though."

God, it would be nice to have someone to talk to. Confide in. Get a damn opinion from, because Mark could not believe he'd been so wrong in his interpretation of Carla's feelings for him.

Maybe she did have a boyfriend. He'd asked that night and she'd said no, and it's not that he thought she was the type to cheat or lie, but it's possible an ex had come back into her life since then. Maybe one night with Mark had convinced her to run back to a former lover. Lovely. That thought depressed him further.

Logan was still waiting and watching. Mark let out a sigh. It wasn't in Mark to tell tales about his sexual conquests, as limited as they were. Maybe it was because he'd been on the chess team with the nerds while in school, rather than the football team with the jocks, but that kind of locker room talk, bragging about what he'd shared with Carla, seemed wrong. Even with Logan.

"There's nothing I want to talk about right now, but thanks." Mark stood. "So, you interested in that cup of coffee? I've even got decaf if you're not man enough for the real stuff this late at night."

"Your fresh ground, gourmet-bean coffee?" Logan laughed. "Yeah, I can handle your 'real stuff.' You forget, I'm in the army. The crap they call coffee is questionable on a good day. Don't you worry about me. Bring it on."

"You've got it." Mark nodded with a smile.

Subject changed and crisis averted . . . at least until later when he was alone with nothing to do except think. And remember.

Mark poured another two fingers of whiskey into the glass in his hand and then went to grind the coffee beans.

Spurring the horse to maximum speed, Carla raced out of the arena, reining him in to a sharp stop at the end of the alley. She turned them in a tight circle and trotted back to confirm her suspicions; she'd knocked every single one of the three barrels down.

"Perfect run, darlin'. You got every one." With a grin he was lucky she didn't kick off, Tuck looked up at her and patted the horse's flank. "Too bad the object of the sport is to leave all the barrels standing upright."

"Smart-ass." Carla blew out a breath and surveyed once more the damage she'd inflicted on the barrel-racing course.

In competition, every one of those three fifty-gallon drums lying on its side in the arena dirt would have cost her a five-second penalty. In a sport where the fastest time took home the prize money, the kind of run she'd just made was totally unacceptable. Particularly for a champion who rode at the level she did. Even the students she was there to coach managed to get through the course cleaner than Carla had today.

"What's on your mind?" Tuck continued to stroke the horse's heaving sides.

"Nothing. I gotta cool him off." She moved to turn the horse toward the exit again when Tuck grabbed the bridle.

"Nope. We're gonna talk." He turned toward the stands, where a few members of the rodeo team were hanging out, waiting for their turn. "Val! Would you mind walking Carla's horse to cool him down?"

The girl stepped off the bleachers. "No problem."

Tuck's gaze focused on Carla. "Get on down here."

Crap. She sighed and gave in. There was no arguing with Tuck when his mind was set. Stubborn as a bulldog with a bone, this man was. Hell, most men were. That thought should make her happy she was without one in her life at the moment.

It didn't.

"What's up with you?"

"I don't know what you mean." Playing dumb was

always the best course of action when there were no other options.

"You know exactly what I mean."

"The barrels? I just had the blacksmith put new shoes on Liberty. I'm wondering if he trimmed him too short."

Tuck laughed. "Blaming the horse? Nuh-uh. Not gonna work. You trained that gelding so well, he could run that cloverleaf without any rider at all. Probably better and faster than you did today, too. You steered Liberty right into that last barrel."

"I was trying to make up some time and cut too close. That's all." She shrugged.

"You can lie to yourself, Carla, but you can't lie to me. What's happening? Something wrong at home? Your ma and pa all right? Is the farm not doing well? I know with this economy—"

"No. Stop, Tuck. The family is fine. Everything is fine."

Tuck leaned back against the rail and folded his burly forearms across his chest. She'd seen this stance before. It was Tuck digging in his heels for a long wait, and wait he would until Carla gave him what he wanted.

She let out a sigh and blurted, "Mark called me the other day."

The only indication of his surprise was a lifting of his brow, which for a man like Tuck, who tended to keep things close to the vest, was pretty big. "And?"

"He asked me out."

"And?" The intensity in Tuck's tone increased along with his obvious impatience at her vague answers.

"I danced around the issue, but basically I let him know I didn't want to see him again." It had been one of the hardest things she'd done in recent memory.

"So what's the problem? Has he kept bothering you?"

Carla watched Tuck switch into overprotective mode. She had to nip it in the bud before he strode over to Mark's house and beat him up for bothering her, or something. She already had two brothers who acted like cavemen. She didn't need another one.

"No. Nothing like that. He hasn't called back or made contact with me at all." In a clear case of be careful what you wish for, Mark had accepted her blowing him off. That he didn't even make an effort to come after her hurt.

Go figure. She'd obviously turned into one of those fickle girls who couldn't make up their mind. She'd always hated that kind of female. One night with Mark and now she'd become one. Maybe she should be a nun. Avoid men altogether since she was obviously no good at this stuff.

Tuck still watched her too close for her liking. "If you don't want to see him again, and he's leaving you alone, what's the problem?"

Maybe a full confession would help her psyche . . . and her barrel racing. It couldn't hurt. "I do want to see him, but I can't."

"All right. Why can't you?" Tuck's patience was pretty amazing. No wonder he was good with the students.

"I googled him."

Nostrils flaring, Tuck drew in a deep breath. "And?" Maybe Tuck's patience was growing short after all.

"And, he's got so many degrees I don't even know what half of them are for. And he wrote a book." Carla was lucky she could write a check without messing it up. Forget about write an entire book.

A deep frown creased the brow beneath Tuck's cowboy hat. "That's what this is about? You're afraid you're not good enough for Ross? Did he say something to make you feel like that?"

The alpha male was back, ready to defend her honor. "No. Stop, Tuck. He didn't say anything. He didn't have to. I know the deal. He's got a PhD. I have a GED."

"So what?"

"*So what?* How can you say that? I dropped out of high school. He has a doctorate."

"And? What's your point? Becca has a doctorate, too." Tuck sighed and reached out to lay his hand on Carla's arm. "Listen. I'm not dismissing your concern. I'm trying to remind you that you're worth more than a diploma hanging on a wall in a dusty frame. Are you forgetting you have a thriving business as well as how many championship buckles?"

"It's not the same."

"No, not the same, but equal. You can't compare apples with oranges, Carla. You and Ross are both successful in your own fields."

"Are you telling me you never feel insecure against Becca's accomplishments?"

He bobbed his head. "I did once. Way back before we started officially dating."

"And?"

"And it turned out we both had misconceptions because we never bothered to talk it out. But all that resolved itself once we took the time and talked to each other."

"You really don't mind she's got the fancy diploma and you don't?"

"Nope." Tuck swiveled his head. "When Becca and I are together, I couldn't care less if the bedroom walls were plastered with her degrees. Don't make one damn bit of difference."

Carla snorted a laugh. "Sex—the great equalizer?"

"Well, yeah, but it's more than that. There's gotta be respect for each other. Good sex don't hurt, though. So . . . was it good?" He waggled his brows.

"Tucker Jenkins!" She delivered a well-aimed punch straight to his shoulder. Carla knew she could pack a good wallop. There'd been plenty of opportunity to practice on her brothers while growing up.

"Ow." Wincing, Tuck rubbed the spot. "Sorry. Just wondering, is all."

The problem was, it had been good. Really good. Her cheeks heated at the thought.

"Never mind. You don't need to answer. It must have been pretty great to make even you blush." He laughed.

"Tucker—" She reared back for another hit, but Tuck backed out of her reach.

He held up his hands in surrender. "All right. All right. No more about that subject. Just one more thing."

Carla sighed. "What?"

"He'd be lucky to have you. Remember that." Tuck leveled his gaze with hers and she realized how serious he was by the tone of his voice. No joking now. Tuck meant it.

"Thanks."

"So what are you going to do about Ross?"

"I thought we were done talking about this?"

He shrugged. "Man has a right to change his mind. You gonna call him?"

She debated a snappy comeback. Something clever to put Tuck in his place, but Carla found she didn't have any fight left in her, so she opted for the truth. "I have no idea."

Through narrowed eyes, Tuck watched her for what felt like a long time before he nodded once. "So, I wanted to see if we could shave some time off Val's runs today. Think you could work with her on that?"

"Oh, uh, sure." Shock at the change in subject from her love life back to the practice was enough to have Carla stuttering over her answer. Though the look in Tuck's eyes as he turned toward the arena told her this was only a temporary reprieve.

Chapter Seven

Mark scrubbed his hands over his face. His frustrated sigh reached no one's ears except his own since he was alone in his office. Hell, he was probably alone in the building, save for a janitor or two working the night shift. Leaving work to go home alone held no appeal.

Funny, he'd worked so hard to make his condo into a home, but it didn't feel very homey lately. It just felt empty.

The phone ringing on his desk had Mark frowning at the unfamiliar number on the caller ID. He reached for the receiver. "Hello?"

"Ross?"

"Uh, yes." Who the hell was calling him at work this late?

"Jeez, man, you're putting in the hours. And during summer break, no less. I tried your house number first but when I got no answer, and saw your cell number isn't listed, I figured I'd take a shot at the office. Listen, don't you get any ideas about making Becca work this late because I'm not putting up with it. Especially after she and I are married."

Pieces started to fall into place and Mark recognized Tucker's voice.

"Don't worry about that." The answer of who was calling raised another question for Mark. Why was he calling? "So, Tucker, what can I do for you?"

There was a pause, then a sigh, which had Mark more intrigued. Tucker Jenkins, stern soldier and big and tough bull rider, wasn't usually one to mince words, yet he seemed to be at a loss now. What in the world could this call be about?

"Look, Ross. I'm going against my better judgment here, and I'm breaking one of my own rules by interfering where I have no business, but I can't stand seeing her like this. I just want you to know, I don't do shit like this. You know, going behind somebody's back."

The more Tuck spoke, the more confused Mark became. "Okay. Is Becca upset about something happening here at work? I would certainly understand if she felt more comfortable talking to you rather than me—"

"Becca? No, this isn't about her. I'm talking about Carla."

Just the name had Mark's heart rate speeding. "What about Carla?"

Had Tuck tracked him down to defend her honor? Just what Mark needed, a broken nose to go with his bruised ego.

"You need to call her."

Huh. Not what he'd expected Tucker to say at all,

but at least Mark could honestly say his not calling Carla after they'd been together was not the issue. "I did call."

"Call her again." Tuck's order came through loud and clear.

Mark would gladly concede the point that perhaps Tucker had tougher skin than he when it came to women, but a man could take only so much rejection. Mark wasn't sure he had it in him to go back for more. "Tucker, I don't know what she told you—"

"Enough."

Tuck was obviously a man of few words, but that didn't change the fact that Carla had blown Mark off. "Look, based on our last phone conversation, it was apparent to me she doesn't want me to call her."

"Ross, listen to me. I'm not gonna betray her confidence any more than I already have by repeating what we talked about. Just trust me on this. Call. Her. Again."

The pounding of his pulse echoed in his ears as a small spark of hope began to grow inside Mark. "You really think I should?"

"Yes!" Tuck's booming answer left no room for further question.

The idea of talking to Carla again had him feeling nauseated and excited at the same time, but he'd do it. He had to. He'd never be able to face Tucker again if he chickened out. "All right. I will."

"Good. Do it now. She's alone in the truck driving home from practice, so she'll be able to talk to you without a house full of nosy family members listening in." Tuck had thought of everything, and

Mark couldn't be more grateful for the unexpected ally.

"I'll call right now. And, Tuck? Thanks."

"Yeah, well, just don't screw it up."

Mark laughed, though his nervousness over the impending call had it sounding more manic than humorous. "I'll try my best not to. Believe me."

He hung up and, with shaking hands, opened the faculty directory online and scrolled to Carla's cell number. He pulled his own cell out of his pants pocket and punched in the numbers.

"Hi." Her informal greeting told him she recognized his number, though her hesitation ramped up his anxiety a bit.

"Hi. I was wondering . . . can we talk?"

She blew out a breath. "Yeah. I think I'd like that. Do you want to meet somewhere tonight?"

God, yes. More than anything. Heart pounding, he glanced at her home address. "If you'd like, I can be at your place in fifteen minutes."

"No! Sorry, just anywhere but my house."

Mark pulled back from the phone at the force of her reaction, until he remembered what Tuck had said about her nosy family. She must still live at home. If she did want to talk so she could let him down gently, he'd prefer not to have an audience of her relatives in attendance. "Do you want to meet somewhere in the middle? Like a coffee shop?"

"I'd rather talk in private."

Hmm. That could be a good sign, or a bad sign. He wasn't sure which yet. "Okay. Where?"

"Can I come to your place?" she asked.

"Yes. Of course you can. Not a problem at all."

Had he remembered to put his dirty laundry in the hamper? It didn't matter. He'd beat her there and make things right before she came inside. Did he have any beer left in the fridge from the last poker game? Mark stood as his mind reeled. "Let me give you the address. The directions are pretty simple."

Carla stood outside Mark's place and tried to ignore the tremble in her hand as she raised it to press the doorbell.

She never got to it. Before she had the chance to ring the bell, the door was flung open and Mark stood in front of her, looking better than she'd ever imagined.

"Hi. Sorry, I'm still in my work clothes." He glanced down at his tie and cringed. "I didn't have a chance to change."

"Don't apologize. I like it. You look . . . professorly." And with that realization, she had to squelch the insecurity she felt all over again. Where was Tuck and his pep talk now that she needed him?

"Come in. Please." He stepped back.

She walked a few feet into his home and realized it really was his. It looked like him—the tailored yet masculine furniture and the accents suggested he'd hand selected every detail. Crystal glasses and bottles of liquor made for a beautiful but practical display on the sideboard. Old leather-bound books sat in stacks on every available flat surface around the room. She had no doubt he'd painstakingly searched for and chosen each one.

The last book Carla had read was—when? Back in high school before she'd dropped out.

Crap. This was a bad idea. She was about to leave when the expression on his face stopped her. A frown creased his brow and she noticed the insecurity and hesitation in him. Mark thought that it was him, that she didn't want to go out again because she didn't like him.

"Mark, I like you."

He let out a short laugh. "I like you, too."

"It's just—"

Mark held up one hand. "Wait, let's sit down for this conversation. I have a feeling I might need to."

Carla sighed. She was screwing this up royally. He gestured toward the sofa, and sat. He followed, but left a good distance between them.

"Go on. What were you going to say?"

"I want to see you again," she began.

Mark nodded. "That's fortunate, since I'd like to see you again as well."

"But . . ."

He waited, his face an expressionless mask but she could still see the turmoil of emotions he tried to hide just beneath the surface. "But what, Carla?"

Frustrated at her inability to express her feelings, she asked, "Why do you want to see me again?"

"Why?" He smiled. "That's easy. You're amazing."

Disappointed, Carla pursed her lips. "I'm not talking about the sex." Good sex couldn't sustain a deep, lasting relationship if there was nothing else there. She'd had relationships like that before. She didn't want that now with Mark, but how could she have more when they had absolutely nothing in common?

"Neither was I, though the sex was amazing, I'll admit." He laughed.

"Then why?" she asked again, hoping with every fiber of her being there was something more between them.

Mark's gaze captured and held hers. "It's everything about you, Carla. How you are as comfortable sitting on the bottom of the lake grabbling for catfish with Tucker as you were holding a conversation over breakfast with the heads of the departments the next morning. How you gave me a chance even when I was making a fool of myself trying to catch a one-pound fish. I know Tucker thinks the world of you, and I don't believe he's a man to give his respect lightly. I know you're smart and funny and kind and patient and beautiful—"

He paused when she wiped away the tears streaming down her face, and then asked, "Do you want me to go on? I can if you'd like."

"No." She swiped at one more errant tear. "But you're obviously brilliant. You spend your days with scholars. I spend mine surrounded by manure."

A frown creased his brow. "Don't you know, it's our differences that make me like you even more. Carla, if I wanted to be with a woman like me, I could be, but I'm single."

It seemed a valid point. One she couldn't refute. She forced herself to meet his gaze. "I guess you're right."

"Good. I'm glad you agree. So, if you're satisfied with my answer, how about if we finally get around to that date? I could take you out for a nice dinner." Mark reached out and took one of her hands in both of his.

Yes, she was satisfied with his answer. Carla glanced down at their fingers, intertwined, and then back up at the sincerity on his face. She smiled. "Or we could order in, and then afterward, maybe you can do that one thing you did to me in the tent again?"

"Uh, of course." His cheeks colored all shades of red as he swallowed hard. "That was just a simple matter of physiology, actually. You see, if you stimu-late—"

"Mark?" She moved closer to him on the couch cushion. Carla didn't need to know how he'd given her the best orgasm of her life using just his mouth and hands, but she did want him to kiss her—and do it again.

"Yes?"

"Stop talking now." She hooked one hand around the back of his neck and reeled him in until they were inches apart.

"Okay." He grinned, and when he took off his glasses and set them on the coffee table, she knew things were about to get wild.

Read more Kate Angell in
No Strings Attached,
available now.

At the beach the rule is no shirt, no shoes . . .

"**B**londe, metallic blue bikini, left side of the pier near the boogie board rental," Mac James said in a low voice as he handed Dune a twenty-ounce cup of black coffee from Brews Brothers. The scent of Bakehouse doughnuts rose from a bakery box. "I'm betting Brazilian wax. She's definitely a two-nighter."

Dune Cates raised an eyebrow. "Brazilian?"

Mac blew on his coffee to cool it. "Women discuss boxers, briefs, or commando on a man. I debate waxing."

Dune shook his head. Mac was his partner on the professional beach volleyball tour. On court, they were as close as brothers and in each other's heads. Off court, their lifestyles differed greatly. Mac was up for anything at any given time. Dune, on the other hand, was more conservative. He had foresight and weighed the pros and cons. He knew when and where to draw the line, whereas Mac had no boundaries. He saw life as a free-for-all.

Mac had dated more women than Dune could count. He'd recently parted ways with a waxing technician at VaDazzle Salon in Los Angeles. The salon was known for its pubic hair designs. Mac now played his V-games with the eye of an expert.

Dune had pretty much seen it all. His bed partners shaped their pubes into lightning bolts, hearts, and initials. One female surfer dyed her pubic hair pink. Another was striped like a zebra. His most fascinating lover had been shaved and decorated with stick-on crystals. She'd sparkled like a disco ball.

His preference was, and always had been, a light bikini wax or totally natural. He didn't need creative techniques to turn him on.

He leaned his forearms against the bright blue pipe railing that separated the boardwalk from the beach. He took a deep sip of his coffee. It was midmorning and the sun warmed his back right between his shoulder blades. The heat never bothered him. He'd grown up at the beach. The sand and shoreline were home to him. It was where he earned his living.

He looked toward the boogie boards. The blonde stood out. She was definitely Mac's type. His partner loved long hair and legs that went from here to eternity. The woman's hair skimmed nearly to her waist and her legs were sleek and toned.

Dune read women well. He knew who liked him as a person and who only wanted a piece of his action. He recognized the blonde as a woman who enticed men and enjoyed their attention. She made a theatrical production of laying out her towel, then rubbing on suntan oil. She was soon slick. Her entire body glistened.

Beside him, Mac opened the bakery box and offered Dune first choice. He selected a glazed doughnut. Mac chose one with chocolate frosting and sprinkles.

"Sweet Cheeks near the volleyball net," Mac said between bites. "Red one-piece, black hair, French wax. Nice walk. I'd follow her anywhere."

Sweet Cheeks was tall and slender, Dune noted. She moved with the slow, sensuous grace of a woman who knew her body well and owned the moment. The lady was hot.

Mac squinted against the sun. "Tattooed chic in a fringed camo thong bikini, third in line at the concession stand," he said. "Is that a tat of a rattler coiled on her stomach?"

Dune checked her out. "Looks like one."

She was a walking advertisement for a tattoo parlor. He saw just how much she liked snakes when she widened her stance. A python wrapped her left leg; its split tongue darted out as if licking her inner thigh.

"Snakebite, Dude," Mac said. "Woman's got venom. I bet her pubes are shaved and tattooed with a cobra."

"She's definitely into reptiles."

Mac reached for a second doughnut, topped with cinnamon sugar. "Sex and snakes don't mix. I'd go soft if I heard hissing or a rattle."

"Major mood killer," Dune agreed.

They drank their coffee and ate their doughnuts in companionable silence. All along the coastline, sunbathers sought their own private space. That space was limited. The expanding crowd was an improvement from the previous summer when the economy tanked and one person had the entire beach to himself. It felt good to Dune to see his hometown thrive.

Mac nudged him, pointed right. "Check out the desert nomad at water's edge."

The woman was easy to spot. She was short and overdressed for the beach. She wore all white. White reflected the sun. A Gilligan bucket hat covered her hair. Her sunglasses were enormous, hiding her face. A rain poncho capped her shoulders, and she wore waterproof pants tucked into rubber boots.

She walked slowly along the compact sand, only to retreat when a splash of foam chased her. It appeared she didn't want to get wet. She bent down once, touched the water, then quickly shook the drops from her hand.

She played tag with the Gulf for several minutes before turning toward the boardwalk. She tripped over her feet and nearly fell near the lifeguard station. The guard on duty left his female admirers and took her by the arm. He smiled down at her. She dipped her head, embarrassed.

The lifeguard gave her an encouraging pat on her shoulder and sent her on her way. Her rubber boots seemed overly large, and she stumbled two more times on her way to the wooden ramp. Sunbathers scooted out of her way.

The closer the woman came, the slower Dune breathed. His heart gave a surprising squeeze. *Sophie Saunders*. He was sure of it. No one else would dress so warmly on a summer day. And Sophie was naturally clumsy.

Ten months had passed since he'd last seen her,

although he'd thought about her often. They'd come together for a worthy cause: to boost the Barefoot William economy.

His younger sister, Shaye, had organized a local pro/am volleyball tournament to keep their town alive. He'd provided the professional players. The pros were auctioned to amateur athletes. Sophie had bid ten thousand dollars to be his partner. She wasn't good at sports, but she had the heart of a champion.

Sophie, with her brown hair and evergreen eyes, had a high IQ but low self-esteem. She was a bookworm, shy and afraid of her own shadow. She feared crowds and the ocean, yet she'd powered through the sports event and made a decent showing. He wondered if she'd ever learned to swim.

Her image had stuck with him. He remembered things about her that he'd rather have forgotten. She had amazing skin, fair, smooth, and soft. Her scent was light and powdery: vanilla and innocence. Her hair smelled like baby shampoo. She hid her curves beneath layers of clothing, yet her body gave off a woman's heat.

She'd bought her very first swimsuit for the tournament. He could close his eyes and still picture her in the cobalt blue tankini. He could hear the male fans on the outdoor bleachers applaud and whistle their appreciation. Sweet Sophie had an amazing body.

Their team had fought hard during the event. He'd tried to shield her when they'd battled through the loser's bracket. His best attempts hadn't saved her, not by a long shot.

Sophie wasn't the least bit athletic and had taken

a beating. Opponents nailed her with the ball, time and again. She'd gotten sunburned, bruised her knees, and eaten sand. Yet she'd never complained. Not once.

To this day he regretted not telling her good-bye when the weekend ended. Instead, he'd watched her walk away. It had been for the best. She was a Saunders, and he was a Cates. A century-old feud had separated the families back then.

The lines of hostility had blurred when Shaye married Sophie's brother, Trace. Both sides had eventually accepted their marriage. Only his grandfather Frank had yet to come around. He was old Florida, opinionated and stubborn, and set in his ways.

Dune figured everyone would forgive and forget once Shaye became pregnant. She and Trace wanted to start a family. Dune anticipated her announcement any day now. No one would want to miss the birth of the couple's first child.

He absently rubbed his wrist. He'd played a big part in Barefoot William's financial recovery, only to suffer for it later. Tendonitis was a bitch. Freak accidents occurred in all sports. Some were career-ending.

He'd taken a dive at the South Beach Open and fallen on his outstretched hand prior to his hometown tournament. He'd suffered a scaphoid fracture.

His orthopedist put him in a short, supportive cast and recommended that he not take part in the event. Dune refused to let his family down. He managed to serve and spike with one hand as well as others could with two. He'd played through the pain.

In retrospect, he knew he shouldn't have participated. He'd aggravated his fracture further. Despite additional surgery and extensive therapy, he never regained full strength in his fingers and wrist.

He was a man of quick decisions, yet the thought of retirement left him feeling restless, indecisive, and old.

Sophie was so young. She was twenty-five to his thirty-six. Their age difference concerned him. He'd dated sweet young things, all worldly and experienced. But Sophie was unlike any woman he'd ever met. She was sensitive and vulnerable, and made him want to protect her.

He preferred no strings attached.

Cat Johnson's Oklahoma Nights series
continues in *Two Times as Hot*,
coming this October.

Read on for an excerpt from Chapter One,
as plans for Becca and Tuck's wedding get under
way.

"This'll be your first time meeting Bec's sister, won't it?"

Logan dipped his head in response to Tuck's question. "Yes, sir. It sure will be."

"I'm not worried about Emma fitting in. Everyone loves her. It's the rest of the relatives I'm concerned about." Becca screwed up her face into a scowl. "My father, Mr. Punctuality, is beside himself they're not here an hour early and it sounded like my mother was already well into her sherry. She bought a bottle at the duty-free shop at the airport."

"Sounds like a hell of a start to a party." Jace walked through the door and scooped Becca into a hug that lifted her feet right off the ground. "Hey there, darlin'. You look great, as usual."

Jace gave Becca a kiss and set her on the ground.

Becca laughed. "Save some of those compliments for later when my relatives from New York are here and I'm tearing my hair out. I may need to hear them."

"You've got it. And just send me the signal and I'll sneak you some booze, too, if you want it." Jace winked at her and slid a flask out of his pocket.

"I'll keep that in mind. A visit with my parents might require some alcohol." Becca glanced at Tuck. "I'm going to go see if your mom needs any help in the kitchen."

"Sounds good, baby." Tuck nodded.

Jace watched Becca leave as he walked over to Tuck. He stuck out one arm to shake the groom's hand. "Hey, man. How you holding up? I've got the truck filled up with diesel and coolers full of ice-cold beer. It's parked right outside, just in case. You ready to bolt yet?"

Logan shook his head. Typical Jace. As changeable as the wind. Sucking up to the bride with one breath, and offering to help the groom escape with the other.

Tuck's gaze cut to the doorway Becca had left through before he answered, "Not at all. I'm loving every minute of it. Nothing more fun than planning a big ol' wedding. You want a beer? I'm getting myself another one."

Logan glanced at his own bottle. He wasn't even halfway done with his own beer yet but Tuck's was empty. Tuck might pretend he was calm, cool, and collected about the wedding and all it entailed, but the empty bottle told another story.

Out-of-town relatives. Nervous bride. Rentals. Last-minute errands. Saying "I do" for the rest of your life . . . Yup, Logan sure was happy he'd be on the ushers' side of the altar rather than directly in the line of fire like the groom.

"Definite yes on the beer," Jace answered Tuck, and turned to extend a hand toward Logan. "Lieutenant Colonel Hunt, sir. What's the status of the Oklahoma State ROTC program?"

Logan laughed as Jace lowered his tone of voice and spoke more like a battalion commander than a bull rider. "A little slow right now since we're between semesters for the summer, but thanks for asking. How you been, Jace?"

"Good. Rodeoing quite a bit now that it's summer. Dragging Tuck with me when I can convince him to ride."

"Just don't break him, please. Tuck may be a bull rider part-time, but full-time he's one of my soldiers, and one of my department's best military science instructors. I need him with two good, working legs for when we go back to working out with the cadets. Got it?"

"Sure thing. Let's just hope Becca doesn't break him during the honeymoon." Jace waggled his eyebrows. "As for rodeo, he usually ends up getting his ribs broken when he wrecks, not his legs, so we're good. Broke ribs hurt like a son of a bitch, but he can still run with 'em."

Jace grinned and accepted the beer Tuck handed him. "Thanks for the vote of confidence, Jace. And I only broke my ribs once or twice, thank you very much."

"Once or twice, my sweet ass. You can't seem to keep yourself out from under hoof. You're too tall for a bull rider, if you ask me. You need to be small and quick like me. You should have stuck with team roping."

Watching the two men bicker, Logan sipped his beer and stayed out of the fray. He wasn't about to enter that debate. Bull riders were crazy.

Sure, Logan had joined the army knowing there'd be times during his career he was going to be up against an enemy who wanted him dead, but to get on the back of a bucking bull knowing you were going to be thrown in the dirt every damn time? Nope. Not for him.

While Jace and Tuck continued to banter—something about which bull Jace drew last time he rode—motion out in the driveway caught Logan's eye. He turned to watch through the window as a hot as hell woman in a short, black dress reached one long, bare leg out of the car. She stepped from behind the open passenger door, and even doing nothing but standing in the driveway, she was sexy enough to make a man take notice. Her blond hair and resemblance to Becca told him this must be her sister, Emma.

Logan glanced at Tuck and wondered how bad of a friend he was that Tuck's soon-to-be sister-in-law was giving him a hard-on. Just from his thinking about what the curves that dress accentuated so nicely would feel like beneath his touch.

Imagine if he ever actually got his hands on her?

An older woman and man exited the front doors of the sedan and joined the blonde. They had to be Tuck's new in-laws. Their presence should have diminished Logan's amorous fantasies about Emma. It didn't. It seemed Emma had captured his attention and she wasn't letting go. He managed to block her parents right out as he wondered what her hair would feel like against his cheek while he ran his tongue down her throat.

"Hey, Tuck. It looks like Emma's here." Jace came to stand next to Logan at the window. He let out a slow whistle. "Boy oh boy, is she looking good."

The tone of Jace's voice made Logan turn to get a good look at him. The man had a knowing expression on his face that didn't sit well at all. "You know her?"

"Ohhh, yeahhh." Jace dragged the two short words out to be obscenely long.

What the hell was that about? Logan's brows rose. He turned to glance at Tuck.

"Emma was here with Becca the first time she came to Oklahoma for the job interview at OSU. You know, the night she and I met at the rodeo." Tuck had answered without Logan having to ask, but that sure as hell didn't explain the rest. Such as why Jace was acting as if he and Emma had done more than just meet that night.

Those were details Logan was more than interested in having. "Yeah, I remember you telling me about the rodeo."

But not that Jace and Becca's hot sister from New York had had a little one-night rodeo of their own.

Of course, Jace liked to exaggerate. It didn't matter if it was about conquering a bull or a woman. Logan had known the man for years through Tuck. Since the two had ridden on the rodeo circuit together before Tuck had enlisted in the army. If nothing else, he knew Jace could throw the shit with the best of them. It was very possible nothing at all had happened between Jace and Emma, except in Jace's own overactive imagination.

He decided to run with that theory and see how things progressed. It was far better than the alternative—assuming Jace had a prior claim and having to back off. A lot could happen over a short period of time. Look at how one night between Tuck and Becca had changed both of their lives. Logan had an entire weekend and a wedding reception to work with. There'd be sentimental speeches and tears, music, and a fully stocked bar. Everything to put the partygoers—and Emma—in the mood for romance.

Not to mention Logan had Tuck on his side, pulling for him, putting in a good word. At least Tuck had better be on his side. Jace was Tuck's friend, yes, but Logan was like a brother. Not to mention his boss and a superior officer. If it came right down to it, Logan would pull rank. Hell, he could order Tuck to put in a good word for him with Emma or else.

When it involved leggy blondes with curves like Emma's, a man had to bend the rules a little sometimes.